SUMMER'S BLONDE BOOTY

CRISTINA CORREIA

FOR EVERYONE
EVERYWHERE:

MAY YOU GET WHAT YOU WANT,
AND STILL WANT IT ONCE YOU GET
IT.

PROLOGUE
The Man

He became a theatrical producer as soon as he got his discharge from the Army in 1975. He, Wade Sellars, had been known as the best craps player in the military, and the many thousands of dollars in wrinkled greenbacks he carried in his gear made him think his reputation was much deserved.

As a teenager, he had decided that the stock market and show business were just big casinos. By the time he reached his late twenties, he came back from Vietnam, received an honorable discharge and he decided he loved women, so he took his craps winnings to the nearest racetrack and quadrupled it in a half-dozen afternoons.

He invested his winnings in a Broadway musical and was named co-producer. The show became popular and he married Helene Vicks, the prettiest girl in the entire chorus.

Helene, more than anything, wanted to become a star, so in 1978 he gave her the opportunity by producing his first musical and casting her as its star. The show succeeded despite her. New York's most influential critics lauded him as an astute producer whose debut featured wonderful performers, an irresistible book and a catchy score. The only problem, if she could be called such, was Helene Vicks.

The morning after the show's final performance, Helene Vicks announced her retirement.

'Sweetie,' Wade had told her, 'you need to know when the cards are good or bad. When they're bad, get up and walk. You wanted too be a star and I gave it to you, didn't I? Now I want you to give me a son.'

On July 4, 1979, she gave birth to a girl. He overcame the temptation to name her Independence or America and settled on Summer, and when the nurse placed the child in his arms, he gazed down at her and thought, *I'm going to give it all to you. You're going to have whatever you desire.*

When she was a toddler and he came home, he would greet his daughter before he even looked at his wife.

By the time she was ready to start kindergarten, he concluded that Hollywood movies were garbage, so he flew out there to make his own.

The following year, he produced two smash hits and received his first Oscar nomination.

The year after that, he won an Oscar and the Hollywood gossip columnists reported that he was dating several beautiful women. Helene then began drinking and seeing other men.

When Summer was about eight, Wade named his yacht for her, and Helene died from a deliberate overdose of painkillers.

Then Summer and Wade were all each other had.

He had a heart-to-heart talk with her as he drove her to a New England boarding school. 'Mommy's gone, sweetie, but this school will teach you to be one fine young lady.'

'You could teach me, Daddy,' she'd said. 'We could live together and you could teach me.'

He shook his head. 'I travel all the time, baby. I'm never at home. Besides, I'm a man. I don't know how to teach a little girl about becoming a lady.'

After a pause, she said, 'Daddy? How come Mommy died?'

'I don't know. I guess she wanted more than I could give her.'

'Mommy said she wanted to be somebody. Are *you* somebody?'

Wade laughed. 'Yeah, I'm somebody. I'm five somebodies.'

'Then *I* want to be somebody, too.'

'And you will. But you need to be a proper lady before you become somebody, and this school if full of nice ladies who will help you with that.'

So she had agreed to spend the rest of her childhood in that boarding school, learning to become a sophisticated young lady. Whenever her father went into the Northeast, they would spend the weekend together.

He became richer and more famous, and, like most other successful gamblers, he knew when to hold them and when to fold them. The pit bosses in Las Vegas hated to see him enter their casinos; once, he lost one of his houses in one evening of baccarat. But he walked away chuckling, because he knew he would win back what he had lost. He always did.

If you were to ask him about the day when his luck ran out, he could tell you just that.

London, June 6, 1997.

The day he learned about his little girl...

PROLOGUE
The Girl

She couldn't have said when her luck ran out because she wasn't a gambler like her father and really didn't believe in "luck." But she was his daughter and thought that if luck existed, she was the luckiest girl alive.

From day one she had felt that life at the New England School for Girls as simply biding her time. The girls, invariably friendly and overprivileged, worshipped the Beatles or Rolling Stones if they were younger or, if older, were "Rikia fans." Rikia was Rikia Saddy, sixteen, an older student. She was boisterous, she could sing and dance, and everyone agreed she was the most interesting thing around. (Years later, while going through the pictures in the yearbook, Summer would be amazed at how much Rikia looked like Peter Frampton.) But at the time, when Rikia was the star of the School for Girls, a place scarcely lacking girls who wished to be noticed and admired, nobody seemed to mind her masculine features, tameless hair and braces. All who knew her predicted that she would go from high school to becoming a major star on Broadway.

In Grade 12, when cast as the lead in the school's production of *The Sound of Music*, Rikia chose Summer as her "personal assistant," which meant that Summer got to do a hundred errands for Rikia. What Summer liked most about spending so much time with

Summer was the older girl's eagerness to learn about Summer's father. "Your dad is Wade Sellars? Really? Will he be in the audience?"

Her father did attend a performance, and afterwards Rikia melted into a blushing and giggling puddle as Wade Sellars shook her hand.

"What did you think of her?" Summer asked later. "Wasn't she spectacular?"

"No. She looks like a boy. She needs to do something with her hair. *You* were the one everyone watched."

"But she can sing so well…"

"You're confusing 'good' with 'loud.' She's a homely girl with very little talent."

"For real?"

"I wouldn't lie to you."

After Rikia graduated, the school seemed boring. Summer, despite what her father had said, knew that even if Summer wasn't beautiful, she had something—she *was* something. A beautiful girl named Gina became the lead for the next school play, but everyone whispered, 'She's no Rikia.'

A couple of years later, the girls started talking about Rikia again when one of them saw her name on the masthead of *In* magazine. 'Rikia's an editor there!' she screamed. Most of the girls looked with bulging eyes at the printed name, but Summer felt badly— why wasn't Rikia following her dream of a life on the Broadway stage?

When she told her father about it, he just shrugged. "So she's a flunky at some fashion magazine. I guess she's lucky to have a job."

"But on the stage, she was so talented."

"Was not. That was just a bunch of kids

performing in a school play. Out there on Broadway, there are a hundred girls as beautiful as goddesses, and those girls can sing and dance, but even so, they are desperate for jobs. Beauty may not be everything, but it's a nice thing to have."

"Daddy, will I be beautiful, too?"

"You already are." He smiled as he ran a hand through her dirty blonde hair. "You have wonderful hazel eyes, just like your mother. I love your hair and eyes."

She loved her father's cobalt-blue eyes, and his deep tan and thick black hair. He was so handsome that females of all ages stopped and stared as he walked by. Her father seemed to go through life having a good time and dazzling the world with his success, while most of Summer's classmates had fathers were gaining weight, losing their hair or fretting over impending layoffs or separations.

But on the weekends Summer spent with her father in Manhattan, his main goal seemed to be making sure she was happy.

Those weekends with her father caused Summer to avoid getting too friendly with the other girls at school. Getting really chummy with a classmate meant holiday dinners at their place and weekend sleepovers—and Summer would be expected to share her father, so to speak, with the other girl. She had no intention of doing any such thing. Naturally, sometimes he needed to be overseas or other faraway places to look after business, but his weekends with her more than compensated for his absences. Those wonderful Saturday mornings when the limousine picked her up and delivered her to Manhattan. Her father kept a set of rooms at the Plaza. When she entered his suite, she would always find him hard at work, doing deals on the phone, a secretary taking notes, flunkies making themselves useful. But then all activity would cease and Wade would jump and take his daughter into his arms. His cologne smelled wonderful and his strong arms around her made her feel as if nothing bad could ever happen to her.

She would eat lunch while he did business that would not wait till later. She would eat her sandwich while she stared and listened. He sat at the phone, his voice deep and resonant, his words forceful. He did deals with people all over the world, every one of them presumably grateful for the opportunity to do business with Wade Sellars. Once in a while, he would look in her direction and shoot her the quickest wink—a gesture that said *No matter how busy I get, I will always think of you* and *It's just life; don't take it so seriously.*

After lunch, the rest of the day was theirs. He would take her to Saks and buy her whatever she wanted. Afterwards, he would take her to Rockefeller Plaza for ice skating (he, a poor skater who did not wish to be laughed at, sat nearby and sipped coffee as she glided around the rink). If he had a new show happening or about to happen, as he often did, he would take her to see rehearsals. Sometimes they saw every show on Broadway, even the smash hits that had been sold out for months (they always managed to find a couple of seats for Wade Sellars and his guest). On one Saturday they saw the matinee *and* evening performances of his show. That evening, as always, he took her to Sardi's, where they looked at the caricatures of celebrities and he shared gossip that made her giggle.

Summer loathed Sundays. No matter how much

fun they had that morning, she knew that the big shiny car would be there to take her back to the School for Girls. And she knew she had to go back to school, just as he needed to go back to his phone calls and business deals. Even at that age she knew he was the only man she could ever love, and that no man her own age, no matter how handsome, intelligent and charming, could ever be, in her mind, half the man her father was.

He was producing a play in Paris when she graduated from high school. He missed her ceremony, but she didn't mind—she wanted to miss it herself, but since they'd made her valedictorian, she had to be there. Then she would fly off to Paris to spend the summer with him.

"What about college?" he had asked.

"What about it? I don't need it."

"Yes you do."

"Why?"

"Because you just do. Why do the other girls go to college?"

"So they can meet rich boys who want wives."

"Aren't you one of those girls?"

"No. If I'm meant to marry, I'll meet that man. If not, *c'est la vie.*"

"A person needs to have a career. What do you want to do?"

She shrugged. "Be an actress, I guess."

"Just try to do *that* without college or some other kind of formal training!"

So they made a deal. He would finish his project in Paris, go on to the next one in London, and while there he would enroll her in the Royal Academy of Drama. She wasn't entirely sure she wanted to study there—fun became work when you took it that seriously—and she wasn't sure she even wanted to become an actress...

The main thing, the thing that really mattered, was that she was going to Paris. *Paris!* All she needed was to get through her valedictory address; under her gown she wore a sensible linen dress, and in her handbag she had her airline ticket and passport. She'd already made sure that her suitcases were in the limousine's trunk, and the car was parked just outside the school. All she needed to do was give her speech, accept her diploma, and run for it.

She got through it fast. Finished her speech, heard the applause without paying much attention to it, strode up the aisle before being blocked by a wall of tearful well-wishers. Shaking hands, being pulled into hugs, promising to stay in touch. Yeah, yeah, yeah. She tore off her gown, tossed her cap and practically dived into the limousine as it pulled out to drive her to LaGuardia Airport.

The 747's first-class section was less than half full. She had four seats all to herself, tried to stretch out for a snooze but felt too excited to sleep, eat or watch the movie. She leafed through magazines, floated away on daydreams and drank one soda after another. Finally, she could feel the jumbo jet start to ease on down at seven o'clock in the morning, local time. When she exited the aircraft, she saw him standing there with some men in dark suits, right on the airfield, with a private car. He took her into his arms, and she knew, as always, that she was the luckiest girl in the world. The most wonderful man in the world was hers. *Hers!*

They got into the shiny dark car and headed straight for Customs. She handed over her passport, the official stamped it, and a couple of handsome French boys handled her luggage.

"Those fellows don't speak English, but they're very conscientious. They'll make sure your suitcases make it to the hotel before you do." He took her outside to a souped-up blue Ferrari. She beamed at him like a little kid on Christmas morning. "I thought it would be better to drive into Paris in something like this. Get ready, beautiful girl. You're about to make your grand entrance."

So they drove into Paris together that morning, with the breeze in her hair and the sun on her face. A few shopkeepers appeared, getting ready for the day. Here and there a horn let out a lame little squeak; as the day picked up, those horns would blast with deafening loudness.

Wade pulled up to a small restaurant whose proprietor rushed out and hugged the man, then insisted that the two Americans go inside for breakfast.

The city burst with activity as they reached the Hotel Cecile. *The City of Light should be called the City of Noise*, Summer thought.

"Is it always this loud?" she asked her father.

"Always." He smiled. "That's part of its charm." Then, "Within an hour, you'll see every American who's in Paris right now."

Upstairs, she giggled with glee as they entered her immense suite with its marble fireplaces and two bedrooms. "I didn't know I would be staying in a palace!"

He smirked. "I thought you might like it. I made sure you got the room on the quieter side of the hotel. Now, here's what I want you to do: Take a bath, get a nap and be ready by four. I'll have someone pick you up and drive you to the studio. We'll drive back here together."

She frowned. "Why don't I just go to the studio with you right now?"

"Bad idea. You look dead tired, and I want you to be fresh and rested for your first evening in Paris. Also, in case you didn't know, dinnertime here is around nine or ten."

He went to the door, opened it, then stopped to gaze at her for several long moments. "You know what? You really are just too damned gorgeous."

When she went to the studio after her bath and nap, she stood far back and watched as Nick Mitchell, the tough-guy actor the movie critics were calling the next Clint Eastwood, did a steamy scene with Christiane Morin, the fiery French actress making her debut in an English-language film. Summer had seen her in a few foreign movies and thought her amazingly beautiful, with her big dark eyes and big blonde smile. But Christiane spoke with a very prominent accent and her English was so poor that she kept mispronouncing words. She would swear, and Wade would come over and put a reassuring arm around her shoulders, and they would do another take. Soon they were up to fifteen takes, and Wade shouted, "Print it!" Then, once the house lights went on, he saw Summer standing there, so he gave her his biggest smile and strode over to embrace her.

"When did you get here?"

"Several takes ago," she said. "Are you a director

now, too?"

He shrugged. "I didn't know that doing an English-speaking part would be that hard for her. Yesterday, the blew one line after another, the director yelled at her in French, she yelled back, and before long she burst into tears. It took so long to do her makeup again, and for her to accept the director's apology, that I just sort of stepped in and intervened. That way, we started shooting again and finally got or two half-decent takes."

Just then a young man hurried up to them. "Monsieur Wade, my workday finished a couple of hours ago but I stayed because I wanted so much to meet your daughter."

"Pierre Lemans, this is Summer. Summer, this is Pierre. Now go home." Wade smiled at him.

Summer smiled, too. Pierre was young, maybe twenty-one, and spoke with such an accent that Summer wondered if he would ever have a chance in Hollywood movies, since that was surely his goal. He was tall and handsome, like a magazine cover boy. "He has only a small part," Wade said as soon as Pierre left, "but who knows? He may get the career boost he needs. I discovered him tending bar and singing in a crappy bar right here in Paris. He's a natural performer—he's already charmed all the women on the set, even Christiane. Sometimes that's how you can tell which actor has the presence and will have the big career. When a European has charm, American audiences will fall in love with them."

They walked arm in arm through the studio on the way to the car. Everyone else had gone home, and it was just the two of them. Moments such as this were her real reason for flying out to Paris—to spend time with him, walking side by side, listening to him talk, sharing his life, maybe even offering solutions to his problems.

"By the way," he told her, "I've set aside a small part for you. Nothing to brag about, just a few lines, but you said you wanted to be an actor. We'll see after a few takes if you still want a career in screen acting." She threw her arms around him until he begged her to stop. "Please! Let me go! I can't breathe!"

As they struggled with traffic jams that were as bad as, or worse than, anything Summer had ever experienced in Los Angeles or New York. As they sat in the sleek car and waited to get to where they were going, he complained to her about this movie—Christiane's frustrations with delivering her lines in English, her dislike of Nick Mitchell, Wade's anxiety over being flayed by the critics if the movie turned out badly…and that damned Parisian traffic! Summer listened and nodded, delighted to be with him indefinitely, not caring where she went or what she did so long as he was near.

When, eventually, they got back to their hotel, another slim, handsome young man stood waiting in the lobby with some large boxes. Summer wondered: Didn't these guys eat their country's wonderful, fattening cuisine?

"Meet Etienne," said Wade, nodding in the young man's direction. Etienne followed them up to Summer's suite. "I was afraid," continued Wade, "that you might not have quite as many outfits as you'd like, so I sent him out to get you a few things. He does the shopping for many V.I.P.s, you see. Take what you need, or take it all. I have to shower and make a few calls to Hollywood and New York." He pecked her cheek and added, "Be ready at nine."

He sat waiting for her when she walked into the living room at nine. He let out a wolf whistle and said, "Sweetness, you're so much more gorgeous than those models…"

She pointed at her breasts. "My girls are too small."

"Nonsense."

"I like this dress because it really shows me off to best advantage."

"You're beautiful in everything, babe."

"I opened those boxes and took out this dress, plus a couple of skirts and shirts and a pantsuit."

"Is that all? Maybe you just didn't find anything you really liked. This city is full of sidestreets with fun places for women to buy clothes. Maybe you can find what you like there. I'll ask Christiane about that."

Summer shook her head. "Daddy, I didn't come all this way to go shopping and buy clothes. I want to watch you make that movie."

He laughed. "Seriously? Sweetie, filmmaking must be the most boring thing in the world unless you happen to be the star or director. Even the producer finds it tedious. Besides, you're seventeen and this is Paris. *Paris!* The last thing a beautiful young lady here wants to do is spend her time loitering on a movie set."

"I don't just want to *loiter* on a movie set. I want to *act* on one. I also want to learn more about that bit part you promised me."

"Well, maybe you *are* an actor after all. You're getting an attitude like one. Come on, let's go eat. I'm famished."

They went to a restaurant in an old section of

town. Summer stared at all the ancient stone buildings. She loved such places; they reminded her of the old houses she had seen in San Francisco. That was the trouble with America, she thought—they knock it down once it starts to age and then they replace it with something brand new and totally boring.

The two of them dined by candlelight in a place called Nicole's. Summer smiled and closed her eyes, then opened them again, not entirely able to take in the beauty of it all. She was there, with him, in Paris—just the two of them, and somehow he, Wade Sellars, the busiest man in the world, had arranged for this evening. She gazed at him as he poured her some wine, as did some other women at nearby tables who pretended they didn't. She sipped her cappuccino and looked up just as Christiane and Pierre entered the restaurant. Wade saw them right away, waved at them to come over, insisted that they sit down. He ordered a fresh bottle of wine. Christiane, knowing she had the attention of her boss, began telling, or trying to tell, Wade about one of her movie scenes. Soon becoming frustrated with her middling English, she began, literally, groping for words, as if those she needed were floating in the air around her. Pierre laughed and said to Summer, "My English, too, is very poor. Will you help?"

"Maybe."

"Your father waits and waits till you come to see him. Do you know this?"

"I had a feeling."

"I, too, ask myself, 'Pierre, how long will it be till you get to meet this charming young lady who is the daughter of Monsieur Wade Sellars?'" He tried to put his hand over hers, but she jerked back and turned to her father for help. But Wade was whispering into Christiane's ear, and she into his. They smiled, giggled and rubbed noses. Summer tried not to notice that Christiane's hand was on Wade's thigh.

"Sometimes," Pierre was saying, "we do not need words to express how much love we feel."

"Your English is good enough," she replied, sitting up straight. She wanted to reach over and yank Christiane's hand off her father's hand.

"My English? I learn it from American Army men." Pierre chuckled. "My mama is widowed very young, so the Army men like her a lot. They come to visit us. They teach English to us both. But now my mama is old and fat, so no more Army men. Just Pierre."

Summer smiled as her father gestured for the check, then took out a thick wad of bills, peeled off more than half the wad and stuck the rest of it back into his pocket. Summer didn't know that much about French currency, but she could guess at how much money her father, with supreme indifference, had literally just dropped on the table. She glanced around and observed that Christiane and Pierre, too, were a bit wide-eyed.

"Well, sweetie," Wade said to Summer, "I guess I've kept you all to myself for long enough. You know what a beautiful American girl needs on her first night in Paris? To go dancing with a handsome young Parisian, that's what." He laughed. "At least, that's what happens in the movies." He patted Pierre and threw his arm around Christiane as they walked out of the restaurant.

Outside, they all stood for a moment. "OK,

Pierre," Wade said, "here's the deal: You're going to take Summer dancing. You don't have to show her the whole city tonight, because we're all going to be here for two months." He put his arm around Christiane and walked to his car.

Summer wanted to cry as she watched them drive off. She couldn't believe it—here she was, standing on an unfamiliar street in Paris with a handsome man who was not named Wade Sellars.

Pierre took her arm and led her down the street. "I have my car here. It is very small, but that's the best for this city." They squeezed into his puny car and he darted in and out of hellish Parisian traffic, saying nothing. Summer's first thought had been to ask him to take her back to the hotel…but what good would that have done? Would she just sit there and wait for Daddy? No; better to go with Pierre and have a nice time so that Daddy will sit in the hotel wondering where his little girl was. He had walked out of that restaurant with that trampy actress on his arm and left his daughter with this French boy. All right. She would show Daddy how that sort of thing felt.

Pierre stopped the car at a chocolate shop at the end of a winding street. "Nightclub is downstairs," he said as they struggled out of his car. "Best of its kind in this city. Private club," he told her with a smile. "Only cool people get in."

The entire building looked as if even the tiniest earthquake might flatten it, but the discotheque itself was a vast cavern of blaring rock music, flickering colored lights and undulating bodies. Pierre shook hands with everyone, including the server, who escorted him and Summer to a table by an alcove. Then Pierre ordered a bottle of white wine on ice and half-pulled Summer onto the dance floor. She didn't want to dance at first, because everyone seemed to know the latest moves, and she hadn't danced with anyone lately, preferring to spend her weekends with her father. She looked around and saw all the other girls twitching their limbs and shaking their shoulders as if they out there by themselves, without partners. But Pierre beamed at her, let his hips sway to and fro, and mouthed *Do like me*. The beat of the music was catchy, and as Pierre pumped his fists into the air and nodded his encouragement, she moved her body, too, and presently gave herself over to the music. By the time the music stopped, both were sweaty and exhausted; they practically carried each other back to their table, where Summer downed an entire glass of wine, grateful for its chilled effervescence. Pierre ordered another bottle as he refilled her glass. Some of his friends came to sit with them, and soon their large table was full of laughing, chattering Parisians. Most of them, even the girls, danced with her, and she would have enjoyed it all if she hadn't kept thinking about Christiane and her father…where they were, what they were doing…why he'd left her with these strangers so he could run off with that woman. Summer walked off the dance floor, and the boy she was with ran up behind her, spun her around and waved his arms in confusion.

"It's nothing personal. I'm tired, that's all," she said to Pierre. He offered the boy an explanation, who just smiled, nodded and asked a different girl to dance. At about one, their group thinned out. Summer wondered where her father had taken Christiane—or where *she* had taken *him*—and what they were doing. Summer hoped her father sat worrying in his hotel suite just then, but she doubted it; he was probably still out, laughing and whispering with Christiane. She finished her glass of wine and wanted another one, so she reached for the bottle but it was empty. Pierre looked at her, and shook the bottle with a frown. He asked their server for another bottle but the man refused. After some bickering and scowling, he said, "No more wine, darling. It's closing time. We must take our party somewhere else."

As they climbed the steep steps of the ancient building, Summer said, "Where to now? Is there another place to go? In America, in New York, we have clubs that stay open till four."

"This is Paris, not New York," he replied. "Here, we don't go out and party till late. After the dance clubs close, we party at home."

"But—"

"We go to my home. I have wine, too." He turned to the young couple behind them. "Jean and Danielle, you come too."

Jean shook his head and said, "Goodnight, *mes amis.*" He threw his arm around the girl and they walked away. Summer and Pierre got into his car and she said, "Pierre, maybe I should go home, too. It's been fun. Really terrific."

"No. We go back to my place for a glass of wine and a few laughs. Your *pere* will think I am a useless date if I bring you home so soon."

She chuckled. "Oh? Are you my date, a little gift from my father?"

He went silent. Summer could feel the car going faster, faster. He took one curve, then another, at a frightening speed.

"Pierre, you'll get us killed! Slow down!" Then,

"Have I offended you?"

"Yes. You call me a whore."

"I did not. Anyway, I was just kidding. I meant no disrespect."

He pulled over to the curb. "Look, we need to understand each other, OK? Your *père*, he is a very important man, here and in America. But I am good actor, maybe the best. I see my scenes that have just been shot. I think the best directors, in Europe and America, look at this new movie and say, 'Pierre is so very good, I want him in my movie.' Most of my part in your *pere's* film is already done, so I have nothing to gain by spending time with you. I am here with you now because your father says, 'My daughter is the most beautiful girl alive,' and I think, 'No, nobody is that beautiful.' But when I meet you this afternoon, I think, 'He is right—she is more than beautiful.'"

Summer laughed. "OK, Pierre, I think I understand. But remember—nobody called you a whore. Don't be so sensitive."

"Then what do you call a man who is bought by someone?"

"The closest I can think of is a faggot or hustler. Some guy who hangs out on the street waiting for some guy to pay him for sex."

"I don't do that. That's not me."

"I didn't say you were."

He resumed driving but went slowly. "Here in France, life is very competitive and we have to fight for everything worth having—money, women, power. But we cannot allow ourselves to be bought by women. A man who lets himself be bought by a woman...well, he is less than a man." Then, "Look, I forgive you if you agree to come to my place for a glass of wine. OK?"

"Well—"

"Or maybe I still feel insulted if you refuse my invitation. Maybe I think, 'Pierre, she's just with you right now to make her *père* happy. She really does not like you.'"

She sighed. "OK. I'll have one glass of wine with you."

He drove this way and that, making a dozen turns or more, and Summer started to wonder if they were lost. But by and by they reached a big, stately old house. "This place? It used to be a rich old woman's house. Hitler and his people stayed here. But things changed and it got chopped up and turned into apartments."

Pierre led her through an unlit courtyard, past crumbling benches and a broken-down fountain. They reached his suite and he slid his key into a huge wooden door. "Come in. This is mine...for the time being."

Summer looked around at this vision of faded opulence and modern indifference—high ceilings, worn marble floor, clothing and debris strewn everywhere.

"No maid service?" she asked.

He shrugged. "No need. Not here that much." He turned on some music and began opening a bottle of wine. "This is the same as we had to drink in the club." He handed her a glass and tossed some newspapers off the sofa. "Sit."

"Beautiful sofa," she said. "You should have it redone—"

"No time for that. As I say, all of this is just for now. in movies, I am soon to be the biggest star.

Once that happens, I will move to America and buy the best sofa in the world."

She frowned. "Christiane Morin is a big star, yet she stays here. She hasn't moved to America."

He laughed. "Christiane Morin already has more money than she can spend. Besides, she's over thirty, so she's too old for America."

"Was she born rich or did she make her money from making movies?"

"No, she made her money from lovers. She has had many lovers who have given her much gold jewelry. She makes good money from movies but lots more from her lovers. Your *père*? He has given her beautiful gold chains—"

She shook her head. "I don't want to hear this. I want to go home."

"But you been here only two minutes. I open whole bottle of wine just for us. We need to drink."

"Pierre—"

"Drink."

They sat together on the sofa and she took tiny sips of her wine. He slid his arm around her shoulders, and she pretended it wasn't there, but she could feel the caress of his fingers.

"Pierre," she said finally, "I want to go home."

He took the wineglass from her hand and set it on the floor. Then he got up and pulled her to her feet. "Let us dance. Nice and slow."

"But I've been dancing—"

He took her into his arms and swayed to the soft music. She could feel his hard, muscular body—his chest seemed a wall of stone—and she tried not to think about the prominent bulge in his tight slacks. Her thin little dress felt like no protection at all.

Suddenly he kissed her, sliding his tongue into her mouth. She tried to pry herself away, but he was too strong for her. He held her still with one hand, while with the other he fondled her breasts. She tried some more to wrench herself away, but each time he just laughed again. Then he picked her up as if she were a rag doll and carried her over to his bed and dropped her onto it. Before she could say or do anything, he hiked up her dress and started pulling off her panties. She cried out when she felt his sweaty hands on her bare bottom.

He glowered at her. "Summer! What is your problem?"

She rolled off the bed, pulling down her dress. Her face felt hot; she swallowed hard and ran into the living room to grab her purse and shoes. He followed her. "Summer! Talk to me!"

She spun around. "*Talk* to you? What do you want me to say? 'Thank you for trying to rape me'?"

He shook his head. "No rape here. Just making love."

"To you, rape and making love are the same thing."

"No. Rape is physical attack. Making love is beautiful thing, two people sharing their bodies. You agreed to come here to be with me. Remember?"

"I came here because you asked me to, and I thought I had hurt your feelings."

"Maybe I have hot French temper," he said. "But right now you are acting like such a snotty little American girl."

"I *am* an American girl."

"*Oui*. But with one big difference: You are Monsieur Sellars' daughter. They say that in America, girls have rules. First date, maybe goodnight kiss. Second date, making out and some groping. Third date, more of the same. No lovemaking till maybe fifth date. The American boys play by the same rules. But your père, he says, 'I am Wade Sellars. I follow nobody's rules. I make my own.' So I thought you were your father's daughter who made her own rules."

She scowled. "So you thought I would just put out for you tonight?"

He chuckled. "Well, yes. You went out for drinks with me…you danced with me…you came back here with me. It's all very romantic and I thought you wanted to make love with me." He reached forward and jiggled her breasts. "No bra. Very provocative. Nipples hard as rocks. Your boobies say, 'Pierre, I am so excited. Please make love to me.'"

"Take your hands off me and take me home."

Instead, he kissed her some more, pinning her against the wall. She fought as best she could, kicking at him and trying to bite his lips, but his only response was a deep, throaty rumble of laughter. Then he reached down and pulled her dress up around her arms. She felt his tongue teasing her nipples. She gasped at the sensation of his fingers in her panties, exploring the arena between her legs. "My little Summer," he said. "You are wet for me. No woman can resist Pierre."

She managed to bring her arms down and push him away. She pulled her dress back over her body and said, with tears streaming down her face, "Please, please just take me home."

"Why those tears?" he asked, smirking. "I am the best lover around. Let me pleasure you, and you will see. Get naked and come to bed. I will show you a real man, not like those pansies in America." He unbuckled his best, dropped his pants and soon stood naked but for skimpy bikini briefs. He grinned as she looked, then looked away, then looked again. "You see how much I want you, Summer? You see how much I offer you? Can you really say no to me?"

"Please...I just want to go home..."

He grabbed her hand and stuck it into his underwear. "Have you ever felt anything so strong and wonderful, *mademoiselle*?"

She whimpered. Then she turned away from him. After several long moments of silence, she heard him say, "Summer, have you ever made love to a man?"

"No." Her voice was scarcely above a whisper.

After some more silence, he said, "I'm so very sorry." Then "What is your age? Twenty-one, twenty-two?"

She choked back a sob. "Seventeen."

"Oh my." She watched as he ran a hand through his thick black hair. "You seem so much more mature." He muttered, "I tried to screw Wade Sellars' virgin daughter."

"Please just take me home," she said again.

"*Oui.*" He got dressed and escorted her back to the car. They remained silent and he drove and drove. Finally, as he pulled up at her hotel, he asked, "Is there a boy you love in America?"

"No."

"Then I want to be your first. I will wait. I will not touch you until you tell me when. Do you trust me?"

"No."

He chuckled. "Listen what I say, Wade Sellars'

beautiful virgin daughter. Women in France and everywhere else want me. They say, 'Pierre, I want your big beautiful cock inside me.' This is no boast; I hear it all the time. So when you say, 'I am not ready for love,' I tell you that I will wait until you want me. I thought tonight you were ready to make love, but you said no. So I think we should just be friends and see each other till you are ready. I apologize for tonight and we forget that this ever happened. OK?"

She said nothing. Her thought was, *The weird thing is, he actually thinks his behavior tonight was appropriate. My dad said, 'Take her out for a good time,' so that's what he did.*

"It's too bad you don't want to be with me," he was saying. "Especially since you have never had a lover. I would be your first, and your best. Till the day you died, you would remember my loving and it would make you smile.

"I was bad boy tonight. I get aggressive with you because I thought you like it rough. One of my American girlfriends? Her thing was for me to chase her around her hotel suite. She would lock herself in her bedroom and scream, 'Break down the door and take me by force!' So I say to myself, 'Pierre, this girl is a freak, but she say to you what she wants, and you must do it.' I break through the door and chase her around. I rip off her clothes because she wants me to and I give it to her nice and rough because she wants that, too. I make her scream. She make me scream, too. We make love all night and then we never speak of this again. Why not? Because she is married to major American movie star and it would be bad news if the world knew about her and Pierre. You see, I am gentlemen about these things—I never kiss and tell."

She smiled despite herself. This evening had been

much too weird. This guy had taken her out, then taken her to his place and tried to rape her. Now he was sitting there, saying, 'Let's forget I tried to rape you. We'll keep seeing each other and I won't stick my thing into you until you say yes.'

He turned and smiled at her. "I know you will say yes soon. I can see your nipples get erect again. When a female gets her boobies and she starts to bleed each month, it is nature's way of saying, 'Girl, you are a woman now. It is time for you to make love.'" He added, "You have small boobies. That's good. They will stay firm for a very long time."

"Pierre," she shot back, "just shut up, OK?"

"Wow! How can the daughter of Wade Sellars be so uptight?"

"I'm not uptight." She looked out the window and saw the hotel's doorman. Her evening was over. Pierre wouldn't try to manhandle her when help was just a scream away.

"I don't have to act tomorrow, Summer. We hang out and party some more, OK?"

"Nope."

"Why not? Are you angry?"

She let out a loud, angry laugh. "Angry? Pierre, you tried to *rape* me tonight."

"No—I just try to make love with you tonight. But you say no, and I respect that. Tomorrow is another day. I call you, we ride my motorcycle all over Paris. OK?"

"I said no."

"Then I will call you tomorrow in case you change your mind. *Au revoir.*"

She got out and he drove away. She entered the hotel lobby, which was deserted at three in the morning. As she rode the elevator up to her room, she wondered about what to tell her father when he asked about why she had come home so late. Maybe he would be facing the floor at that moment, and when he heard the click of her key into the lock, he might jump to the floor, throw it open and pelt her with questions. She smiled as she pictured his handsome face grave with concern. Well, she wouldn't tell him what really happened—she'd just say that their goodnight kiss had been a bit too friendly and she didn't want to see him again.

"Hello…? It's me," she called out as she opened the door. Nobody was home, although she found a wad of cash and a note on the coffee table.

Waited as long as I could, sweetness. Sleep late and dream well. Remember, this is not the United States, so the stores close in the afternoon. This city is full of fun places to see and things to do, so ask the concierge for a few suggestions. Here's some money to keep you going. If you end up in a store and fall in love with something that costs more than you have, just get them to send it COD to the hotel. Sleep well, my special girl. XO, Daddy.

She read his note a couple of times, then looked over at his closed bedroom door. He had already gone to sleep! He wasn't fretting over her at all! Of course, he surely had no idea what a pig Pierre was, so that explained his lack of concern for her.

She went into her bedroom, already feeling better about things. She liked it that Daddy was asleep in the other bedroom, and that he had gotten home at a decent hour; he hadn't gone and spent the night with Christiane, as Pierre had suggested. Pierre had sex on the brain all the time and assumed the same of everyone else. Well, what did that horny Frenchman know, anyway?

Just as she began to undress for bed, she decided to open her father's door, to see if he was still awake; if so, she wanted to wish him a good night. She left her bedroom and walked across the large living room and, with a burglar's stealth, turned the doorknob and pushed it open. Seeing nothing but darkness and hearing no breathing, she crept closer to his bed. After several long moments of utter blackness and silence, she reached down to touch him. Her hand felt nothing but linen; she groped about some more and, in frustration, turned on the bedside lamp.

The bed was empty. It hadn't been touched.

She stomped out of the bedroom and returned to the money and note in the living room. Pierre had been right all along about her father and Christine— the two were together somewhere, probably making love in the actress' apartment.

Back in her bedroom, she reminded herself that her father had every right to spend his time with the person of his choice. His reputation as a womanizer was legendary; she knew that, of course, and thought it none of her business. She turned out the light and waited for sleep to come. It did, and she had crazy dreams about her father, Christiane, Pierre and herself.

She opened her eyes and the vestiges of her weird dreams dissolved. As she yawned and stretched and cleared herself of sleep, she saw patches of sunlight on the floor of her bedroom. Then she heard the infernal racket of Paris' notorious traffic. Listening more closely, she picked up the sound of her room's telephone. Her bedroom clock said eleven. She hurried into her living room and answered the phone.

"Summer, this is Pierre. Good morning!"

Click.

She ordered coffee from room service and went into Wade's room so she could make his bed look slept in. She didn't want the housekeeper to get the wrong idea—or the right idea—about where he'd spent the night. *Like they give a damn one way or the other.* She was in a big old hotel in Paris that catered to rich, powerful people like Wade Sellars, so they knew perfectly well that such guests did as they pleased, and screwing around was certainly part of the program.

Her phone rang again. She hoped it was Wade but guessed it wasn't. It it was, she would try to sound sleepy and insist that she'd had a wonderful time last night.

"Summer, it's Pierre again. I guess we were cut off."

She groaned.

"Dumb woman on switchboard."

"No, Pierre, I did it."

"Really? Why?"

"Why not?" Then, "I don't really want to talk to you. I just want to drink my coffee and wake up."

"I call you because it's a glorious day and you should be outside, not inside drinking coffee and waking up. I come get you and we eat lunch at this nice little place—"

"No. Pierre, the way you treated me last night was too awful. Don't contact me ever again."

"Last night I didn't know better. I think, 'Pierre, she is grown woman, so you must make love to her.' Then I find out you are still a child, so now I think, 'Pierre, she is a little girl, so you must treat her like one.' Understand?"

"Sorry, not interested."

"You know what I do for you? I wax my motorcycle for two hours. Just for you! So today I take you somewhere you would like and we do things your way. *Au revoir.*"

Click.

Her room-service coffee did not arrive, which surprised her very little, so she decided to let Pierre buy her some. After all, she loved to drink coffee in the morning. She gathered up the cash her father had left, then put it back down on the table, along with his note. She called housekeeping and asked to have her bed made immediately. She knew her father had more games going than Toys R Us, and she had inherited his love of playing head games with other people. Well, let him come back here and wonder what *she* had been up to!

She could not stay mad at Pierre. He ordered her coffee and croissants. He spoke loudly and smiled often, and it seemed that half the people in the place stopped by to speak to him. His charisma got to her, and soon she began laughing and giving him girlish backtalk, often with a mouthful of food. His big, open smile and exuberant enjoyment of such a simple thing as breakfast made her start to forget his abominable behavior from the night before. She knew that he, in his own way, was trying to apologize, and that she, when getting dressed, had put on Levi's because she unconsciously had chosen to go out motorcycling with him.

His bike was navy blue. He insisted that she wear a helmet with a face shield. "You sit behind me and hug me or you will fall off," he told her, laughing.

He drove her with much care as he pointed out buildings he thought might interest her. At one point they stopped in at a mom-and-pop shop for bread, cheese and wine. "You could drive through Paris every day for a year and still not see everything worth seeing," he said.

Soon they walked back to his bike. He threw a friendly hand over her shoulders, and she turned to face him.

"Pierre," she said, "I want to thank you so much for this afternoon. I've had too much fun."

"Tonight I take you to dinner. Really great place. Authentic French cuisine."

She shook her head. "No. I can't have dinner with you."

"Why not? I promise I keep my hands to myself."

"I always have dinner with my father."

"Always? But you live in America and don't see him very often."

"Well, he's here and so am I. So I want to spend time with him."

"You can go back to your hotel, chat with Daddy for a bit, then have dinner with me."

"I want to have dinner with him every night. And he wants to have dinner with me."

"Is that so?" Pierre asked.

"What's that supposed to mean?"

"It means," Pierre said as they climbed onto his bike, "that Monsieur has had dinner with Christiane every night for the past month."

"Well, I'm here now, so that changes things."

"Does it? I'm not sure that your presence changes anything at all. Do you expect to have dinner *every* night while the two of you are here?"

"Well, yes."

He revved the engine. "I understand it all now."

She asked, "What do you understand?"

"No beautiful young lady wants to eat with her *père* each night. You must have other plans you don't want to tell me about."

"I have no other plans."

"Then you dine with me tonight?"

"I said no."

"I'll take you home. I don't call you again. You know what your problem is? You just don't like Pierre. And that's too bad."

They took off in the general direction of downtown Paris; he drove faster and faster, indifferent to her screams of protest. The bike bounced as he drove over bumps and potholes, and half a dozen times they nearly collided with other vehicles. He ignored her pounding fists on his back, and finally she just closed her eyes and waited to arrive at her hotel or fall off Pierre's bike. She could hear insane honking and enraged yelling just before the bike's front wheels went airborne and Summer felt herself thrown off the vehicle. She felt grateful to be without pain as her body slammed into a hard, hard place and everything went black.

As soon as she opened her eyes, she saw her father—or thought she did—and reached out for him, but her arms felt as heavy as wrought iron. She blinked a few times, to clear up her vision, and saw her leg in traction. Then she remembered Pierre's crazy driving and being thrown off the bike. Now here she was, in a Paris hospital, and it didn't look as if she would be going anywhere anytime soon. But hadn't medicine improved so much in the past few years? Didn't they have casts that allowed you to walk comfortably…? She tried to sit up, but her entire body seemed to be encased in plaster. She saw her father in the room whispering to some nurses, but when she tried to call out they just ignored her. Or had they not heard her? Had she made any sound at all? That bit of exertion tired her out as if she'd just finished a marathon. She closed her eyes and sank into a long dreamless sleep.

She woke up to see a nightlight and a nurse sitting at her bedside. How long had she been asleep? No matter; she watched her father come in and shoo the nurse. At her bedside, he smiled with sadness and said, "Don't worry, sweetie…We're gonna beat this thing."

She tried to open her mouth and say, *What are you talking about? What's wrong with me?* But no words came out, and she just lay there.

"Sweetie, the doctors say…well, what do they know. They don't know everything, right? And they sure as hell don't know Summer Sellars!"

She wanted to cry. Here she was, all busted up in a hospital bed because of that simpleton Pierre, and now her father was away from the studio, worrying about her for no good reason. She wanted to say all these things to him…but why couldn't she speak?

This was all too ridiculous. She moved the fingers of her right hand, and that worked. She raised her arm and that was OK, too. Her father sat there, zoning out, so she reached out and touched his arm. He jumped up and beamed at her.

"Summer! You moved your arm! *Nurse!* She moved her arm! Come see!"

She tried to tell him she was OK and that she was thrilled to see him, but then she felt that heavy, dopey sleep pulling at her. She didn't want to sleep; she wanted to talk to her father. She blinked and took deep breaths…anything to stay awake. A moment later the room seemed crowded with white coats. Well, she thought, that was Wade Sellars for you—he yells and they come running. One of the white-coated men moved her arm and leg. Then he started to move her other arm and she felt sleep covering her like a thick, heavy woolen blanket.

"Oh, sweetie," she heard him say as she drifted off, "we're going to get through this thing together…"

When she woke up, he was still there, with tears streaming down his face.

"Here's how it is, sweetie," he said. "You were real banged up from that motorbike crash. The doctors had to shave your head because of a concussion. You had a fractured skull, and they had to release some blood. They were afraid of clotting, I guess. Anyway, I guess that worked out OK, although your back is broken, but that'll mend over time. You have several leg fractures, so they have you in casts so you can't move. Your concussion affects your arm movements, but that'll be OK over time. Just stay optimistic, sweetie…"

She nodded and fell asleep again.

1

September, 1990

When Wade Sellars walked into the V.I.P. room at Kennedy International Airport, the hostess looked at him with the wide-eyed wonder he'd seen in so many other women's faces. He was tall and handsome, charismatic and magnetic. Wade Sellars was *somebody*.

The hostess told him that Summer's flight would be half an hour late. He nodded and sat down with a cup of coffee. He had plenty to fret over besides his daughter's recovery. Wade's movie had opened to savage reviews. He blamed himself for that, but considering what had happened to his kid, the Christiane Morin movie seemed trivial. He had gotten Summer the best medical care available, and they all said the same thing: She needed physiotherapy as soon as possible to maximiz4e her chances of a full recovery, but the physiotherapy couldn't happen until her bones had healed.

Wade had confronted Pierre about the accident. The Frenchman had insisted that Summer wanted him to go faster. Wade fired him from the picture and ordered the editor to delete all of Pierre's scenes—which seemed to displease Pierre fairly little, and Wade suspected that the young man knew the movie wasn't much good anyway. It opened in Europe and America to abysmal reviews and closed fast; in New York, it ended up in a Times Square grindhouse.

The man did his best just to shrug it all off. He'd started out with a foreign star who couldn't speak English and a script that was scarcely a masterpiece. Besides, he was due for his first flop; since getting out of the Army in 1975, he'd had one success after another. So he told the press, 'Now the world knows the awful truth: Wade Sellars is only human.' They all laughed, but at Summer's bedside, he asked himself, *Was it just one flop, or will there be others?*

He had two more movies in the works, and if either of them was a hit, its earnings would make his Christiane Morin flop a relatively insignificant matter. Also, he felt absolutely sure that one of his new movies, a tearjerker based on s runaway bestseller, would be big, even huge. He tried to convince himself that everything would turn out well as he went to the Paris hospital to see Summer. He affected a big, happy smile for her because he knew she would have a big, genuine one for him. He tried to be enthusiastic about whatever progress she'd made in her rehabilitation, but in truth he felt heartbroken that she, Summer Sellars, his daughter, the girl he believed would skate and dance through life without a scratch, had been reduced to cheering and clapping because she'd walked six inches further today than yesterday.

Wade flew in to wish her a happy eighteenth birthday, then he had to go back to America to shoot some scenes in New York and San Francisco, then go to Los Angeles to score and edit the film. He looked forward to the release of this picture; he had convinced himself that it was just the kind of thing moviegoers were waiting for.

They had a huge, lavish premiere in New York with klieg lights and everyone who was anyone. A local TV personality interviewed some of the V.I.P.s. Once the film began, the audience laughed and cried in all the right places. When the house lights came on and the final credits rolled, Wade and the top guns from the studio strode up the aisle with smug chuckles. They went to the Plaza for the after-movie party and learned that teenager initial TV reviews had been poor. But everyone said that only *The New York Times* mattered. At around midnight, they learned that the *Times* had trashed their movie, and then the top studio people left the party. The studio's publicity boss, Bob Blumenfeld, said it was all good. 'Who reads the *Times*, anyway? The *Daily News* is what counts when it comes to movies.' Ten minutes later, they found out that the *Daily News* had given their picture a mediocre review. Blumenfeld said, 'Well, I'll bet that the first-string critic at the *Post* loved it. Anyway, word of mouth will give our picture its legs.'

But the *Post* and word of mouth were very poor. 'Just wait for it to run across the country. They'll love it in other markets,' Blumenfeld insisted. However, in Los Angeles, Detroit and Chicago, people stayed away in droves and Wade's movie, after a month in general release, had minuscule box-office grosses.

Wade shook his head in despair. This picture had *smash hit* written all over it, and his name was on its posters and everywhere else. He remembered the old showbiz adage—everything happens in threes—and knew that this was flop number two for him. Wade Sellars, for whom even the busiest of studio heads stopped what they were doing to take his calls, now discovered that everyone was in a meeting or out of the office. Finally, the top guys in New York gave him a budget of only five million dollars for his next picture. 'Two million,' Wade groused to himself. 'That's chump change.' He knew that such resources would buy him only actors on their way up or down—he had little confidence in them—and a director who, like Wade himself, was struggling to overcome some recent slops. Wade liked working with the most gifted people who were in their most productive years, just as he enjoyed keeping company with women who were still young and beautiful…but what choice did he have as a movie producer? He had signed a three-picture deal, so he had to deliver that crucial third movie.

If he was a risk-taker, he was also a realist…and he certainly was no fool. So he told himself that his success in movies, such as it was, had been due mainly to luck, and if you really wanted to be brutally honest about it, Wade Sellars really didn't know what the hell he'd been doing as a movie producer. His tearjerker that bombed? It just proved that success on Broadway didn't guarantee success in Hollywood. If his third picture crapped out—and he thought that such a thing just might happen—he'd just go back to Broadway and resume his career there. He had enough money of his own to do a new show there, but he would need to make sure that he had a hot new book with a great new score.

He was ambivalent about Hollywood and movies in 1998 as he started shooting his third picture. He felt full of eagerness to see Summer as he flew out to Paris, but his exuberance faded as he watched her struggle with her right leg and he started to realize that she might never recover fully. Her big blonde smile and vivacity only hurt him further. She asked a dozen questions about his new movie. Who would direct it? Did he have any famous actors cast, or would it be with lesser-known performers? Did he have a script? Etc. & etc. As a movie producer, he lied often and well. But with his daughter, he could only tell her gossip he knew she would enjoy and share stories about the weird people and things he had seen in Times Square, a place that had always fascinated her. He saved all of his rage for the doctors. 'What's this crap about her making progress? I've been visiting her all this time and she's still all busted up!'

The doctors empathized with his frustration and acknowledged that her recovery had disappointed them, too. But they reminded him that there had been a delay in her physical therapy due to her leg fractures…she would walk again, yes, but always limp and probably need crutches.

That evening he went out and got falling-down drunk with Christiane Morin and, back at her apartment, threw a tantrum about his daughter's medical care.

"Wade," she said, "I am your biggest fan. My appearance in your movie humiliated me, but I don't say it was your fault. But now you have made two bad movies. I know that Summer is in bad shape, but you have your own life to live, your own career to salvage. Do not throw it all away. Your next movie must be good."

"What are you saying? 'Just go to work and forget that you have a daughter'?"

She shook her head. "Never forget. Just remember that you need to maintain your career, too. Stop fretting that a miracle may not happen to Summer."

His anger sobered him up. She wanted him to stop hoping for miracles. Well, his whole life had been one big dung heap and miracles, albeit little ones, had gotten him every good thing in his life. His parents hadn't lasted long. His mother had decided that family life was less than gratifying, had taken off when he was a toddler. His father, a boxer, had been beaten literally to death in the ring by a stringy kid he should have taken out by the third round. Wade had joined up with the Army and gone to Vietnam because that seemed no worse than life in New Jersey. He had survived the war, mentally and physically, for reasons he could not fathom. Dozens of times he had watched as guys he'd eaten and slept with were taken down by bullets that missed Wade by inches. He had watched them die, and they watched him live, both surely wondering why they had been blown away and not him, since they had families and sweeties back home who wrote to them and sent them goodies while they knew he was a lone wolf who would be missed by no one back home if he get blown to smithereens out there…

But no. He decided that if *he* lived and *they* died, it was because he was meant to return home and do what must be done and only he could do it.

"Summer will recover," he said to Christiane.

"You have options."

"Do I? Tell me."

"You can try Lourdes. If that doesn't work, and you want to spend some money, there is the Clinique."

"Never heard of it."

"In Switzerland, near the Alps. I understand they

have done great things to help people like Summer."

The next day Wade flew out there and drove to a large chateau. He met with Dr. Jonasson, a skinny, pale man who inspired very little confidence in the rich, powerful American. Wade had his daughter in the best hospital in Paris—he would have her flown to the best one in the U.S. if he thought it would do her any good—and brought in the best European doctors to consult with the best French physicians. They all said the same thing: *Her injuries were very bad; the human body is what it is; we're doing the best we can for her, but we're not magicians—we can't just snap our fingers and make her all better.*

By the time he reached the Clinique, Wade had written it off as just another rehabilitation center that did its best to make its patients comfortable. He and Dr. Jonasson walked past smiling, waving stroke victims. Inside a room, disabled children sang.

"We always do therapy. Always," said the doctor. "It gives them a sense of accomplishment that is crucial."

"Where are the TV and radio?" asked Wade. "How do you get your news?"

"We don't need news. It's all bad, anyway—wars, murders, disease. Here, we have each other, and it's all good."

"My daughter just turned nineteen. Everyone here is very young or very old. I'm not sure she would have anyone to connect with in this place."

"Oh? And how many people in that Paris hospital has she been able to 'connect with'?"

Wade sighed. "Nobody. But she's not surrounded there by stroke victims and amputees."

The doctor frowned. "Many times, being around

those less fortune helps a person recover. The child who loses an arm comes here and sees a boy missing both arms; the one-armed boy starts to see that his disability does not mean the end of the world for him. The boy missing both arms meets a legless boy. Each says to the other, 'I'll help you if you'll help me.' It's what we do here."

"Do you really think you can help her?"

"We can try. We cannot, of course, make promises beyond that."

Less than a month later Wade chartered a plane and flew Summer to Switzerland. He told her how it was, especially about the amputees and Thalidomide victims. What he left out was how much skepticism Dr. Jonasson, after reviewing her file, expressed about her prospects for a full recovery.

After getting Summer checked in, Wade took a room at the nearest inn, about five miles away. Each day he visited her, she smiled and laughed often and seemed to find comfort and strength in her surroundings.

Convinced that his daughter was receiving the best possible care, Wade flew back to Los Angeles to check on the progress of his latest film. He knew he had another disaster; he also knew he could do nothing to improve it. He said to his director, 'Cut and score it; just do the best you can.' He had already announced his return to Broadway, so he locked himself in his Beverly Hills home and read countless scripts. By the time his movie was ready to be released, he had mostly forgotten about it. He sold his Beverly Hills house but kept his suite at the Plaza. He liquidated many of his investments and used the money to buy toys for the kids at the Clinique.

He'd bought Summer CDs of the biggest Broadway shows of the past few years. She promised to dance with him on her twenty-first birthday.

"That's a long time from now, sweetie," he said. "Maybe I'll be too old to dance."

"My leg is still in pretty bad shape, but I'm working on it. That's still my main goal."

That was Dr. Jonasson's main goal, too. 'I'm dissatisfied with Summer's progress,' he had told Wade. 'So I want a top orthopedic surgeon from London to fly in for a consultation.'

Dr. Sam Raney accepted that request for help. 'The girl's broken leg has healed improperly. Best thing to do is break it and set it again.'

"Let's do it," said Summer to her father. Simple as that.

She underwent surgery in Zurich; presently she returned to the Clinique, where she greeted everyone with a big smile and two thumbs up. Inspired by her courage, he went back to America determined to produce another Broadway hit. He cleared out his office in Los Angeles, went to Santa Anita and won a pile of money on a few long shots, then flew to New York, moved back into the Plaza and soon found the play he wanted. He called a press conference and said, "I'm back!"

He did a year's worth of work in the next few months, meeting with set designers, actors and directors. He had lunchtime interviews at Sardi's and sat up half the night talking on the Larry King Show. Wade joked that his "comeback" had people so fascinated, it was as if the Beatles had planned a reunion. The media liked him—his gruff charm went over well. He kept Summer apprised of it all; he said,

'This one's your as much as mine, sweetie.' One thing he conveniently failed to tell her was that the new actress he'd cast had moved in with him.

The play opened in autumn to ambivalent notices. Wade ordered revisions; his new girlfriend and roommate lost a couple of her longer scenes, so she stopped speaking to him. The production opened in other cities, where the critics said things like "Nothing new here…" "It doesn't know what it wants to be when it grows up…" and "Dreadfully miscast." The playwright did interviews, saying that Wade had "fixed something that wasn't broken." The actress who'd moved in with Wade said that the playwright deserved a Pulitzer for his work and Wade should be ashamed of himself for tampering with it (she had since moved out of his home and was now shacking up with the playwright).

Wade said, 'I won't close it.' He reduced his actors' salaries and spent hundreds of thousands of dollars on publicity—billboards, bus boards, full-page ads in *Variety*—and did more radio and TV interviews. He flew to Switzerland and told Summer that his play had standing-room-only audiences and would continue forever.

Later that year, after a long and difficult meeting with his accountant, he closed the play and sold off a bundle of stocks at a loss. Still, he flew out to Switzerland with plenty of toys and walked into the Clinique like Mr. Broadway.

Summer walked into the reception room without a limp, and he remembered: To hell with Broadway and Hollywood; his daughter was all that mattered.

At dinner, she said, "Daddy, why did you tell me that your play was a hit?"

"Well, I liked it. I guess it was just too good for the people out there, the masses."

"You invested lots of your own money in it."

"Sure did."

"And you've had three movies die."

He frowned. "Who says?"

"The trade paper."

"I didn't know they read *Variety* here."

"They don't. You forgot your copy after a visit. They gave it to me to give back to you. I read it all. Why did you tell me that your misses were hits?"

He shrugged. "That doesn't seem too important right now. Your doc says you'll be ready to go home in six months."

"Hello?" She leaned across the table and waved at him. "I'm twenty years old now. No longer a teenager or a child. I know how much this clinic costs and that you're not as rich as you used to be. Some of the people here have actually gone home because their families just couldn't afford to keep them here. So—"

"So maybe you should just stay put and keep feeling better and let *me* worry about paying the bills." He added, "Even when the pictures didn't make money, *I* did. I got my cut right away."

"For real?"

"Absolutely," he lied.

Back in Beverly Hills, determined to make a hit movie, he found a property almost immediately written by a guy who'd had successes early on but nothing recently. He contacted and sweet-talked everyone who was anyone in the movie business, but nobody showed any interest. The studios had fired some experienced executives and hired kids who had never heard of Wade Sellars and couldn't have cared less. He gave the screenwriter back his work and thought of maybe writing a bestselling novel himself. After a dozen frustrating attempts at writing fiction, he gave up and flew to New York, where he hoped his name still meant something to showbiz. But the doors he'd once kicked open were now bolted shut. He decided to walk away from all of it. How could his career as a showbiz mover-and-shaker have declined so much so soon? He hadn't changed; maybe the business had. Or maybe the business had stayed the same but *he* had changed. He was in his early fifties now, with his daughter soon to rejoin him, and for the first time in his life, he didn't know what to do or where to go.

Wade sat in the airport lounge and looked with disdain at the airborne gray muck outside that made it impossible for anyone to see anything. His daughter would be flying through that crap to rejoin Daddy. Welcome home, sweetie.

He spotted her right away—tan, tanned, blonde, blue-eyed, sashaying past men and women who stared at her. Presently they started laughing and crying in each other's arms.

"You look terrific!" She linked arms with him and they started walking. "I'm so happy to be home. Wade, what have they done to Times Square?"

"Did you just call me *Wade*? I'm your father."

"You look too young to be called 'Daddy.'"

Outside, she stared in amazement at the car he'd hired. "A Rolls Royce. You're here, I'm here, this is New York. Nothing's changed."

"Oh, everything's changed," he said.

"If you say so. You know what I want? Champagne and caviar. I want to see some Broadway and eat at Sardi's. But first I want to hear about your new hit."

"Huh?"

"Is it a movie or play? I still want to act—can you put me in it?"

"Summer, are you aware that there is more to life than acting and showbiz and hanging out with me?"

"Not for me there isn't."

"You're a very beautiful young single woman. You should be dating, falling in love, getting married and making children."

"Ho hum. You know, this chick has just spent a long time learning to walk and talk again." She squeezed his hand. "Wade, Wade, Wade...I just want us to do all those things together that we'd planned. This is our time."

"Times change. People change. We need to be flexible and adaptable."

"Yeah, whatever."

"As you know, I went to Italy, but not for a movie."

"Then a TV series," she said. "Or maybe you've gotten into popular music. Am I right?"

He sighed and looked out the car's window. "I've done many smart things in life, and I think lately I did one of the smartest things ever. I have some big news for you. I hope you'll be happy with what I have to tell you."

"Wade, I don't like where this is going. I don't want any big surprises tonight. You know what I want? I want you and me at the Plaza, just relaxing and making small talk. I want it to be the way it was before Paris and my accident."

"We'll be staying at the Amsterdam."

"Why not the Plaza?"

"It's all booked up for the next ten years."

"We'll talk tomorrow," he told her once he got her settled into her room at the Amsterdam.

"Why wait? We'll talk now."

"We have all day tomorrow and the days after. Get some sleep. I can see that you're beat."

Summer got up when she heard the key slide into the lock. She could hear a woman's voice.

"Wade, why do I have to sneak in here. I know she's a woman, not a child."

"Beth, she had firm plans as to how to spend her first night back, and this isn't what she had in mind."

Summer then heard nothing and knew that Wade was kissing Beth. She just stood there, unsure of what else to do.

"She and I are having breakfast tomorrow. I'll tell her what's happening," Wade was saying.

They opened the door and threw on the light. Summer stood in the living room in her bathrobe.

"Summer! Why are you up?" Wade asked. "You should be sleeping in."

"I got up to get a drink of water," she said. "Well, I'm here and you're here, so do you want to tell me who she is?"

Beth nodded. "I think that would be a very good idea."

Wade said, "Summer, this is Beth. Beth, this is Summer."

"Oh, you can do better tan that," Beth said.

"Summer," Wade said, "Beth is my wife. We were married a couple of weeks ago."

Summer stood there, her legs wobbly, and heard herself murmuring some sort of congratulations. A few moments later, she excused herself and rushed to the bathroom, where she vomited again and again.

2

Summer lay in bed for many hours, staring into the darkness. She remembered that Beth, whom she had seen occasionally over the years, was Elizabeth Rogers Stainton, one of the world's richest women. Beth liked men, and she liked marrying them, at least for a while. She'd wed one or two industrialists, then a playwright, a fashion designer. The last one had died in a car accident, and Beth said he was the only man she'd truly loved and she would never marry again. But then she'd apparently taken a nice long look at Wade Sellars and said to herself, 'I want *that* one.'

Maybe, Summer thought, I have it the other way around. Wade, broke and clueless as to how to rebuild his fortune, had decided to marry someone who already had too much money. Good for him, then.

She fell asleep at some point, woke up, went back to sleep and finally woke up again, eager to get out of bed. She put on sneakers, Levi's and a sweatshirt and went outside. Summer wandered into Times Square, where she saw family shops and restaurants instead of porn theatres and arcades.

"Summer…!"

She turned around and saw her father.

"I've been waiting around here for the past half hour," he said. "I figured you'd be here. Let's go get some coffee."

They went into a Midtown restaurant, and Wade

said, "Why were you walking around in Times Square? That's still a dangerous place for a young lady. I was worried about you for hours. I must've smoked fifty cigarettes."

"You shouldn't smoke. It's bad for you."

"And *you* shouldn't be all alone in Times Square. When I went into your room and saw that it was empty, I didn't know what to think. Beth calmed me down and we just started to think about where you might have gone. I thought, 'She's probably gone off to Times Square. She's always been fascinated by that place.'"

When she just shrugged, he reached over and placed his hand over hers. "We need to talk about some things."

"So talk."

"I wanted to tell you about Beth—"

"Then why didn't you?"

"Because I didn't think I would actually *marry* her. So we started dating, and all the newspapers made a big thing of it—"the filthy rich widow and her newest beau"—I knew that that clinic in Switzerland gets no news, so you would never find out about it. But I needed to tell you about it anyway, so I thought I'd tell you during the drive from the airport. But you said, 'All I want is some caviar and champagne and the two of us,' so I decided we'd have our little celebration that evening and I would tell you the next morning. Unfortunately, it didn't work out that way."

"When did you fall in love with her?"

He chuckled. "Hasn't happened yet. Probably never will. The only woman I've ever loved is you."

"Then why did you marry her?" she asked in a matter-of-fact voice.

"Because," he told her, "I'm poor and she's rich."

"*What?*"

"My showbiz career has flatlined, sweetie. Nobody on Broadway or Hollywood has any confidence in me because of my three consecutive movie flops. They treat me like I have AIDS or something—actually, the treat the AIDS people better than they treat me. Right around then, the Swiss doctors said, 'We're discharging Summer in September.' Just when I had no way of supporting you. Do you know where I was when Switzerland called me about you? I was living with Claire Tinsall as her gigolo."

"You cast in in a couple of your movies. She's very pretty."

"Yeah. Too bad she can't act. She's got her own top-ten TV show now, probably run for another decade. She makes piles of money, has a big house with plenty of hired help…including me for a while. My job was to work on my tan, keep my muscles firm and be close at hand whenever Claire got horny." He paused. "This is an awful way for a father to speak to his daughter, but I'm pretty much out of options now, so I'm just saying to you, 'Here's how it is—deal with it.' So I'm at Claire's house, lying by her pool, getting a suntan like a nice little rent boy while the servant brings me cocktails and I can sleep sixteen hours per day if I want. I'm thinking that this is a perfectly OK way for a grown man to live, except for the fact that I have about thirty-five cents in my pocket, and that's all the money I have in the world. So I start thinking, 'Is there some way I can hook up with somebody else who won't treat me like a boy toy?' So I go to a premiere with Claire, and I get this idea. I'm her escort for this event, and the Hollywood reporters are polite enough to say, 'Here is actress Claire Tinsall with her date, film and Broadway producer Wade Sellars.' Well, we get to our seats, and she leans over and whistles, 'Wade, I'm so happy you've moved in with me. I would be so lonely without you. Hollywood is so full of faggots and I think you're the only real man left. I'd been celibate for *so* long before we hooked up.'

"Anyway, things sped up a little bit. I got a phone call from Beth. She said, 'I saw you at the premiere. *I* was there, too! Why didn't you come over and say hello? No matter—are you free for lunch?' So I said yes; Claire was out getting her nails done or her boobs fixed, so I let Beth buy me some lunch. She said, 'We should get married because I've done some checking on you and know you're tapped out.'"

Summer made a face. "How did you feel about that?"

He laughed. "Well, sweetie, the shortest distance between two points is a straight line; in other words, sometimes the best thing to do is to ask for what you want. She also said, 'I will never finance any of your movies or plays. Do you still want us to marry?'"

"So you married her. Where and when?"

"London. August. Her people did a good job of keeping it a secret. I'm glad."

"So she's our only source of income?"

"Afraid so."

"At least you're no longer Claire's beefcake boy."

He smiled. "Well, there's that. Beth said, 'Now that we're married, we need to make ourselves look respectable. I'm going to make you the director of one of my companies. Just show up, look good and act important. You'll need to sign some forms to authorize this or that.' Easy enough. I put on a suit, have breakfast, go into the office and shut the door. Then I read *Variety* and *The Hollywood Reporter*. Takes up my whole day."

Summer grimaced. "It sounds awful. What I had in mind was for us to get a Manhattan apartment together. I could get a job to pay our bills."

"Oh? Doing what?"

"Acting, maybe. Or helping with productions, reading scripts."

He shook his head. "Those jobs are hard to get and they pay almost nothing. Plus, that's not the kind of life I want for you."

"What kind of life is that?"

"I want to you to have the very best of everything. And that costs money."

"That's why you married Beth."

"At least now you have a rich stepmother who can give you a wide range of options. Her world is full of people who don't necessarily talk about showbiz. For you, showbiz can be a fun hobby, something you enjoy whenever you feel like it—but it shouldn't be your life and livelihood. Also, you saw that world as Wade Sellars' daughter. I was the boss; I introduced you to the biggest stars who had the best dressing rooms. Those performers had the most talent and luck, and often it was luck more than talent. You didn't see the lesser people with the cramped dressing rooms because I made damn sure I kept you away from that. You grew up around showbiz success, not failure, so naturally you turned to me and said, 'I want to be a showbiz success when I grow up. Make it happen, Daddy!'"

"I loved showbiz because you loved it. Don't deny it."

He shook his head. "I *didn't* love it. I loved going to the racetrack and betting on horses. I loved gambling on a horse or a movie or a play. I loved the money and fame, the applause, the women. You don't think I took you to the theatre every weekend because I loved it and wanted you to love it, do you? I did it because I had nowhere else to put you. Now, don't get upset," he said as he watched her face redden. "I had this little girl to raise and I didn't know anybody I trusted enough to take care of you, so I just took you to work with me. I was a widower with a little kid, and most of the women I knew where chicks I was banging, and they had kids who called me Daddy, just like you. So I raised you that way because it was the most convenient for me. Now I'm asking you to try something different."

"And what's that?"

"Make friends with Beth. Meet her friends; see her world. If you refuse, you will break my heart."

"Then I'll give her a chance."

"She's a great chick. I don't know why she wants me."

"She wants you the same way that Claire Tinsall wanted you. And Christiane Morin, and all the other chicks you meet."

"Sex doesn't mean that much to Beth. I guess she wants companionship, and she just thinks that a woman should be married. She's arranged a dinner party in your honor, so she really wants to have a great relationship with you. Her cousin Stephen will be there as your escort, and it wouldn't be the worst thing if you two got to know each other very well."

"Is Stephen one of the world's richest men?" Summer asked.

"Not even close. Beth's father had the megabucks. He—"

"Died when she was a kid, and her distraught mother committed suicide a year later."

He frowned. "How do you know about her?"

She laughed. "Are you kidding? I went to the New England School for Girls, where the other kids used to say, 'Who's Beth Rogers Stainton going to marry this week?' I just never thought the answer would be, 'My father.'"

He sighed and signaled for the check.

"I'm sorry, Wade. I didn't mean to sound like a bitch. So tell me about Stephen."

"Oh, he's a handsome man in his late twenties. His father was the brother of Beth's father. Stephen is a Rogers, a family with no huge money, but they do just fine anyway. He works as one of Beth's money managers, and his father is a managing partner at one of Manhattan's bigger law firms. Stephen is Beth's principal heir."

"Sounds like a catch," Summer said. "You got yours and I'm getting mine."

"Not funny."

"Yes it is."

"First of all, you and Stephen Rogers aren't exactly engaged yet. I have a feeling he knows he's considered an eligible bachelor and he has some ideas about which woman *he* wants to marry, so it's not like I'm saying, 'Summer, meet Steven—he's yours if you want him.' The truth is, I want you to enter Beth's world and meet a man with breeding and class. I'm sure Stephen has a wide circle of friends. If he doesn't want you, he'll certainly introduce you around and you'll meet a man that way." He paused. "I'd love to see you married, with a child or two or three. What I would hate is for you to become a female Wade Sellars."

"Too late. I'm already you, and I like it."

He snarled. "Why? I'm the worst role model ever. I've never played fair with a woman in my life. But I'm going to do my best with Beth. I'm going to make up for all the times I've treated women like second-class citizens."

Summer smiled. "I'm sure I'll like Stephen Rogers just fine. I'll make eyes at him so that he'll introduce me to all of his overprivileged, snobbish friends. But that means I'll have to wear something very special to this dinner party."

"I can help you with that." He reached into his wallet and withdrew a business card. "Go to the bank and ask for a Miz Colleen Annis. She'll have you sign some documents. They have a trust fun in your name. You have money. You can open a checking account immediately."

"Wade, that's not necess—"

"Relax. It's your money, not Beth's. Your mother put it aside for you, and I put it in trust, which was smart of me because if I'd allowed myself access to it, I'd have spent every dime of it by now." Then, "Look, it's not a fortune, but it's about twenty-five thousand dollars. So go to Bonwit or Bloomie's and get yourself something nice."

They left the restaurant and walked until they reached the Amsterdam Hotel. They stood there for a few minutes.

Summer said, "I wonder if Beth is up there,

watching us."

"Hell no. She took a Seconal before I left. Anyway, she rarely rises before noon." He reached into his pocket and took out a plastic card. "This is your passcard. You're already registered. Always ask at the desk for messages."

She laughed. "No need. You're the only person I know in New York."

3

Summer's bottom was dragging by the time she got back to the Amsterdam. She checked her watch—four o'clock—and she had only one large box. After trying on many outfits, she'd decided upon a black skirt and cream-colored blouse that she knew would be appropriate for Beth's dinner party.

"Miz Sellars?" asked the desk clerk. "You have two messages."

She went upstairs to read them. In her suite she found maids dusting things. She headed for her bedroom to read her messages. Picking up the hotel phone, she dialed the number.

"Miz Runnalls' office."

"Who is this?"

"Her receptionist. Who is *this*?"

"Summer Sellars. I got a message from you."

"Oh, sure. Let me put you through." Presently another voice came on. "Summer! Is that you?" The woman sounded eastern, with perfect diction, like so many of the women in those parts who had gone to the best schools.

"Do I know you?"

"Summer, it's me, Rikia. Rikia Poole."

"You mean from the New England School for Girls?"

"That's me."

"Jeez, Rikia! It's been eons! How did you find me? What are you up to?"

"Well, for starters, I want to know why your father was so nasty to my photographer last night."

"Not sure what you're talking about."

"I sent him out to get a picture of you for our magazine, Summer."

"Which magazine?"

"*In* magazine."

"Oh, do you still work there?"

"I run it now. I'm editor-in-chief."

"Fantastic!"

"Summer, have you been on Planet Fringus or something? I've been on all the radio and TV talk shows plugging the magazine. Have you heard of computers or the Internet? They're becoming very popular, you know."

"Well, I've been in Europe for the past while, just doing my thing…"

"I'm the youngest and best-paid magazine boss in the world. I've done wonders for *In*; for years it was a joke but I've remade it into something people take very seriously."

"Congrats, Rikia. I remember back at the girls' school, we went bananas after you graduated and we saw your name on the masthead—"

"As junior editor." She laughed. "In other words, I was a flunky. Well, I toughed it out, and now I'm the boss."

Rikia suggested doing a story about Wade and Summer, but Summer declined, adding that a leisurely, friendly lunch might be a better idea. They hung up, and Summer took a bath. She fell asleep in the tub and was awakened by a maid.

"Miz Summer, Miz Elizabeth say you gotta dress for dinner."

Summer was already dressed by the time Beth appeared. They stood there for a moment, eyeballing each other. Then Summer extended her hand and said, "Congratulations. I think I forgot to say that last night."

Beth embraced her. "I don't think either of us knew what to say last night." Then she released the girl and held her at arm's length. "You are just too gorgeous. Blonde hair and blue eyes…lovely tan…beautiful dress. But you need some gold." She sent her maid for the jewelry box and weighed down Summer with eighteen-karat-gold neckchains. "That's better," Beth said.

"I'm nervous about meeting Stephen," Summer said.

"Don't be. You two will *adore* each other. Now, I've told everyone that you've been away at the University of Geneva."

"Why?"

"Wade tells me you're fluent in French."

"*Oui—*"

"Then good. There's no point in having anyone know that you were in that awful accident and had a concussion and broken bones. It's time for you to start your new life with some *quality* people. Just forget about your time at that clinic. It didn't happen. Understand?"

"O.K."

"Now, Stephen will arrive a few minutes early. You will come out to meet him when I give you the signal. You must always make an entrance, and you can make only *one* first impression. As I say, you and he will adore each other. Even women who don't like men find him irresistible. Turn on the charm and let him admire your good looks. You seem to have inherited many of your father's finer points. Well, nice for you. You just stay here until it's time to meet Stephen."

4

At just after six in the evening, Stephen Rogers ran home to get dressed. Damn that Beth! Damn her to hell! Whatever she wanted, she got. If he wasn't such a gentleman, he'd punch her in the nose! Well, all he could do was smile and try not to get on Cousin Beth's bad side. She had gotten him that job at Dewey, Cheetham and Howe, and made sure that he personally looked after her vast investments, which really looked after themselves. Damn her, and damn his father for not having a fortune of his own! He admonished himself not to be so hard on the old man. After all, he worked hard and made six figures every year. But with their big townhouse near Central Park and another house in Connecticut, well, there wasn't going to be much for Stephen to inherit. But then, there was no pressing need to worry about money; Cousin Beth had enough to pay everyone's bills for a dozen lifetimes.

Beth's marriage to Wade Sellars had traumatized them all. His mother coped in her own way, with three days of tranquilizers and crying jags. Beth's previous husbands had been harmless enough, but Wade Sellars? He was a tough guy, a Vietnam vet, a movie and Broadway producer, lover of a hundred or more women—in other words, the guy was no fool. Stephen felt anxious about Beth's failure to do what their family called "the old switcheroo." Beth's thing with each fiance had been to go to her lawyer with him, draw up a will leaving millions to her betrothed, then present him with a copy of that will on their wedding day. The day after, she would go back to her lawyer—alone—and get him to do a new one, leaving very little money to her new hubby.

As one of Cousin Beth's money men, Stephen knew that "the old switcheroo" hadn't happened to Wade Sellars—yet. He wondered if Wade had sweet-talked her so much that she'd decided to leave millions to her new husband.

'Stephen,' she had said on the phone, 'did I tell you that Wade has a daughter? She's delightful, and she's flying in from Europe today. Would you mind showing her around? I hate to ask, but I know what a kind person you are and how you're always willing to help in my time of need.'

She hates to ask? Stephen thought. Beth never asks; she figures out what she wants to says, *Get to it! Chop-chop!*

Damn it all to hell. He hated everyone who kept him away from Hana. She was Beth's friend. She was also his lover.

Hana! How many times had he beaten off to a picture of her? He wanted only her. The first girl he screwed had reminded him of her, but from that time, as he grew up, he thought of Hana as an unattainable dream girl while he tried to have fulfilling relationships with women his own age.

But then, nearly a decade ago, he had seen a picture of Beth and Hana together on the beach.

Hana, a woman old enough to be Stephen's mother, was in a skimpy bikini, looking svelte and lovely. He instantly got a boner and wrote to Beth: *Please introduce us!* She ignored his message, but he tried again and again, and finally she replied, *Hana and I are going to the opera in New York. Want to escort us?*

Part of him regretted getting what he wanted. He'd changed clothes many times that day and felt overcome with anxiety as Beth introduced him to Hana. He remembered her firm handshake, her big toothy blonde smile. He felt his penis stiffen as his eyes wandered down to her pushed-up breasts. While not a particularly famous actor, she had been in many movies, and he spent most of the evening in a daze as she made a point of holding hands or linking arms with him. He couldn't understand why Beth was so casual and blasé about being in the company of such a goddess. But then he supposed that when one had as much money as Beth did, everything—and everyone—could be bought and sold. To her, Hana was just another friend to hang out with.

The day after their evening at the opera, he sent Hana flowers and his phone number. She invited him over for a drink. He could feel perspiration streaming down his back as he rang her doorbell.

The door opened, and Hana said, "You're right on time, my under-thirty admirer. Do come in, because I want to make love with you."

Afterwards, as they lay naked together, she said, "Nobody must know about us. Understand?"

"Yes." Hana was in her fifties. Her tummy was tight; her breasts and butt were remarkably firm. She smelled good and kissed him deeply with her tongue. He knew that she had come from Scotland; he'd heard rumors that she was a lesbian. Well, everybody had secrets. He decided to value their time together and not ask too many questions.

"I will call you when I want to be with you," she said. For a while, she did. When she didn't call, he wondered if she'd started menstruation. Then he wondered if women her age still did that.

"She's gone," he said to Beth.

"She does that. She gets bored and flies away."

"Her apartment is mostly bare."

"That's so she'll never feel that she lives there."

"Oh."

He didn't hear from Hana again, and as he prepared for Beth's dinner party, he reminded himself that he and Hana were not meant to be and that Beth still had enough cash to keep them all happy forever.

Damn, I hate you, Stephen thought again as he pressed on Beth's door's buzzer. Her butler opened the door and Wade greeted him. He accepted a martini, kissed Beth's cheek and sat with Wade, waiting for his beautiful daughter to come out so he could get a look at her.

He'd drained his drink and sat there waiting for Beth to offer him another one, and that was when Summer Sellars came out. He stared and stared like an imbecile but couldn't help himself. Damn, she was beyond beautiful! He sat back and closed his eyes for a moment. Summer was drop-dead gorgeous…but she wasn't Hana, the woman with whom he was still deeply in love with.

A few more people arrived, and Stephen observed that Summer and Wade kept observing each other's whereabouts. Occasionally the father and daughter winked or grinned at each other, as if saying, *Are we having fun yet?*

You should be having fun, Stephen thought. You're now Mr. Beth Stainton, and you've managed to keep yourself in her will.

People kept fawning over Summer, lavishing compliments on her. She just smiled, and Stephen concluded that she'd heard all that praise a thousand times already. Maybe she had no use for Beth's friends. Maybe she had no use for Stephen either.

"Summer has been studying abroad," Beth was telling everyone. "I think it's a wonderful thing for an American girl to study overseas; it gives her a perspective she might not otherwise have. Plus, she's been studying languages. Fortunately, she's been privileged enough to devote himself to personal enrichment. Nobody's been saying, 'Summer, personal enrichment is a luxury you can't afford. Now go get a job and bring home a paycheck so you can help feed your family.'"

Not long later, Stephen went up to her and said, "You're my date, right? Let's leave and go somewhere else."

"I don't think I can."

"Oh, I'm sure you can."

"I'm taking her out to meet a few of my friends," he said to Beth and Wade. "Thank you for a lovely evening."

Minutes later, they were in a taxi heading for a place called Ruby's.

The nightclub was packed and the music audible from three blocks away. Stephen seemed to know everyone there. They joined a few of his friends at the bar. Summer danced with a few of them, then with Stephen. He said, "I want to spend the night with you."

Summer wondered if she should be offended by being spoken to that way. But this was Stephen Rogers, a man desired by many women, so she guessed that he just told them what he wanted and they probably put out for him most of the time.

After a few more dances, he said, "Time to go." She nodded, eager to leave. The music had given her a headache. They remained silent on the way to the Amsterdam.

"Thanks for a terrific evening," she said as they stood at the hotel's front entrance.

"We'll have many others." Then he pulled her in close and kissed her long and hard. She felt him trying to force his tongue into her mouth, and she wondered why she didn't enjoy being kissed.

When it became clear to Stephen that he wasn't going to get his tongue into her mouth, he ended their kiss. "We're going to be great together," he murmured. "I just have a feeling about it." Then he got back into the taxi and went away.

When Summer entered her suite, Wade and Beth looked up. "Isn't Stephen wonderful?" Beth asked.

"While you two have your girl talk," Wade said, "I'm going to get a beer. Are you thirsty, Summer?"

"I'm fine, thanks." Summer began unclasping Beth's jewelry. "Thanks so much for lending me your gold, Beth."

"Happy to do it. Now, tell me about your evening. Where did Stephen take you?"

"To Ruby's."

"The most exclusive hangout in town."

"He knows everyone there," Summer said.

Beth nodded. "They're people worth knowing."

Summer went to bed and stared at the wall. Stephen, so tall and handsome, was every woman's dreamboat. She probably shouldn't have been so offended when he said he wanted to go to bed with her. Throughout their evening, he hadn't tried to feel her up or do anything else unacceptable. Most of the time, she forgot that she was no longer an innocent young thing at the New England School for Girls. Wade had changed; so had the rest of the world. She needed to change, too. She would start changing in the morning.

Wade sat on the sofa with a cup of coffee and a copy of the *Daily News* when Summer came into the living room the following morning. He poured her a cup and said, "There's not much breakfast around here. Beth sleeps till she's all slept out, so if you want steak and eggs, you'll have to go down the street."

"It's early," she said. "Why are you up?"

"I was going to ask you the same thing."

She sat and sipped at her coffee. "Wade, we need to talk."

"Isn't that what we're doing?"

"I don't want to live here in this hotel."

"Why not? You got a better deal somewhere else?"

She shook her head. "It's just that, when I came back from Switzerland, this wasn't what I had in mind."

"And what was that?"

"Just you and me in some modest little Manhattan apartment."

He chuckled. "It seems to me that I got you a better deal than that."

"But this isn't just the two of us. That's what I wanted."

He took her hands in his. "Look, sweetie, just give it some more time. We'll have this talk in a month, and if you still want to move out, I'll respect that." Then, "How did you like Stephen?"

She shrugged. "Very handsome."

He arched an eyebrow. "Is that all?"

"Isn't 'very handsome' a good thing?"

"I hope you're going to keep seeing him. I want you to meet a good man, fall in love and live happily ever after. All fathers want that. Of course, when you finally say to me, 'This is the man I'm going to marry,' I'm sure I won't enjoy hearing that. I'll probably say, 'He's not good enough for you.'" He added, "Never mind me. I'm always a grouchy bastard in the morning. So, what do you have going today? Want to have lunch?"

"Wish I could. I need to go shopping today and get some new outfits. Stefan told me where to get my clothes, and later I'm meeting Rikia Poole."

"Never heard of her."

"You met her at the girls' school," Summer said. "She was the star of the school play."

"The homely chick who looked like she was about to wet her pants when I shook her hand?"

"Yes. Well, she's now the editor-in-chief of *In* magazine."

"Oh, *that* rag. That takes care of your day. Beth and I are having people over for cocktails at seven, then we're going out for steaks. Are you seeing Stephen again tonight? How did you like Ruby's?"

She shrugged. "Ruby's was so crowded and the music was so noisy that I couldn't hear myself think."

He smirked. "Maybe that's a good thing." He added, "You know that I think your dating Stephen Rogers isn't the worst thing in the world, but take it nice and slow."

"Wade, I know you want it to work out with Stephen and me. But you've got something else on your mind. Tell me."

"It's just that you're in a very vulnerable place right now. Pierre and the accident, the rehabilitation...then you finally come back here, ready to say to me, 'Let's get an apartment together,' and then finding out I've just gotten married."

"Go on."

"Well, it's nice that you like Stephen Rogers, but this town is full of chicks who are saying, 'I want him.' There's some competition for that guy."

Summer frowned. "Do you know something I don't?"

He shrugged. "Just that I've seen him with Hana a few times, and they looked very chummy. I envied him because, just between you and me, I would dump Beth in two seconds for Hana."

"So he's dating Hana," Summer muttered.

"Beth and I may have inadvertently sent you the message, 'Summer, this is Stephen. He's yours if you want him.' Beth would love it if you married him, but he's no pushover; nobody's going to hurry him. I just don't want you to spend the rest of your life sitting on your butt, waiting for him to call."

Summer let out a bitter little laugh. "I'm not going

to sit on my butt waiting for him—or any other man. What I want is to go into showbiz because that's all I've ever known. I want to act. I've never actually *done* it, but I've watched so many of them who've won Tonys and Obies, and I've thought, 'I'm *sure* I could do that!' I need to work, to feel useful and maybe even fulfilled."

Wade nodded. "Most of the producers and directors I knew best are now in Hollywood. I don't know anyone involved in Off-Broadway. Here's what I can do for you: I'll call the Harris Johnson Agency. It's a terrific talent firm. Tubby Samuels is the vice president in charge of film. He owes me half a dozen favors, so I'll get him to introduce you to whoever handles legitimate theatre for them. I'll call him in an hour."

She smiled. "Sounds good. Maybe you can get me in to see them tomorrow."

"Maybe. In the meantime, you should go out and buy some clothes."

"Great idea."

5

She went to Fifth Avenue and bought everything she wanted—slacks, blouses, skirts, shoes, suits. She had the many boxes delivered to the Amsterdam and thought, *Now I look like the hippest chick in New York.*

In was a place of chic clothes and controlled insanity. The receptionist walked Summer down a long hallway where staffers half-ran with armfuls of documents and other items. At the end of the hallway, the two women stopped at an office whose door bore the name RIKIA POOLE in big block letters. The beautiful woman behind the desk was on the phone, but she waved Summer in. Summer wondered who this woman was and why she'd parked herself in Rikia's chair. Where *was* Rikia.

The woman hung up the phone. "Well, that took forever." Eyeing Summer, she added, "You are gorgeous. I think it helps that you're the daughter of Wade Sellars."

Summer frowned. "I'm sorry, I don't know you. I came to see Rikia Poole."

The woman extended her hand. "Pleased to meet you. Rikia Poole."

Summer burst out laughing. "How can it be you? You've...*changed*."

Rikia smirked. "We haven't seen it each other in ten years. I've lost weight, had my teeth and nose fixed and go to the gym to keep everything where it's supposed to be for as long as possible. Did you really think I was willing to go through the rest of my life looking like that?"

"You look fabulous," Summer said. "Back in school, you had so much charisma and presence that everyone thought you were beautiful."

"I was ugly before ugly became fashionable. So, I can see you're all dressed up. Want to pose for some pictures?"

"No, I just want to sit here and rap."

"All right. I understand you have a stepmother now whose name is Elizabeth Rogers Stainton."

Summer nodded. "True."

"Know what I would love? To do a story on her and your father. Our readers always love getting peeks at the filthy rich, but Beth Rogers Stainton has always said no to us. I'm amazed that the other chick mags haven't approached you yet and said, 'We'd like to something on you. How about Summer Sellars comes of age?' You see, in this business, the stories don't come to you; you have to think them up for yourself, then go out and find the people whose help you'll need to *do* those stories. I work probably sixty-five hours per week, and you want to know why? Because I want *In* to be the publishing phenomenon of the universe."

"Are you dating anyone?"

"I'm shacking up with Hank, my photographer, who's really an actor. Photography, acting—he's quite good at both. Trouble is, the poor dude just can't seem to get the break he needs."

"Back at the girls' school, I thought you would become a Broadway star by age twenty-five. When they did those plays, you really owned the stage. The audience couldn't take its eyes off you."

Rikia shrugged. "Hey, I did my best. I was dumb to get that rhinoplasty because it made me look like just another cute chick; before the surgery, at least my face had some character. I also did that 'starving artist' thing—auditioning during the day and working at Denny's or HoJo's at night and eating and sleeping once in a while—but then one day I saw this actress chick applying at HoJo's and she was, like, in her thirties! I thought, 'Phooey on this nonsense; I'm not going to spend the next decade of *my* life struggling to get occasional acting jobs.' That was when I started having more realistic goals and got a job at *In*. The mag was dying, but I said, 'I have a dozen great ideas on how to save it.' Trouble was, everyone said, 'Who the hell are you? You're just a flunky. Shut up and fetch me some coffee.' That went on for a couple of years until someone whispered, 'The big bosses are closing us down.' So I thought, 'Here's my chance,' and went to Hamish Johns, who was chairman of the board of the group that owns *In* and a bunch of other things. I ran down for him what I knew the mag needed: 'We need to start going after the working girl, the housewife, the younger woman; and why are we trying to compete with *Vogue* when it comes to high fashion? Let's go after ads for new bras and panties; let's run stories that don't have conventionally happy endings; we can print articles about couples whose marriages have ended despite help from counselors and shrinks. If you want *In* to survive, we'll need to go in new directions and try new things.' He just sighed and said, 'OK, we'll do things your way and see if you can save this magazine. Your new title will be Editor of Special Subjects, just so there's no confusion about how much power you'll have; if you believe in something, we'll do it.' Within a year we had doubled our readership and I became editor-in-chief. We've covered abortion, gay marriage, medical marijuana and many other touchy topics. But if I want to keep the party going, I have to think up new stuff all the time. So I'm sitting here, thinking, 'If I can't get Elizabeth Rogers Stainton, I'd like to get her stepdaughter, Summer Sellars.' What I have in mind is, 'Summer is not a season; she is the girl with everything.'"

Summer shook her head. "Absolutely not."

"Then why are we having this conversation?"

"Because, well, we've known each other since…and I'm back in town after all that time in Europe…and I don't know anyone else here."

Rikia smirked. "Poor little rich girl? Please. That was your stepmommy's trip. Or it was till she married your dad. He must be the lay of the land. When he and I met that time at the girls' school, I nearly came in my pants."

Summer got up to leave. Rikia pulled her back down. "Lighten up. You're back in town and you're lonely, huh? Welcome to the human race. If I didn't have a live-in boyfriend to scratch my itch every night, my right hand would have fallen off long ago. If you can fall asleep in a man's arms and wake up with him still there with you, you've got something. So my thing is, I've got something with Hank, and if I can get him to take pictures of you for *In*, that would be a great career boost for him, and he would take photography more seriously. That way, I wouldn't have to worry about his leaving me to go off with some theatrical road company." As she spoke, her face changed, and Summer could see the exuberant, needy little girl from the girls' school. All the cosmetic surgery in the world couldn't change that, she supposed.

"Rikia," Summer asked, "if you and Hank are so deeply in love, why don't you get married?"

"Because I don't believe in marriage or most of the other institutions I've grown up around." She lifted her chin and instantly became the editor-in-chief of *In* again.

Just then a man entered the room. He had longish dark hair, wore a Yankees cap, an Army jacket and tattered Levi's. Summer knew he had to be Rikia's photographer/lover. Only such a person could walk around that place so poorly dressed.

"Hank," Rikia said, "this is Summer. She said no."

"Hard luck." To Summer he said, "I could use the scratch, and boss lady here tosses and turns all the night if the magazine has a bad month."

Summer watched Rikia shoot him a dirty look, and she sensed that Rikia desperately needed this story, and that it might improve things between this couple.

"Rikia, why don't I call my father?" she said.

"Why?" Rikia sat glowering at Hank.

"About the story you want to do."

"I thought the answer was no."

"I'll talk him into it. He knows better than to refuse to give me what I want."

Rikia smiled. "Then do it! Use my phone."

Summer dialed the usual numbers but could not locate Wade. Finally she tried the gym where he often exercised. He came to the phone. "I hope this is important."

"Wade, I'm at *In* magazine. Rikia wants to do a story on me. OK with you?"

"Yeah—as long as it's about *you*. That magazine has been after Beth for years, so maybe they're trying to get to her through you. Just be sure you get to approve the story before they print it."

"I hear you."

"Good. Also, I got you an appointment with Tubby Samuels at the Harris Johnson Agency at ten tomorrow."

"Thank you, thank you, thank you."

"You're welcome, sweetie."

Click.

Summer said "Here's what my father wants…" and ran it down for her.

Rikia said, "I can work with that. I'll have a letter written immediately giving you copy approval. I'll give the story to Renée Kulis. Hank, let's do the photos *tout de suite*." She pushed the intercom button and said, "Paula, come in here and takes some notes." She pushed another button. "Elaine, hold all calls unless it's someone I really need to talk to, and I think you know who those people are. Also, I'm going to need Noel to show me his new artwork before I leave town. Yeah, that's all." At that moment a tiny, homely young woman stepped into the room.

"Have a seat, Paula. This is Summer Sellars. Summer, Paula is a wizard at shorthand. I'll ask the questions because I know how the story should flow.

Then, after we've got a bunch of answers to those questions, I'll hook you up with Renée.

Hank had finished loading his camera and began snapping away at Summer. His lights hurt her eyes. She wondered why they had to do this annoying stuff *now*.

Rikia smiled at her like a child who was getting what she wanted but was only halfway through. "Now, Summer, where did you go after the New England School for Girls?"

"To Switzerland."

"To which college?"

Summer couldn't remember what Beth had told her. "I don't wan to talk about the girls' school, Europe or college. Couldn't we just deal with what I'm doing back here in New York? I'm here and I need a job."

Rikia guffawed. "Your father just married the richest woman in town and you're looking for work?"

"Sad but true."

"Then come work for *me*."

Hank started snapping pictures just inches from Summer's face, and she shot him a look. "Please just keep talking to Rikia," he said. "Do your best to pretend I'm not here. It looks more natural that way."

"Work for me as a junior editor. All of our reader know damn well who Wade Sellars is, and I'm sure they know that you're his daughter. They would love to see your name on our masthead. Don't worry—I would never let Summer Sellars be a flunky or anything. I'd pay you decent money you certainly don't need. You would show up, look good and act important. I'd get you to write the occasional story."

"But I've never written for any publication. I'm

not sure I could—"

Rikia waved her off. "All you'd have to do is draw up a list of questions, do the interviews and give your notes to me. I'd have one of my staff writers compose the actual story."

"I have no degree, no practical experience, no nothing. Why hire me?"

"Because you're Summer Sellars and your father is Wade Sellars, who knows everyone worth knowing. Look, last year Michael Jackson was in town and we had no way of interviewing him because we had no access to him. Your father may be retired, but he could probably make a phone call and get us in to see the King of Pop. As for you, we want you to do stories on the up-and-coming actors who are beautiful. Plus, your stepmother knows the amazing Hana. Wow! If we could do a story on her, the actress who doesn't do interviews!"

"Good luck with Hana," Hank said.

"Or maybe Summer is at a party with Hana and overhears that sexy screen legend say something that's worth printing…"

"Summer," said Hank, "I've got lots of pictures of you frowning and pouting. Please switch to a different emotion."

She stood up and moved to a corner of the office. "This is just too weird. I come by to visit an old friend, and what happens? She calls in her photographer to take pictures of her magazine, then she says, 'I'll hire you because you have a father who can get us access to A-list stars.' Not gonna happen."

Rikia asked, "You've said you want to work. What kind of work do you want to do?"

Summer placed her hands on her hips. "I want to

act."

"Surprise," Rikia muttered.

"Can you act, sing or dance?" Hank asked her.

"I don't know. I've never tried. But I'm great at listening and looking and, you know, observing."

Hank snapped some more pictures of her. "I have a photo session with Roman Nabokov, a big director. I'll take you with me so he can get a look at you and tell you if you're wasting your time."

When they left the office, Hank said, "There's this thing in New York for unemployed actors. It's called the subway. Ever heard of it?"

"Vaguely," replied Summer.

"Well, poor little rich girl, it's time you checked it out."

They rode the train downtown and Summer decided that riding in a limousine was much better. They walked a couple of blocks to a grimy building and climbed a few flights of stairs. "Roman keeps his office here," said Hank. "He doesn't care about luxury because he lives in his head." They both stopped to rest a couple of times before reaching Roman's door. Hank knocked a couple of times and a deep, resonant voice called out, "It's unlocked."

Summer then met Roman Nabokov, a skinny little man who needed a shave and haircut. He wore soiled jeans and a red sweatshirt.

"Hank, who's she?" he asked, by way of a greeting.

"Summer Sellars." Hank starting taking pictures again of Summer, who eyeballed the loft as if looking for an escape hatch.

"You still looking to act on Broadway?" Roman asked Hank.

"Always."

"Broadway is nowhere," Roman told him. "Off-Broadway exists for a reason. It's for artists to present their true visions. Broadway? That's for ass-kissing sellouts who just want to make money and win Tonys. Off-Broadway has *integrity*."

"You got a part for me? I'll take it. I'm an actor. I need to act. Photography is what I do to pay my bills."

"You still shackin' up with the *In* boss?"

"Sure am. Why wouldn't I be?"

"Well, I'm under the impression that she's your vocational counselor as well as your main squeeze. You've turned me down before, and I thought it was because your old lady said, 'Roman's Off-Broadway, and you're too good for that. If he offers you something, say no.' So now you're telling me, 'Roman, I want to work for you. If you have something for me, I'll take it.' What's the deal?"

Hank checked his light meter and reloaded his camera. "Frankly, I wanted to work for Andrew Lloyd Webber, but that isn't going to happen. Consider you and me a done deal. When do rehearsals start?"

"Next Monday or Tuesday. You won't be the star of the show, so you'll have relatively few lines to learn. You could probably call it in."

"I'll be there." Click, click, click.

"Why all the pictures?" Roman asked. "Who *is* she anyway?"

"We're putting her in the mag. She's Wade Sellars' daughter." He added, "She acts, too. Do you know anyone who knows anyone who wants to cast a tall, blue-eyed blonde about twenty years old?"

Roman frowned at her. "Can you act? Are you

any good?"

Summer shrugged. "I think so."

"You know something? One of my supporting players is leaving me and I haven't yet found a replacement. I was thinking of calling Kia Lizandos but she probably wouldn't want the gig. It pays chump change. By the way, do you have an Equity card?"

"No, not yet."

He smiled. "Perfect. Go with Hank and see the play tonight. Pay close attention to the part played by Davida Irmas. I'll need you to read for me tomorrow." He tossed a copy of the play to Hank and said, "Kill it, dude."

Back on the street, Summer whirled around and said, "Hank, did he mean that? Will I really have an Off-Broadway acting job right away? How terrific!"

Hank looked up. "Got some weather happening. It'll rain hard for a few minutes, then stop. Let's duck inside somewhere and get a sandwich and a cup of coffee. We can kill time before going to the theatre. You need to call home to tell them you won't be there for dinner?"

"No, they probably won't notice my absence."

They entered a restaurant and sat down. After a few moments of watching fat pellets of rain pound the Manhattan sidewalk, they ordered cheeseburgers and coffee. Hank took out his Olympus and took a few more pictures of Summer.

"Rikia says you're a pretty good photographer," she said.

"I'm as good as I need to be."

"She says you have the potential to be the very best."

"I'd rather be a mediocre actor than an elite photographer," he retorted.

"Oh."

"Rikia makes six figures. She pays me decently. But I'm interested in any more of her handouts."

"But she says you're good. *Very* good."

"She meant I was good in the sack."

Her face reddened as she busied herself with her cheeseburger. He told her about his acting career—summer stock, Off-Broadway, a commercial that kept him in residuals for the longest time. "But that's all gone now. Everyone says I have looks and talent, but that's worthless without luck, and I seem to be a very unlucky actor. As for photography, I have no intention of breaking my balls to become a world-class picture-taker. It just doesn't interest me that much."

They are in silence. As they finished up, Summer said, "You were right—the rain stopped."

"We'd better get going. I'll pay this time."

Back on the street, everything was wet and some of the more annoying smells had been washed away. Summer, sensing Hank's ambivalence about Rikia, tried to think of something good to say about her old friend. She thought Hank was handsome in a granola kind of way, and she suspected that his relationship with Rikia would improve if his acting career got a major boost. Wade Sellars had always said that he felt best about his life in general whenever his career was going well.

It started to rain, so the two broke into half-runs. He pulled her into a storefront and said, "Whew! We made it."

Summer looked around. "Where's the theatre?"

"I'll show you." He walked her through the store, which was vacant but for a couple of benches and a table stocked with Kool Aid and chocolate-chip cookies. He pointed to the snacks and said, "That stuff is called 'intermission refreshments, Off-Broadway style.' A girl stood behind a rickety ticket box. She waved and smiled at Hank; he returned the greeting as he took Summer into a long, narrow room filled with aging folding chairs facing a stage without a curtain.

"Is this…*it*?" Summer asked.

Hank nodded. "It's called 'theatre without an ego.' This used to be a store. Someone came along and converted it into a playhouse. The dressing rooms are upstairs, and Roman keeps a room on the third floor for homeless actors. You know that myth of the starving artist? It's not a myth, especially for actors. Unless you're getting checks from home, poverty and starvation are always imminent concerns." He turned and looked at her. "You still want to act?"

"We'll see."

By ten minutes to eight, the house was packed. Someone brought in extra chairs and they, too, were occupied till virtually every inch of space was taken up by the audience. Summer noticed that no one complained; they sat packed together, practically on top of one another smiling and talking as if they'd known each other for years.

"Quite a hit they've got here," Summer said.

Hank shrugged. "Roman's plays always get attention. Everybody is asking, 'What's Nabokov's latest play about?' Even the Broadway big shots come down here sometimes. Roman's so unconventional, you never know what he's going to do."

The house lights went down and the entire cast came on stage. Then all but three exited. Those remaining—three women---were dressed to honor America: One wore in red, the second in white and the third in blue.

"That girl in red," Hank whispered to Summer, "is the one you'll replace. Those girls are the past, present and future of America. They remain on stage throughout the performance."

The three girls chanted some stuff, and then a man appeared. He said some things Summer scarcely understood. Then another man entered, and the two men stared at each other for the longest time— Summer swore they were checking out each other like a couple of guys at a gay nightclub—before the stage filled with artificial smoke.

When the smoke cleared, the two men, and the patriotic girls—were naked. The two men began having simulated sex as the girls sang songs Summer didn't know.

"I gotta go," she blurted to Hank as the house lights went up for intermission. She marched up the aisle but he caught up with her.

"You can't go yet. Your big scene is coming up."

"Really? Who will I be screwing?"

"Oh, is that your problem? Did you get freaked out by the nudity?"

"Yeah; didn't you?"

"Look, the theme of this play is AIDS in America. Kind of hard to do such a play without nudity or sex."

She walked fast and hurried through the lobby, where people were lining up to pay three dollars for two chocolate-chip cookies and a cup of Kool Aid.

Out on the street, Hank grabbed her arm and said, "I'm not that thrilled with sex and nudity on stage either. Besides, I'm very straight, so I it would be a real challenge for me to get naked and physical with another guy. It would be a real challenge for Rikia to see me on stage with another guy, too."

"So you can empathize with me when I say that there's no way I'm going to do that play," she said.

"But you saw how popular it's becoming, and it's a *Roman Nabokov* play. It would be a great thing for my career as an actor. As I've said so many times, I would rather be a decent actor than a first-rate photographer."

She shook her head and strode away.

"Yeah!" he shouted. "That's it! Poor little rich girl! Go run home to the Amsterdam and cry to your daddy who's pimped himself out to Miz Beth! Fuck her, fuck him and fuck you, too!" He darted back into the theatre. She stood on the sidewalk, frowning; he had sounded close to tears. She wanted to go up to him and say she respected his feelings, she wasn't mad at him…but he had gone. People were shuffling back into the theatre. She didn't know its name—did it *have* a name? Looking this way and that, she could not locate a taxi; wrong part of town for that. In front of the theatre, some limousines sat parked. Summer, who knew a few things about such cars, checked out their license plates' configurations and figured out that they were rentals. She walked up to one and said to its driver and said, "The play won't end for another hour. Could I hire you—"

"I don't think so." He turned up his radio.

She swallowed hard. Reaching into her bag, she

pulled out a fifty-dollar bill and went to the next limo.

"Excuse me, sir. Would you take me home?" She held up the money.

"Where do you live?" he asked, licking his lips at the bill.

"At the Amsterdam."

He reached up and plucked the banknote out of her hand. "Get in."

As they crept north, he said, "What's the deal? Your boyfriend acted like a jerk or the play was boring?"

"Something like that."

"All the big wheels are coming down to see that show. What's so special about that play?"

"The guy who wrote it. Nabokov. Everyone thinks he's a genius."

"Years ago, I wanted to be a performer on Broadway. I'm a lifelong New Yorker, so the big time was always just a few minutes away. But then I got married and had kids. I'm too normal and sane for showbiz, anyway."

By and by they reached the Amsterdam. Summer hustled out of the car and into the hotel's lobby. On the elevator ride up, she told herself, *I don't want Off-Broadway. I want to starve and sleep on the grimy floor. I want to be applauded by thousands and make Wade and Stephen proud of me. I want to act in front of clean, beautiful people in a lovely, sparkling Broadway playhouse. I want to be more than just Beth's new stepdaughter or Wade Sellars' child—I want to be Summer Sellars, Broadway star.*

6

After giving her a big hug even though they had never met, Tubby Samuels asked, "How's your dad? He was smart to retire; wish I was that smart myself. You should meet a nice fella, get married and forget about this showbiz stuff. But since you're here, I'll see what I can do for you."

He walked her down the hallway and introduced her to a fresh-faced young fellow who looked to Summer like a high-school sophomore. The youngster had a large office and a bulky desk. On his desk sat a multiline telephone, and each time a call came in, his elderly secretary would holler, "Mr. Tyler, line two is from the Coast. Please answer it." He would holler back, "Lighten up, Joanne," and roll his eyes at Summer as he took the call and spoke in arcane showbiz jargon that flew right over Summer's head.

When not on the phone, he managed to set up a few appointments for her. "I know of two shows that are being cast right now. You're too tall for one of them, but maybe go there anyway and let them get a look at you. The other thing is a musical. Can you act, sing and dance? No? Well, I'll send you out there anyway. You're gorgeous, and that means a lot. Even if you can't sing, they may have average-looking chicks in the cast who can sing and drown you out. If that doesn't work out, at least you'll get to meet you, and the heavies—the guys in charge—will probably remember you if something else comes up. I'm going to give you a list of producers to visit just so they'll know you exist. Also, I know one of the Amsterdam agencies is about to shoot a commercial. That's not my thing, but it's a lead you should pursue."

"Thank you so much!" Summer beamed as she stood up and shook his hand.

"Don't thank me, thank Tubby! He asked me to help you. Gotta love Tubs! Gotta love him! He tells me that your father was one of the heavies in this town. Well, let's hope you make it big and make your dad proud. That's one of your goals, right? To have you dad point at you and say, 'That's my girl!' Check in with me once a week. Make sure you leave your phone number with Joanne." Then he went back to his telephone and frantic secretary as she left his office.

Summer made a top priority of following all the leads Tyler had given her. One was for a play; she'd cleared her throat repeatedly while stumbling through her lines; they'd sent her away with, 'Thanks for coming in.' At the Madison Avenue ad agency, she discovered a few dozen girls competing for a cigarette commercial. The client was launching a new brand or trying to make an old brand attractive to young women—she wasn't sure which. They asked if she smoked; she said she'd never even tried it. They ordered her to buy a pack, learn to smoke and return in a couple of days. She did as told, lit one up in her bathroom, felt dizzy and nauseous. She took a second drag, felt even worse and vomited into her toilet.

Then Stephen called. "What are you doing?"

"Smoking."

He laughed. "Why?"

"For a TV commercial. They said I have to inhale."

"Well, don't inhale. Just pull it in a little and blow it out. It will look like you're inhaling. No use rotting your lungs with cancer sticks. After you're done with the commercial, don't ever smoke again."

They made a date for the following evening, and Rikia called to tell her to be at a producer's office at ten the next morning. But when she arrived at the office, she said, "Mr. Tyler sent me."

The producer shook his head. "Why does Tyler do these things? You're all wrong for the part. Tyler thinks he's doing you a favor by sending you everywhere, but he's just wasting everyone's time."

"Make love with me tonight," said Stephen as they sat in the restaurant. The place was packed, but he knew the manager, so they were seated right away.

"Excuse me? What do you mean?"

"Just what I said. Come home with me."

"Why not come back with me to the Amsterdam?"

"Because your, uh, roomies might be there."

They got a taxi. Summer told the driver, "I'm going to the Amsterdam."

Stephen frowned.

"It's not that I don't like you," she whispered to him as she climbed out of the car. "We just don't know each other that well yet."

She crawled into bed and turned on the radio to a music station. She liked Stephen—or at least she thought she *could*, if only he wasn't so smug and full of himself. But she wanted to keep seeing him because she was starting to feel so lonely.

She felt as if she'd been asleep for maybe fifteen minutes when her telephone rang.

"Up and at 'em!" Rikia said.

"What time is it?"

"About seven-thirty."

"I've got blackout curtains. Feels like midnight."

"Well, it's not. Summer, I need to see you *tout de suite.*"

"Is it about the story?"

"Hell yes! Let's have dinner tonight."

"Fine," said Summer.

"Where," Rikia asked, "is Anya Semko?"

"On the phone with someone in London," replied one of her flunkies. "She's got this idea that the Nancy Boys aren't really British."

"Nonsense. They're one of the U.K.'s biggest exports since U2."

"She says she has a hunch he's from Detroit."

"Whatever. Send her in when she's done."

Summer, who had been sitting on the sofa, said, "I've heard Anya Semko is difficult."

"That she is. We'll make this brief."

Presently a woman well over six feet tall ambled into the room. She pulled a handful of frizzy, dishwater-blonde hair out of her eyes and pumped

Summer's hand. Then the big woman reached into her well-used denim handbag and pulled out a tattered notepad. She sat down, asked Summer a few questions and scribbled away. Anya seemed amazed that Summer's parents had named her for a season. After a few more questions, she got up and stalked out of the room.

"I wouldn't want to punch it out with her," Rikia said. "On the other hand, *she's* the one I would want on the premises if anyone started getting an attitude with me and threatened me with violence. Her father was a good newswriter and she's learned plenty from him. She loves attacking people in print. She's a little disappointed that this piece on you will be 'up,' not 'down.'"

"Why does she love attacking people?"

"Well, when you're as ugly as she is, you have a big grudge against the world."

Summer smirked. "But *In* keeps saying that ugly is the new pretty."

"Not in her case. Anyway, don't sweat a thing. You will have complete approval of the story, and I had our lawyer write something saying that we'll keep your father and stepmother out of our story." Then, "You didn't get that cigarette commercial, right?"

Summer shrugged. "There'll be others."

"But you're pretty bummed out about it."

"Why should I be bummed out? I have a terrific life. I'm here the greatest city in the world. My father is here. I have a generous stepmother and a beautiful room at the Amsterdam…"

"Blah, blah, blah."

Summer narrowed her eyes. "Excuse me?"

"You heard me. You hate living in that hotel, and

you hate the fact that your father married Elizabeth Rogers Stainton. When you got back here from Switzerland, that was exactly what you *didn't* want—to hear your father say, 'Welcome home! I'm broke, but guess what? I've married Beth, so you and I will be rooming with her at the Amsterdam for the foreseeable future.'"

Summer sighed. "I *am* ambivalent about our arrangement. It's her apartment. I want my own place."

"Then move out."

"He says, 'Stay as long as you like. Stay here as a favor to me.'"

"Do you always do as he says?"

"Most of the time, yes." She added, "My mother died when I was young, so in my early years it was just me and him. I liked that just fine. Trouble is, he's the only man I've ever been able to relate to. I don't know how to date. Mainly, I don't know what I want from life right now."

"Sounds like someone needs a shrink."

"No thanks. I had enough psychotherapy in Switzerland."

"Then *I'll* be your shrink for the next five minutes. Your father is a handsome, charming man— *I'd* like to hang out with him, too. If you're looking for a younger version of Wade Sellars, that would be Stephen Rogers. One of my people saw you and Stephen at Ruby's not long ago. I don't like that phony nightlife scene, but Ruby's is the most exclusive place in Manhattan, and if you're going to do hang out with the beautiful people, Stephen is the man you want on your arm."

"I went out with him last night. He asked me to

go to bed with him. I wouldn't, so he didn't even try to kiss me goodnight."

Rikia stood up. "Time for a drink. Let's go to Peggy's. It's not far."

Summer like Peggy's. The restaurant had a warm environment, and their server told Summer she was a beautiful girl who surely would become a star soon. Summer ordered a glass of Chardonnay and Rikia a double martini. They sat in silence for a few moments.

"So," Rikia said, swallowing a mouthful of gin and vermouth, "what did you think of Hank?"

"Nice enough guy."

"Have you seen him since the play?"

"Nope. Was I supposed to?"

Rikia snarled. "Well, I live with him, and *I* haven't seen him lately, so I was wondering if *you* had."

Summer shook her head. "No, ma'am. Haven't seen the guy."

"Just be straight with me: Did he hit on you?"

"Oh, please—"

"Well, didn't he?"

"No way. We went to the play and—"

"Yes?"

"I left. I got freaked out by Nabokov's play. Hank seemed to find it very profound. He went back inside to watch the rest of it. He said it was this symbolic thing about AIDS in America—"

"I didn't like it either. I went down there to check it out myself. Hank was there but he didn't see me. I got weirded out by seeing a couple of naked guys make out. I'm tolerant enough, but there is a limit. I also like plays where I'm able to understand what's going on. I don't like plays where I ask, 'What's it about?' and they say, 'It's whatever you want it to be about' or 'Figure it out for yourself.'"

"Do you see a future for yourself and Hank?"

"You want to know his big issue with me? It's that I went to work at that rag called *In* and said, 'It's broken; let me fix it.' So, as a reward, I make six figures per year. I pay four figures per month for my apartment, but it's big and comfy and in a good neighborhood. Do you want to know something? I sometimes work eighty hours per week to make *In* the best mag possible. For that kind of effort, I think I deserve a comfortable lifestyle. But there's Hank, whose main message seems to be, 'I'd rather be a starving artist than a sellout like you!'"

"Really? Isn't he happy about your success?"

"Never. He admires people who have taken vows of poverty and are contemptuous of those who have made it and are enjoying themselves. I wish we could work out a compromise. All I can really say is that I want him, adore him and love him."

"At least you know who you are and what you want," Summer said.

"Beth said you went to some Swiss university. Didn't they teach you any life skills?"

"If they did, I've already forgotten them."

They sat and lingered over homemade pecan pie and coffee as Summer told Rikia about her time recuperating in Switzerland.

"That's tragic," Rikia murmured. "To get busted up like that, thrown off the bike. Then all that time in rehab, and finally flying home to Daddy, only to hear him say, 'There have been a few changes. I know you wanted us to shack up in a Manhattan apartment, but I don't think like that.'"

"'Shacking up'? Rikia, it wasn't like that."

"Oh, but it was. That guy Pierre who crashed his bike? And Stephen Rogers? You didn't go to bed with those two gorgeous men because to you it would have been too much like cheating on you-know-who."

"Ridiculous," said Summer with a shake of her head.

"Not at all. You want to know the secret to happiness for Summer Sellars? Move out of the Amsterdam."

"That's one of my top priorities."

"Then do it. Living in that hotel room with Beth and Wade is the worst thing in the world for you. You won't grow up and have satisfying relationships with men until you get your own pad and start living as an adult." She paused. "As for your aspirations for a career as an actor, I'm not the one to give you any advice…"

"Look, I'm not Hank. He's totally obsessed with acting, and that's just not me. Besides, I'm sort of under the impression that I have very little talent. So many people think that everyone can act, or learn to, but I know that isn't true. It takes training and dedication that I lack. Still, I do want to work and live as a normal person."

"I can always make room for one more at *In*," said Rikia.

"Thanks, but I really don't want to be an office flunky."

"Already got enough of those. I would expect you to work."

"Tell me more."

"I would imagine you'd enjoy working for me, here, than going to auditions and getting turned down and taking acting classes from a bunch of temperamental, aging actors. If you're ambivalent about acting now, you'd grow to hate it soon enough. Only thing about working for me is, I couldn't pay you much at first."

"Not a problem. I'm not rich, but I'm not poor. Plus, I have a stepmother who is eager to buy my affection. I'm going to move out of the Amsterdam."

Rikia frowned. "I think I can help you with that. There's a guy in my building named Bart Edgars. He teaches Faggotry one-oh-one at Columbia and he's going to Europe for a year. He said to me, 'You know of anyone who would want to sublet my suite?' It's really puny—just a studio—and his rent is chump change because he's been in it for so long. Want me to find out if it's still available?"

"Please do. In fact, its not terribly late now. Let's go visit him."

Barton Edgars beamed at Summer as they shook hands. He showed her his antique furniture and Murphy bed, his spacious walk-in closet and kitchen with a window.

"Isn't it all just too *marvelous*? I really *hate* to leave it."

Summer agreed with him and the three of them sipped sherry in celebration of the girl's new, albeit temporary, home.

"Well," Rikia said, "at least now we've gotten you out of the Amsterdam."

7

Summer sat up on the Murphy bed, reading through a stack of back issues of *In* magazine. She had received her first assignment, *Hollywood North*, an article about Vancouver, Canada, a city that recently had become very fashionable as a location for Los Angeles filmmakers due to the weak Canadian dollar and Vancouver's relative closeness to Los Angeles. Also, that Canadian city had many homes and neighborhoods that rich American movie people found irresistible and affordable. She called a realtor in Vancouver and got a couple of decent quotes, then went online to gather more information on Vancouver's appeal as a filmmaking hub and second home to California showbiz folks.

After perusing articles from a variety of all the current articles in leading print and online magazines, Sumner observed that those stories she liked most and paid most attention to had strong first paragraphs that got her attention right away. She had tried a dozen approaches, but all seemed wrong. Naturally, she assumed that Rikia would get a staff writer to revise it, but Sumner wanted to send her friend the message, *I don't need a rewriter; I can do this thing without anyone's help.* Working on the magazine had given her a true sense of purpose for the first time in her life. Her minuscule excuse for an office was *hers* and nobody else's. The puny apartment she sublet was *her* pad; her paychecks went towards her rent.

Her past few weeks had been difficult but rewarding. Three weeks of being her own woman and making her own decisions. The first week had been the worst. Telling Wade and Beth that she was moving out. Beth had glowered a bit, but before she could say anything, Wade said, "I knew this day was coming. People your age all want their own places to live. I hope you'll be happy in your new home."

Beth said, "I want to check it out before you commit yourself to moving in." Barton Edgars looked about ready to faint when Beth and Summer entered the apartment. "Why, Ms. Stainton—I mean Sellars— I didn't *know* that Summer was your daughter!" Summer could tell that Barton was ready to kick himself for settling on such a half-decent rent.

"Where's the rest of it?" Beth asked.

Barton threw out his arms. "It has only one room. But it's a big room, and I'm pleased that Summer will be living here among my precious things."

Beth shook her head and walked past him. She drew the drapes. "Ugh! No view, Summer!"

Barton thrust out his chest. "There is a beautiful garden out there to look at."

"No sunlight and only one room. Well, I guess you young people would say, 'Less is more.' If you want to leave a luxury apartment for a slum, I can't stop you."

Barton's face went red. "Mrs. Sellars, this is as fine a building as you will find in Manhattan."

"We could make it a bit more comfy," said Beth. "Get rid of those drapes—"

"Absolutely not! I had them custom made!

Nothing must be removed!"

Beth headed for the kitchen, and Summer said to Barton, "Don't worry, I won't change anything."

She had moved in on the first day of October; her father brought over a bottle of champagne, which they drank over ice. Wade looked around, nodding and smiling. "You've made a good choice, Summer. A young lady needs her own space. After all these years of living with the old man, you need a home to call your own...even if it really belongs to someone else."

Beth came by at seven to collect him. They were going to an exhibition of some kind at the Museum of Modern Art, the sort of thing that Summer knew her father loathed. Beth brought her a basket of cocktail *hors d'oeuvres*. "They're yummier than you think. Smoked oysters to be eaten with these little crackers. Stephen adores the. By the way, how are you two getting along?"

She shrugged.

Beth smiled. "Wade and I are flying to London for a few days for a chess tournament I'm entering. We'll be back as soon as possible, but I still don't like your awful little apartment and wish there was something we could do for you—aside from giving you a quote, 'No, I don't own a house in Vancouver—yet.'"

Summer swallowed. "Is...Hana here?"

Beth frowned. "Why?"

"Because I'd love to interview her for *In*."

Beth's face hardened. "She never does interviews. It's not like she's trying to be reclusive, either; she just doesn't want to sit there and answer questions about her personal life. She's a dumb broad from overseas who can barely spell her own name. She never votes and she never thinks about anything except her own well-being. Yes, she is in town, and she called me the other day, but I've just been too busy to hook up with her. I really can't take Hana for more than fifteen minutes at a time. I mean, who is she, anyway? Just some aging actress who, for some reason, continues to attract the interest of everyone."

Well, Summer thought, *I guess I won't be getting my interview with Hana. Rikia won't be happy about that.*

Steven called to say he would be going away for several days. After a week and a half, she still had not heard from him. She went out to dinner with Rikia and some of the ladies from the office, but mostly she just went back to her apartment and worked on articles, and was quite content with such a lifestyle. Hank had moved back in with Rikia, but Rikia wasn't sure how permanent his residency was. "I think," Rikia said, "he's moved back in because my pad is so much better than anything he's ever lived in." Adding, "We're together...but I don't know for how long." She would not go to see his show, but she did share his new diet—organic food, two dozen vitamins plus huge vitamin injections twice each week from a doctor Hank said was quite magnificent. Summer wondered what kinds of pills and shots her friend was taking because Rikia, who always had been full of energy, now seemed capable of going sleepless for days. Once or twice she telephoned Summer at some ludicrous hour—"Are you up? Good! There's a great old Gary Cooper movie on!"

Wade had sent her a postcard saying that Beth had become a finalist in her tournament. Summer thought it odd that her father, the quintessential gambler and chance-taker, standing off to the side and observing as his wife did the competing.

Now as she sat up in the Murphy bed, trying to compose a lead paragraph that didn't offend her. She wondered if it was possible to sound clever without sounding smartalecky. She read, for the twentieth time, the quote from the sharp-featured model turned actress who had just appeared in her first (and quite likely last) movie. The director and editor had cut her part to almost nothing, but the lady seemed not to mind. "They were much too kind to me. They fed me wonderful food and practically wiped my nose after I sneezed." Summer smirked, thinking of what Anya Semko could do with such a quote.

She blew out a huge breath and sat at her computer. Even Beth's quote sounded a bit cheeky, but Beth always had a way of making her snide remarks sound charming.

Summer deleted what little she had written and stared at her blank screen for several awkward, frustrated minutes before starting again. What could she say about why America's rich people chose to buy homes in Canada? "Beth Rogers Stainton, like most other fabulously wealthy people, loves a bargain…" No, no, no.

Then her telephone rang. She couldn't guess who it might be, but she welcomed the chance to stop writing that impossible article and talk to someone.

"Hey, beautiful girl!"

"Daddy! Where are you?"

"Back in town. Want to go have chili with us?"

"Wish I could, but I'm sitting here in my undies and I'm trying to write a story that Rikia wants done by Friday."

"Is she really letting you write it?"

"Well, if I goof it up, I'm sure she'll have someone rewrite it. How did Beth do in that tournament?"

"She placed third and won five thousand dollars she didn't need. I better get back to her before she gets lonely. Say, do you want to have lunch with me tomorrow?"

"Sounds terrific!"

"Wait a minute; Beth wants to say hi."

"Summer…"

"I heard you did O.K. at that tournament." Summer wasn't sure just yet if she liked Beth; she was quite sure she disliked the woman's voice.

"We had *such* a fun time. Are you going to get a taxi and come out here?"

"Can't. I'm up to here in work."

Beth laughed. "You're starting to sound like your boss."

"I envy you. You're about to have a big, yummy meal. I'm going to make do with a sandwich and soda while I work on this article that doesn't seem to want to be written."

"I'm sure you'll do fine with it. I don't know if we're going to be fed anytime soon—it's so crowded tonight! Maybe some V.I.P. is coming in tonight and everybody is here to gawk. Tell me something, Summer—are you happy with your busy new life?"

"I'm getting used to it. I think sooner or later I'll actually learn to do my job. If I had spent the past few years studying journalism at Columbia, or even some humble state college, I'd probably be better prepared for this gig."

"Well, you got this job because you're a very intelligent, ambitious young—"

"No, I got this job because I'm a childhood friend of Rikia Saddy," Summer said with a laugh.

"The main thing is that you have a job you like most of the time and now have a sense of purpose that you were lacking before." Beth's voice faded and Summer could now hear nothing but a grand well of voices she scarcely recognized.

"Beth? Beth…?"

"Yes, dear, I'm still here. Say, when was the last time you saw Stephen?"

"Let me think—"

"It doesn't matter. He's just walked in with Hana."

"Is Hana really there?"

"Yes. She does that sometimes, you know—goes to the place where people least expect her. But don't be concerned, Summer; Hana is no competition for you."

"I'm fine with it, Beth. I'm glad Stephen is dining tonight with Hana. It will give us something to talk about later."

After making plans to have Sunday brunch with Beth, Summer hung up. She went to her refrigerator, took out a Coke, drank it down and drowned the house plant Stephen had given her.

Beth deliberately collided with Stephen and Hana as the two headed towards the back of the restaurant.

"Hana! You're eating in public!"

Hana smiled. "Yes. There was a double bill I really wanted to see at an art house. Plus, it was such a wonderful night for walking. Finally, after the movies were over I got hungry." She looked at Wade. "Is this handsome man your new husband I have heard so much about?"

Wade nodded. "Yes, and you are a lady I've heard so much about."

Beth asked, "Hana, how long will you be in town?"

Hana shrugged. "One of the finest things about unemployment is that I get to make no commitments or obligations to anyone but myself. I shall be here till I decide I would rather be somewhere else."

"We're opening the house in Florida next week," Beth told her. "Why don't you fly down and stay with us? We've plenty of room."

"What a kind offer. Maybe I will…or I will fly to Europe for some skiing. But I really can't say. Next week is too far into the future. Right now, all I have on my mind is my empty stomach." To Wade she said, "It was quite lovely meeting you." Then she headed towards her table, with Stephen following.

Beth and Wade settled down at their own table. "Wade, I don't like sticking my nose into other people's business, but don't you think that Stephen and Summer aren't quite as, you know, *friendly* as they should be by now? After all, they're a wonderful-looking couple."

"Beth, I've done business on Broadway and in Hollywood long enough to know that 'they look wonderful together' isn't nearly the same as 'they are wonderful together.'"

"Stephen shouldn't be spending so much time with Hana. She's old enough to be his mother. Summer should be paying plenty of attention to Stephen. She's nearly twenty-one, old enough to enter into a serious, even permanent relationship."

"Maybe she doesn't believe in marriage. Many girls today don't."

"Maybe she would marry if the right man came along," Beth said. "Maybe Stephen is the right man for her."

"Summer will do her thing, as the hippies liked to say. So will Stephen. So will you and I. So don't fret." He added, "Hana is one sexy woman. Big dark eyes, big blonde smile."

"She's an aging, illiterate peasant."

"But she seems to be one of your closes friends."

"*Seems to be*. I invited her down to Florida because I always like having famous people as houseguests. Besides, I really pity that poor woman. She's lost and lonely."

Wade started to laugh.

"What's so funny?"

"You. A minute ago you were worrying about Summer and how she's an old maid at twenty. Then you started calling Hana 'lost and lonely.' I think you're very wrong about both women. Hana is…Hana."

"If Hana is such hot stuff," Beth wanted to know, "why did you end up with me?"

He smiled and squeezed her hand. "Dearest, don't forget that by the time I met you, I dated and bedded the most ravishing women in Hollywood. I married you because you're very, very special. Why did *you* marry *me*?"

"Because—"

"Yes?"

"Because I fell in love with you." She paused and looked down on the tabletop, as if the words she sought were written there. "Oh, I know we could have done without getting married—you could have moved in and we could have 'shacked up' and of course nobody would have thought any less of us because it's such a common arrangement these days. But I think that sort of thing is vulgar. I'm very old-fashioned. If you have any money, you're supposed to hide it. If you have a big home or a fancy car, you're supposed to be ashamed of it. Well, I won't be ashamed of it. I put many people to work because of my opulent lifestyle. Entire families depend upon me. I want Summer to live the way I do. I want her and Stephen to be married and to live the way I do."

Wade looked over and saw Stephen whispering something to Hana. "Looks like Stephen is doing all right for now."

"Summer could have him in two minutes if she chose to do so."

"Oh, really?"

"Wade, don't you know how easy it is for a woman to change a man's mind?"

"Is it?"

"Of course it is."

"I'll bet you thought you'd swept me off my feet."

"Didn't I?"

She smiled and shook her head. "I swept you off yours."

"Why?"

"Because I always get what I want. I looked at you and thought, 'I want that one.' When you're Beth Rogers Stainton, you get what you want. Period."

Stephen arrived at Earl's Bistro at one the next day.

Beth had called him a few hours earlier and said, "Stephen, sweetie, let's have lunch today." For the rest of the day, he swore at himself for not declining her invitation.

They sat at a corner table and he asked all the questions he knew she wanted to hear: About her tournament, London and the great shows in the West End. He sat there, smiling and nodding, and at some point she began repeating herself and he knew she had run out of things to say, so he sat back and relaxed.

But then she said, "By the way, Stephen, what is the nature of your relationship with Hana?"

He swallowed and said, "I like her. She's fun to spend time with. A very funny lady."

Beth laughed without mirth. "Nonsense. She's the gloomiest soul I've ever met. Most of your girlfriends have had something going for them, if only physical beauty. But Hana doesn't even have that. She's old enough to be your mother. When people see you together, they talk."

"Oh? And what do they say?"

"That he's a gigolo or queer."

"Well," Stephen said with a smirk, "if they say that to you, I hope you'll tell them that I'm neither."

Beth thrust out her chin. "I don't see this as any cause for levity. People talk, and we need to be concerned when it's you or me they're talking about."

"They would be bored if they knew the truth. I spend time with Hana because she's fun, and that's all."

"No. She's not fun. She's a vile woman who is totally incapable of enjoying anyone or having fun. She knows that you're related to me and that I'm filthy rich—everyone knows that and I'm sure she feels she has plenty to gain by knowing you." Then, "What do you think of Suem, Settel and Kashin?"

Stephen shrugged. "Big powerful law firm. Why?"

"Because I'm thinking of hiring them to do my new will."

He let out a small, nervous laugh. "Why? I mean, didn't my dad already write one for you? Just leave it alone, all right?"

"You're just biased because I'm thinking of doing business with your father's competition. But I'm serious about this. I need the best legal advice in New York. After all, I'm now married and have a stepdaughter. I want to make sure that they get theirs when the time comes."

"I understand that. But you know it would break my father's heart if you betrayed him by going to another law firm."

"And would it break yours if I switched to another brokerage house?"

He stared at her for a few long moments. Then she said, "Oh, relax, Stephen. I'm just thinking out loud. I haven't actually done anything yet."

"I'm glad," he said, hoping she hadn't noticed how profusely he had begun to sweat.

"I enjoy our get-togethers," she told him. "It means a lot to me to see my family often and for us to remind ourselves that we *are* family."

He walked her to her car, waited till it disappeared down the street, and then he called Summer.

8

Wade was mixing cocktails when Summer arrived at the Amsterdam for Sunday brunch. This was the first time she had seen Beth since their return from London. Beth put down her copy of *The New York Times* and accepted an air kiss from Summer. "Ninety-five percent of what's in *The Times* is nonsense but I read it because it entertains me. But enough about me. How about your job? Are you enjoying it?"

"Well, Rikia accepted my article, so I'm proud of that. She put a staff editor on it for some minor things—I'll never be the world's greatest speller—but no major changes. Rikia likes to call stories like mine 'bowel-movement journalism'—a story just long enough for the average reader to take the average crap."

Wade and Beth laughed. Then Beth said, "I hope you aren't taking your new career so seriously that it leaves you no time for a social life."

"Well, I get up at seven and leave the office twelve hours later."

Beth tsked. "All work and no play make Summer a dull girl."

"You're too skinny," Wade said. "You need to eat more."

"Oh, I have a *wonderful* diet," Summer said. "Just the other day I went out to eat with Stephen. We both made pigs of ourselves and even shared a huge, gooey dessert."

"And how is my handsome young cousin?" asked Beth.

"He's the usual Stephen. He took me out to see Edwina, the female impersonator."

"Edwina? Is that tired old creature still around?" Beth shook her head.

"She certainly is," said Summer. "Afterwards, Stephen and I went upstairs to say hello to her."

"How did you get up there? Does Stephen know Edwina?"

"Not Stephen, Hana."

Beth's eyes bulged. *"Hana knows Edwina?"*

Summer nodded. "Yes. Let me explain. When Stephen and I got to the nightclub, they stuck us behind this big post. Then this swarthy young man came up to us and said, 'My friend and I are with Hana and we would like you to join us.' So we did, and Hana's party had a wonderful alcove with a terrific view of the stage. Hana is so beautiful that I just kept staring at her and nearly forgot to watch the show. Afterwards, Hana took us upstairs to say hello to Edwina. Rikia would love it if I could get Hana or Edwina to consent to an interview for the magazine, but that won't happen."

Presently they began having lunch, and Beth said, "Summer, please continue with your story about Edwina and Hana."

"It was weird. Everyone in the room spoke with a weird accent, but virtually all of us spoke French, so that's what we did." She giggled. "Poor Stephen speaks no French, so he just sat there and sipped his wine. Isn't that odd? A rich American man who doesn't speak any French."

"Where did you go then?" Beth asked.

"We didn't go anywhere. Hana left and Stephen took me home."

Beth swallowed a mouthful of food. "I'm so angry I can't stand it!"

"Angry about what?" asked Wade.

"That Stephen would dump Summer off at home and then go hooking up with Hana."

"He did no such thing!" exclaimed Wade.

"Oh, but he did. I spoke to Hana yesterday and she said she was going to Connecticut for a day in the country before the weather turns bad. Don't you understand? This was all planned. Hana never goes to nightclubs or anywhere else. Yes, she knows Edwina, but normally she wouldn't go out to see such a show because the crowds really unnerve her. But she knew that Stephen was very eager to see Summer, so she thought, 'I'll go with Stephen to see Edwina, and that way, Stephen can take Summer out on a date. Then Stephen can ditch Summer at the end of the evening and catch up with me later and we'll drive off to Connecticut.'"

Wade's face grew taut but he kept eating. "If Hana and Stephen had plans to drive off somewhere, I don't see that it's our business. Last time I checked, they were both consenting adults."

"Hana is an adult who consented to making a fool of your daughter," Beth told him.

Wade's face grew red. "Beth, maybe you should mind your own business and let others mind theirs."

Summer took a long drink of water and cleared her throat. "Look, Stephen and I had a wonderful time last night—"

"Then why did you let that old bitch steal him

away from you?"

Summer and Wade stared at her for several long moments, and Beth said, "Summer, I'm only acting in your best interests. Wade, wasn't that one of your reasons for marrying me? You wanted to provide for her but couldn't because of your career setbacks, so you hooked up with me because I could provide those goodies."

"But that doesn't mean you get to run her life and make her decisions. If she and Stephen were meant to be, fine. But if he is interested in someone else, you need to respect that."

Beth hooted. "Stephen told me that Summer is one of the most beautiful girls alive. Do you really think he prefers Hana to her? I seriously doubt that." She added, "No good deed goes unpunished, I suppose. I fixed up that bedroom just for Summer, and she couldn't wait to move out. I wanted for all of us to spend the holidays down in Florida, but nobody else seemed very interested. I also wanted to have a big party down there at Christmas with all my famous friends. I thought by then that Stephen and Summer would announce their engagement…"

"How nice for you," Wade said. "But maybe that's not what Summer wants."

"She has no clue as to what she wants." Beth's voice went cold. "She has to be taught to want the right things. That's what separates us from the vulgar masses out there."

"She spent three years learning to walk and talk again," Wade said through gritted teeth. "Let her live her own life."

Beth rolled her eyes. "Wonderful. Let her work at that ridiculous magazine. Let her live in that dreary little apartment. Why should I try to do nice things for a couple of people who show me no gratitude? If she wants to spend her winter freezing in New York instead of partying in Florida, I'm fine with that."

"Maybe," said Wade, "I'll stay up here and keep her company."

"You'd do that," retorted Beth. "What else would you do? Move out of the Amsterdam and move into Summer's puny, dingy apartment? What would you do for money, produce a Broadway hit? I don't think do. Let me remind you of something, Wade. You used to be someone; you used to have something. But you frittered it all away, and the only reason you live so comfortably now is that you're married to me and I share what I have with you and Summer. As a favor to both of you, I'm trying to get her married to someone who can allow her to continue with her life of privilege, which is far, far more than *you* can give her."

Summer watched the color drain from her father's face. "Wade," she said, "you've been a wonderful father to me and you don't have to do anything more. I'm a woman now, and I have a job I really enjoy. As an adult, I'm totally in charge of my own life and if I want to make my dreams come true, I have to do that by myself. Beth, I would love to spend Thanksgiving with you in Florida. I will be there and I'm looking forward to it. Even if I don't seem full of gratitude all the time, I *do* appreciate all you've done for my father and me. I love that beautiful bedroom you had all fixed up for me—but I think what I need now is to be on my own. Stephen is a delightful man, one of the most likable people I've ever met. Who will I fall in love with and marry? I don't know; but what I *do* know is that it will happen or it won't, and I suppose I'm O.K. with that." She got up, pecked her father's cold, stony cheek and said, "Gotta run. Rikia wants to meet with me about some *In* things."

As soon as she left, Wade said, "Proud of yourself? You just castrated me in front of her."

"I did no such thing. Anyway, let's not fight. Other couples do, but we can be better than that."

"I'm starting to think we shouldn't even be a couple." He got up. "I'll be packed and out of here in an hour."

Beth stood up and grabbed his arm. "No! Wade! Please don't go! If I've offended you, I apologize. Don't leave me."

He stopped and glowered at her. "Tell me something, Beth. Why did you marry me?"

"I married you for love." She threw her arms around his neck. "Wade, this is our first fight and it's my fault. Please forgive me and say you love me, too. I want us to be a happy couple, to show Summer how a man and a woman can really and truly love each other. You know, Wade, I've never had a child, and maybe that's why I'm so aggressive in treating Summer as the daughter I've always wanted. Sometimes I try too hard to do the right thing and show everyone how much I care."

He said nothing as he continued packing his suitcase.

"Wade! Listen to me! I love you and want you and Summer to be my family! What do you want from me? Whatever it is, the answer is yes."

He stopped packing for a moment and eyed her. "Do you really want to know what I want?"

"Tell me."

"Do you remember our prenuptial agreement?"

"Do you want me to tear it up? I will."

He shook his head. "No, I don't want your money. But I want it for Summer. You want her, and everyone else, to know how much you love her? Then make damn sure that you leave her some money."

Beth nodded. "Yes. I'll be happy to leave her a million dollars."

He let out a little laugh. "A million is chump change. Let's say a billion. You're worth about three billion. You can part with one of them"

She took a deep breath. "All right, one billion."

"And no more playing matchmaker. If she's not interested in Stephen, you need to accept that. If he has a thing going with Hana, well, that's his business. You can't say to him, 'I order you to dump Hana and marry Summer.' Understand?"

"Yes, Wade. Whatever you say."

"And remember the billion."

"Of course."

He picked her up and threw her onto the bed. "I had fights with my other broads. This is how we always made up."

Stephen arrived at the Midtown Racquetball Club fifteen minutes early. On the phone, his father had sounded nervous. That was bad. Stephen sighed. Everything had been going so well. Normally he disliked Monday mornings, but he woke up feeling great after his weekend with Hana. His date with Summer had gone perfectly; when they "accidentally" met up with Hana and her clique at that nightclub,

Summer seemed to suspect nothing, and she surely was unaware that he and Hana had driven off to Connecticut at midnight. He still felt giddy as he thought about it. That was his first full night with Hana, and if he lived to be a hundred he would remember the sight of her in the kitchen the morning after, fixing him bacon and eggs for breakfast. She had given him the finest twenty-four hours of his entire life. She had borrowed the use of the house from a friend—for a recluse, Stephen mused, she certainly had generous friends—and the estate, set far back from the property line, guaranteed maximum privacy. Even the weather had been better than decent, considering it was autumn in New England. Stephen had convinced himself that he was now a member of Hana's inner circle, the highest compliment he had ever received.

He saw his father enter the club and rose to greet him. Both men sat and his father spoke right away.

"Tell me something. What does Summer Sellars look like?"

Stephen frowned. "She's gorgeous. Why do you ask?"

"Is she? Then why is Beth so worried about her?"

"I have no idea what you're talking about."

"Beth came into my office this morning to change her will. She seems very anxious about getting her stepdaughter married. I thought Summer might be an ugly duckling nobody wants."

Stephen chuckled. "Quite the opposite."

"Beth wants several changes in the new will."

"Do they concern me?"

"Yes. You are no longer an executor of the

estate."

Stephen groaned.

"She has also decided to have my firm share the executive powers with Suem, Settel and Kashin. But don't despair, Stephen. There's a provision that if by the time she dies you are married to someone she approves of, you will become an executor and head the foundation."

"What a bitch," he muttered.

"It gets worse. Her stepdaughter, Summer Sellars, will receive one billion dollars on her wedding day and a hundred million more to be put in trust for her and to be collected by her when she is orphaned."

"Unbelievable," said Stephen, shaking his head.

"Of course, it's not irrevocable, so Beth can change it. I'm not sure that Wade Sellars knows that it's not carved in stone. He may be an astute Broadway and Hollywood guy, but in financial matters I think he's probably a little bit naïve. In this case, however, I believe Beth is in love with him and will let this will remain valid for the time being. Beth's generosity towards Summer is obviously intended to keep Wade happy, and it made me think that Summer was somehow so repulsive that she would need a nice big bank account in order to attract a husband."

Stephen smirked. "Beth has tried to fix me up with Summer from the moment I met the girl. Beth really wants Summer hitched and out of her way. Beth for the first time is in love and she wants no one to come between herself and the man she loves. She likes to be the boss, to run things and be in charge. That's just the way she is."

His father made a face. "Stephen, I'm getting the impression that you think Summer wants to screw her father and that Beth is jealous."

Stephen shrugged. "Well, that's been my impression. I'm not terribly comfortable with saying so, but I think they have a sort of inappropriate relationship. To Beth, everything would become very convenient if I married Summer so that Beth could have Wade all to herself."

"How do you feel about Summer?"

"She's a beautiful, charming girl."

"Is there another woman in your life?"

Stephen nodded.

"Anyone I know?"

"Hana."

The older man let out a small laugh. "She's much too old for you. I used to have a thing for her when I was your age."

"She's fifty-two. Not so old."

"Too old for you."

"Age is immaterial when she and I are together. Anyway, I'm about as interested in marrying Hana as she is in marrying me. She and I will just keep running around together until one or both of us gets sick of the other. When that happens, I'll probably run up to Summer Sellars and say, 'Marry me!'"

"Oh, and do you think she'll still be available?"

"Maybe. I can hope, can't I? But right now, I can't let go of Hana. She makes me very happy."

"Are you two playing I've Got a Secret or do people know about you?"

"Only a few know. Hana's so reclusive, you know. We rarely go anywhere, but tonight I'm going to dinner with her at a director's house."

His father nodded. "If you keep it up much longer, you'll be known as the gigolo of a washed-up movie star." Then, "Suppose you remain an acquaintance of Summer, but that isn't enough. Maybe she'll meet someone else, a man Beth wants her to marry, and this man happens to work at a brokerage house. Would *Hana* allow you to manage her money?"

"Nope."

"Do you think that being with Hana rather than Summer will do you any good in the long or short term?"

"I think," Stephen said, "that I better start romancing Summer before she meets someone else."

"Then get busy, son. Go out there and do what you need to do."

9

The dance floor at The Edge was packed. Stephen and Summer clung to each other for fear of being trampled. He had taken her to Lutece for dinner and held her hand. When he smiled, she smiled back. Beth and Wade would be flying down to Florida the following week, and Stephen wanted to be sure that Summer would tell them wonderful things about her relationship with him. His goal was for Beth to convince herself that Stephen and Summer were practically engaged. Which he believed was quite an attainable goal; Beth, more than anyone else he'd ever known, could make herself think that things would turn out her way.

Naturally, much depended upon Summer herself. He needed to win her love utterly and completely. Summer was no ditzy model like Voreen Kimmer, the chick he'd been dating. To Voreen, Stephen was the most virile of studs, of course, but also a member of a prominent New York family and the sort of man who could keep her happy for the longest time. Summer didn't share Noreen's needs. Stephen had to figure out the ways in which Summer was needy and exploit those areas. He, a world-class lover, needed to get Summer into the sack a few times and make her scream the same way he'd done a hundred other cuties. Once you found the woman's G-spot, she was yours. Voreen? Hell, he could neglect her for two weeks and when he finally did call, she would jump his bones as soon as they were in the same room.

Stephen just needed some time to do his thing. He had said to Hana, 'Beth wants me to hang out with Summer once in a while. She gets lonely.' Hana said, 'I understand. You're good to do that for her.' Stephen added that he might have to fly down to Florida for Thanksgiving. Hana said, 'Beth invited me, too.'

He panicked for the briefest instant. He could never cope with both women at the same time; around Hana, he always acted like a lovesick schoolboy. The evening would be pure torture. 'Are you going?' he asked. 'No,' she said. 'Thanksgiving is insignificant to me. While I believe in having gratitude for the good things in my life, Thanksgiving is such an American holiday. I became a citizen, yes, but I do not embrace American customs. It is just my way.'

Stephen saw her as the most ambivalent of people—about America, him and everything else. He knew he could never leave her, but she could do that to him, and he wasn't altogether sure that such a thing would happen. He also knew that he would need to separate from her forever, and somehow overcome the agony of such an event, before he could settle down to the business of living his own life.

Even now, as he held beautiful Summer in his arms on the dance floor, he fantasized about Hana. His obsession with that woman made him feel sick, depraved; in his love life, he had always been the boss, the one in charge…the man. Even in his wildest, most reckless affairs, when being under the woman's thumb was little more than part of the fun and games, he allowed his better judgment to prevail and soon his paramour wanted him far more than he did her. But such a thing hadn't happened with Hana, and he knew he could never get enough of her.

But he knew he needed to become the sun, moon and stars to Summer. He needed for her to look at him with eyes that said, *I want you, I need you and I will wait for you.* He wanted a little more time to date her, talk to her and figure out what she wanted so that he could promise it to her. He had looked at her a hundred times already and admired what a beautiful woman she was—she was even more gorgeous than Voreen. If he tried to seduce Summer tonight, would he scare her off? He certainly thought not. This was now November, and they had known each other for a couple of months. Voreen had bedded down with him on their first date, and Hana on their second. He had planned his seduction of Summer for tonight and even found out which kinds of music she liked.

For a moment he felt awkward and uncomfortable. Seducing women was a new thing for him,; usually *they* seduced *him.* He wasn't altogether sure of what to say to begin this seduction; when was the last time he had done such a thing? Also, when was the last time he had pursued a woman so *worthy* of him? Summer didn't make eyes at him or say, 'I want you to take me home and jump my bones.'

He stopped musing when he heard her soft but loud voice in his ear. He shook his head and she repeated herself.

"I said, 'It's too bad that *Rent* is always sold out, but a friend of a friend knows someone in the cast who can get us tickets.'"

He smiled. "Don't worry—*I* know people, too. I'll get us tickets for next week."

He concluded that he needed to get her into the sack that evening. They had to be a couple by the time they flew down to Florida for Thanksgiving. His father said that Beth's new will had been witnessed and signed and therefore official. If Stephen married Summer, Beth would certainly change her will; even an engagement would bode very well for him. He told himself that he needed to speed things up. He took her by the arm and led her off the dance floor. "We should talk more. Can't do that in here. We're never alone."

He pulled out her seat and got her settled in. She said, "Want to go to Bea's?"

He shook his head. "I know the bartender there. We're both sports fans. I'd end up talking to him and neglecting you."

"Then where?"

"How about my place? We can listen to music, drink champagne and talk."

He felt amazed when she beamed and nodded. He signed the check and took her outside. A handful of his acquaintances ogled her for several moments and gave him a discreet thumbs-up. He nodded, feeling very pleased with himself for being the date of the most beautiful girl in Manhattan. Tall and lithe and young...so *young*! He had to stop being horny for Hana all the time; otherwise, he might not be that great a lay for Summer in a couple of hours. Certainly, she'd already had her share of lovers; he bet she'd been romanced by some slick European men while living overseas. In fact, s*he'd* probably taught *them* a thing or two about lovemaking. Any chick who'd been born to, and raised by, Wade Sellars had to be wise to the ways of the world. She'd sure gotten her own apartment fast enough, and that was probably so she could be alone with a man. He thought about that artsy-fartsy crowd she hung out with at that pretentious magazine, and to him they were like a bunch of rats—eventually everyone would do it with everyone else.

Well, tonight he would win her over, and then would do his best to see her two or three nights each week. Maybe by spring they would be more or less engaged. All the while, he wanted to continue his affair with Hana, the woman to whom he meant about thirty-five cents. Summer meant *everything* to him now. Winning her over meant getting back to basics. If he wanted her, the first thing to remember was keeping a cool head and maintaining control of his emotions.

Summer sat beside him in the taxi as it cruised up Park Avenue. She knew he was going to try getting her into bed…and she was going to let it happen. She was fascinated with sex by now and wanted to experience it. She also believed that Stephen would be the best lover imaginable. The moment she lay naked in his arms, she would fall deeply in love and live happily ever after. She *think* he was the handsomest man alive, and Rikia assured her that he was the one who could make all her dreams come true. Rikia could scarcely believe Summer was still a virgin, and during their frank lunchtime talks about sex and men, the women at *In* made themselves quite clear: Being a virgin was something to be ashamed of.

Rikia was doing it with her layour artist now. Hank

hadn't called in a couple of weeks and Rikia, as she put it, was keeping company with Mr. Right Now in Mr. Right's absence.

The cab pulled up and Stephen and Summer got out. Stephen felt nervous as he fumbled with the half-dozen keys it took to unlock his front door. Then he led her inside and switched on the lights. She took off her coat and had a look around, envious that his place was so much bigger than hers. He had a fake fireplace, six-foot-tall stereo speakers; his bedroom door was open and she almost giggled at the sight of his round bed and red walls—Stephen's idea of a brothel!

He turned on his sound system, and a classical piece swelled, filling up the room. Summer grinned— Ravel's *Bolero*, one of the finest pieces of sex music ever written. If that didn't get her in the mood, nothing would. Then he ducked behind the bar and came up with a bottle of Dom Perignon. "You mentioned liking this, so I bought a bottle that day," he told her as he unscrewed the cork. "I've been saving it for tonight. Actually, I didn't think tonight you would be here with me, so I didn't chill the bottle. No matter—we'll drink it over ice." Then, "So, what do you think of my apartment? Wait—don't answer that. I'll bet you don't like it, if only because it's bigger than yours. Come, let's sit and drink."

They took their places on the sofa and Summer sipped her wine. Dom Perignon; wasn't that supposed to be for special occasions? Well, wasn't *this* a special occasion? She was about to get screwed!

She looked up from her wineglass and considered Stephen for a moment. Was he trying to get her drunk and loosen her up for sex? That seemed pretty unromantic; she'd expected him to be more mature and sophisticated. Staring at his face, she also decided that he was less handsome and suave than Pierre, the Parisian kid who'd tried to rape her. Of course, Pierre's sole functions in life were to look good and have sex; Stephen had actually *made* something of himself. When Pierre felt her up and forced himself upon her, she'd panicked and fled; so why was she now here with Stephen? She could leave now, her hymen still intact, but would she ever get a better offer? Did she wish to remain a virgin forever? What would she say when Rikia grilled her afterwards—that she had gotten up and walked away from Dom Perignon and Maurice Ravel and a round bed? She drained her glass and Stephen went to refill it. She thought it was all just too crazy. Was she going to put out for him because Rikia told her to do so? Or to prove to Wade that she could compete with Hana? Why, exactly, was she here with Stephen? Not out of love, because she hadn't yet decided if she really even *liked* him all that much. But what did she know about love, anyway? How much of it had she seen in her young life? Rikia had told her, 'Summer, the kind of love *you* want happens in the movies, not real life.' Even her father had said, 'I don't make love, I only have sex.' She allowed Stephen to pour her some more wine. She sipped it and gazed at him, admitting to herself that he *was* handsome. Once their physical intimacy got started, she would simply follow his lead and do her best to enjoy it—and him—and learn to love him and spend her life with him, if that's what he wanted. She drank some more and held out her empty glass for a refill. Well, he wanted her buzzed and loose, didn't he?

Presently the wine was gone and the music played on. Summer set her wineglass on the coffee table, lay back on the sofa and closed her eyes. She felt Stephen kissing her neck as Ravel continued filling the room with music for lovers. *Am I supposed to enjoy this, Maurice? Are Stephen's kisses supposed to thrill me the way your compositions do?*

Stephen finished with her neck and began kissing her ear. *Oh, yuck*, she thought, *his tongue is in my ear! Why is he doing that?* Then he kissed her lips for the longest time, which she mostly liked, and he forced her lips apart and slid his tongue into her mouth, which she liked less. She jerked away, repulsed, but he kept his mouth glued to hers. He squeezed her breasts and groped for the buttons of her blouse. She wanted to slap his hands away and say, 'Thank you, but I can undo my own buttons. This is a new blouse, you know.' But she closed her eyes and waited for him to turn her on, as if there was an arousal switch on her body he could flip.

She thought for a moment of his bedroom not twenty feet away, and was unsure why he lay sprawled on the sofa, sticking his tongue into her orifices instead of just walking her into the bedroom so they could undress and do…what?

"Beautiful girl," he murmured as he removed her blouse and brassiere. He kissed and sucked at each of her breasts. Soon her had her naked and picked her up. She wanted to say, 'I'm not a paraplegic. I can walk just fine.' But she said nothing.

Minutes later she lay on his bed as he pulled off his own clothes. He stood before her nude, his long member standing at attention. His smug smile reminded her of the men at the Oscars who stood at the podium clutching their statuettes.

"So, how do you like the boy so far?" he asked her.

She frowned. Summer had seen her share of porn movies and all those erections looked ugly, with their blue veins and sweat.

"Touch him. Kiss him." Stephen tried to stick his penis in her face. She pulled away.

He laughed. "O.K., you're shy. I understand that. But before we're done, you'll want to deep-throat me."

She wanted to get up, run into the next room, gather up her clothes and run home. Where was the romance, the sweet talk, the loving? All she was getting now was another horny male wagging his thing at her and bragging about its size.

He got on top of her and kissed her breasts some more. Then he spread her legs and bussed the insides of her thighs. She instantly drew her knees together.

"Got a problem?" he asked.

"Too much light in here."

He chuckled. "Really?"

"Yeah. Not very romantic."

Sighing, he got up and switched off the light. She watched him, not quite believing that they were naked together in his home and he, an experienced seducer, seemed to be treating her as just another of his one-night stands.

Back in bed, in the darkness, he yanked her legs apart and started stabbing her with his big stiff thing.

"Stephen," she said, "I'm not on the pill. I don't use *anything*..."

"No problem. I just won't come inside of you."

After much pumping and sweating and groaning,

he mussed up her hair as if she were a little boy. "Well, that was pretty good, huh? I've had better, but that was pretty fucking nice all the same." Then, "How about some head? I can get a boner and we'll do it again."

"What do you mean?"

"Just what I said. Head. Fellatio. Blow job."

"Not *this* chick!" She jumped out of bed and threw on the light.

They got dressed and he hailed a taxi. As they cruised towards her building, he whispered, "Dammit, Summer, why didn't you tell me you were on the fuckin' rag? There was blood everywhere." He added, "Those were Versace sheets, you know."

"I'm not 'on the rag,' *Stephen*," Summer whispered back.

He thought for a moment. "Oh, wow, Summer. I'm so sorry. I didn't know you were…"

"A virgin? Why are you sorry?"

"Because I don't go around deflowering young girls. It would make me feel like a perv."

"It's a dirty job, but someone's gotta do it." Summer smirked.

When they reached her neighborhood, Stephen told the driver to let them out. "Let's go into that bar," he said to Summer. "I want to drink and talk right now, not sleep."

They went inside and Stephen ordered Scotches over ice. Summer sipped hers, grimaced at its dreadful taste but hoped it would make her sleep. She really wanted to go home, flop into bed and sink into a coma for eight or ten hours.

Stephen swallowed some Scotch and said, "I'm still freaked out that I was your first, but I guess I'm flattered, too. Summer, I really do care for you a great deal."

"Do you?"

"Yes, I really do."

"Well, I think that's very nice."

He placed his hand over hers. "Just 'very nice'?"

"Well… " She wanted to say, *I don't know you very well*, but he would have laughed at her. They'd just had intercourse, after all.

"Summer," he said, "I want to marry you."

"Oh."

"And…?"

"I know that Beth wants you to marry me. Isn't this just too ridiculous, Stephen? We don't know each other at all. We sit here and try to have a conversation but it's awkward because we have nothing to say to each other. If we were in love, we'd get up here in the bar and sing and dance. We would embarrass ourselves, each other and everyone else with our crazy bliss. But we're sitting here talking about love and marriage as if they we were doing a business deal."

After a long pause, Stephen said, "You make it sound as if love were a Hollywood movie with the lovers walking into the sunset while the romantic music plays."

"Well, it *should* be that way. Being in love ought to be an overpowering experience."

"Summer, will you marry me?"

She looked this way and that, then at him. "I don't know, Stephen. I just don't feel anything for you—"

"Do you know the difference between *realistic* and *idealistic*? That Hollywood crap I just talked about is a fantasy, just for entertainment, not to be taken seriously. I've got a deal for you right here. I can certainly offer you more good things than any other man." Then, "Marry me, Summer. I love you."

She smirked. "You love me."

"Don't you believe me?"

"You don't know me. I *do* believe that marrying me would make things very convenient for yourself and Beth."

He ignored this. "Do you love me?"

"I like you."

"Then why were you intimate with me tonight?"

"Because I wanted to fall in love with you. I thought that sex would make that happen."

"I'm sorry it was your first time and turned out badly. The next time—"

"Won't be a next time."

He frowned. "Do you mean you won't see me anymore?"

"No, I mean I won't go to bed with you again."

He slapped a few bills onto the bar to pay for their drinks plus a tip. "This has been quite an evening for you. You're saying things you don't really mean." They both stood up and he helped her with her coat. He took her arm as they left the watering hole.

"Summer," he said, "I'm not going to pressure you at all. I won't ask you to have sex with me again; we'll just keep seeing each other like any other couple, and if it takes months for us to be intimate again, I'm O.K. with that. We'll do it your way—get to know each other better. *But you will marry me.* You will fall in love with me and want to be with me forever—but we'll take it nice and slow. We'll fly down to Florida for Thanksgiving. We'll have several days and nights together to hang out and talk, which should get us off to a pretty good start, and I promise never to try to seduce you until you're absolutely ready. When it does happen, it'll be because you'll tell me when. As you go to sleep tonight, remember to dream of me."

Back in her apartment, she stripped and climbed into her bathtub. She soaked for the longest time and thought about the things Stephen had said.

Much later, as she lay in bed, trying to sleep, she realized that he was probably right—she *would* fall in love with him and marry him.

The next day, her telephone rang, and it was Stephen. He said, "Would you meet me for a drink?"

"Can't," Summer said. "I'm up to here with work."

"Too bad. There's a meeting in Los Angeles next week, so I'll be away for a while."

"Good luck with that."

"I'll call you, of course, and as soon as I get back, we'll go out. I can get us tickets for *Hair.*"

After their call, she lay in bed in the partial darkness and enjoyed the floaty feeling of the sedative she had taken. She could understand why so many people became addicted to those pills. But then it wore off and she got up, determined to get some work done. She thought of getting something to eat but then decided she wasn't hungry.

She thought of a story idea: *Should Turning 30 Freak You Out?*

The week before, Rikia, seeking a new secretary, had declined on an applicant with impeccable credentials and hired a nineteen-year-old with virtually no qualifications. "Summer, I don't want a fortysomething broad working for me. *In* is a hip, swinging magazine. I want cute, exuberant *kids* working here." Summer knew what she meant: The low-paying, junior-level jobs were reserved for kids. The better jobs went to the slightly older folks who had some clue as to how to run a magazine. Rikia herself was nearly thirty, but as the boss of *In*, she was remarkably young to be an executive.

Summer genuinely liked Rikia, but apart from the magazine, they had very little in common. At *In*, Rikia was Boss Lady; whenever she walked down the hallway, people stood up straight and nodded at her with what looked to Summer like fear, or respect, or both. At the weekly editorial meetings, Rikia sat at the head of the table, detached and crisp and eloquent, her word unquestioned. But away from the workplace, she happily shed her stature; Hank's wants and needs always supplanted her own, and in social settings, Summer felt that Rikia seemed grateful for any attention she received from any male.

Summer needed to talk to someone. Rikia was out; she'd say, 'Summer, take some vitamins or go see a shrink.' So she called Wade, thinking they might have lunch the next day. What would she say to him? 'Daddy, Stephen broke my cherry the other night, and I don't know how to feel about it'? No, that wouldn't do. So she picked up the telephone and called him, knowing he wouldn't be home.

But he answered it, and for a moment she wondered if she had just interrupted him being romantic with Beth.

"Are you watching CNN or something?" she asked.

"No, I was asleep. You woke me."

"So sorry. Tell Beth hi for me."

"What time is it, anyway?"

"Nine-thirty."

"Well, I'm awake now, and damn I'm starving! Why don't I jump into a taxi and come get you? We can get a burger somewhere."

"Where's Beth?"

"Oh, her. She gave me some backtalk so I strangled her to death. I'm going to dump her body into the East River when I get around to it."

"Wade!"

He chuckled. "Be downstairs waiting for me in fifteen minutes. We'll talk then."

They ended up at the bar Stephen had taken Summer to right after they'd had intercourse the night before.

"I'm getting old," Wade told her. "Don't have the stamina or resiliency I used to. I played some golf, went home and fell into the deepest sleep of my life. Beth is saying, 'Come on, get dressed. I want to go out for dinner and dancing.' But I'm a zombie. I can't move. So she says, 'Phooey on this! I'm going to play cards with one of my girlfriends.'"

"That's when I woke you. Sorry about that."

"Don't apologize. I'm glad you got me up so that we could eat together. We don't see each other often enough." He swallowed a mouthful of hamburger and said, "So how come you're with your old man tonight?"

"I went out with Stephen last night. He's flying out to the Coast next week to take care of business."

"You two getting serious?"

She made a face. "He asked me to marry him."

"I hope you said no."

"I told him I liked him."

"I bet that put him in his place. He's used to getting what he wants."

"Tell me about it." She crossed her legs. She still felt sore down there.

"So are you sure you're not about to become the next Missus Stephen Rogers?"

"Very sure. I'm sorry if I disappointed you."

Wade chuckled. "Say that to him, not me."

She smiled and looked down at her partially eaten meal, wanting to believe that there had been no sexual intimacy between herself and Stephen. She wanted to think they were just friends, or acquaintances, if that's what she wanted, and she wasn't sure she wanted to know him at all.

"Wade, do you think I have, you know, sex appeal?"

He laughed. "You have far too much."

"I guess I got it from you."

"Your mother was pretty damn sexy, too."

She let out a big breath. "Whatever it is that turns us on, I don't feel that way about Stephen."

"Not at all?"

"Nope. Beth would just love it if I wanted him." Then, "Why are you smirking?"

"Because we're talking about the one guy in Manhattan who can have any and every chick in town, and he's decided he wants you, but *you* don't want *him*."

"I think I like him. I just don't want to marry him. I want someone much more like you."

"Well, too bad. Beth got me first. Anyway, if you and I got married, people might think we were a little weird."

"People already think we're a little weird."

"So maybe we shouldn't get married to each other," Summer said.

"But I thought you had some really deep feelings for Stephen."

"Not deep, just superficial. I think he's too fair and blond. His hair is too wavy."

Wade rolled his eyes. "You're going to reject a hundred men just because they don't look quite enough like me."

"Are you getting upset? There's no reason for you to feel badly just because I've decided I don't want Stephen."

"Not just Stephen. It's going to happen again and again. You'll even be at the altar and you'll look at the groom and say, 'Naw, I don't want this one, either.' I've seen that happen a hundred times." He leaned forward and lowered his voice. "Listen, I'm going to give you some good advice. Do not nurture your false images about me, images that other men can't live up to because they're totally unrealistic. If you want to know the truth, Wade Sellars is not a big deal. You've only known me as Daddy, and Daddy is about as real as a Hollywood hero on the movie screen. It's time for you to understand that Daddy Wade and Wade the man are very different people."

"I've known Wade the man for years and I love him," she said.

"No. You saw only what I showed you. Yes, I was charming and attentive when we hung out together, but you want to know the truth? I was a bad father and a pitiful excuse for a husband. I was a good date and sex partner but I've never loved any of those women and I didn't make them happy for very long."

"But you loved me...you always have..."

"Yes. But I sure didn't spend my nights doing Daddy stuff with you and tucking you in at night even though I should have. Why didn't I? Because I didn't want to. I went off and did my own thing."

"It's such a shame that Mother died."

"Your mother killed herself," he muttered, his face taut with anger.

Summer blanched. "I didn't know that. Why did tell me?"

"To toughen you up. If you want to be *my* daughter, learn to handle yourself. If you love me as much as you say you do, love me for who I really am, not for who you like to *dream* I am. Once you do that, you'll find your own man and fall in love with him. Shit, you'll fall in love two dozen times—but only if you face reality. Figure out what you want and go get it. Don't walk around with your head up your ass, living in a dream world. Don't be a loser like your mother. She traipsed around with her big sad eyes, never actually accusing me of anything but always giving me those suspicious looks. You want to know something? I started to get a little respect for her when I found out she was having an affair—because for once she'd figured out what she wanted and gone out to get it. I started feeling jealous; I was going to start romancing her and trying to win her back. Then I found out he dumped her! She'd get drunk with him and cry about how much she loved me!" He paused. "So now I'm with Beth. We're not in love, but I think we have a viable marriage. I got into it for you as much as for myself."

"I thought you married her for my benefit alone."

He shrugged. "O.K., I'll admit that in the beginning I married Beth because she had the resources—the money—to make many of my biggest problems go away. But you've done all right by her, too, even though you've looked at those goodies—especially the bedroom at the Amsterdam—and said, 'No, thanks, I'd rather sublet a little apartment of my own.' But you *know* those goodies will still be there whenever you want them. Beth said, 'I know a man I want you to meet,' but you said, 'I don't like his blond wavy hair.' He's said he wants to marry you, but that doesn't mean he's in love with you. If he gets lonely and you're not there, he'll probably keep company with someone else."

"You mean Hana?"

"Could be—if he's lucky. Any man with the opportunity to have an affair with her would be a fool to say no." Then, "Maybe you're not in love with Stephen because he doesn't want you to be in love with him right now. It would be a bad deal for you to be in love with him while he was getting it on with Hana."

"Would you 'get it on' with Hana if you had the chance?"

"Like I said, I'd be a fool to say no." .

. "But you're a married man."

"Then I wouldn't tell my wife."

"Maybe she's too much competition for me."

Wade smiled. "You're a girl, she's a woman. Stephen wants to marry you, not her. He will marry you when he's ready to make that commitment."

"'When he's ready to make that commitment.'" She guffawed. "He's already proposed. He's so ready it's ridiculous." She added, "It would sure thrill Beth if we got married. She introduces me to her cousin Stephen and acts like I'm this Barbie doll who says, 'Golly! Is he for me? Let's get married and live happily ever after!' And I really tried to go along with her nonsense. I've also wondered if you wanted that for me—to marry a nice Ken doll in the season's most talked-about wedding; *Wade Sellars' daughter marries Beth Rogers Stainton's cousin*! Is that all there is for me in this life? And if so, should I be grateful?"

He paid the check and they went outside.

"You asked me if that's all there is for you in life and if you should be grateful. I'm fifty-two now, and the more I know, the less I understand. I'm wise enough to know that *I* don't matter anymore—Broadway and Hollywood rejected me a long time ago, and I accept that, and because of my age, I know that I won't be here for you *that* much longer, so your future has been very much on my mind. Not too long ago, I discovered that most of what I had to offer you—my wealth and professional status—had lost most of their value, so when I hooked up with Beth, I thought, 'Well, at least now Summer has a filthy rich stepmother, so my kid should be set for life.' Then Stephen Rogers became interested in you and I thought, 'Summer can have a handsome, much-admired husband, too.' I think you should count your blessings, kiddo."

Hours later, as she lay awake in the darkness, she thought about what her father had said. She felt sorry for him—Wade Sellars, that dashing, womanizing risk taker of Broadway and Hollywood, had gotten old and afraid—afraid of life, afraid of death, afraid for himself and her. She knew she needed to be grateful for her blessings, figure out what she wanted from life and use her beauty, charm and smarts to get it.

She grinned in the darkness and whispered, "Daddy, you and Beth don't need to worry about me and my future. I'm my own woman…I can take care of myself."

10

Summer's future was probably the last thing on Beth's mind as she walked away from her slumbering husband, wrote a brief note and took off. She instructed her driver to take her to one hotel, then she entered the lobby, exited on the other side, got into a taxi and went to the Plaza. There, she took the elevator to the tenth floor and entered a suite.

"Hello?" she called out. "Are you here? Why are you always late? Dammit!"

About half an hour later, the heard the door open. "About fucking time."

Hana smiled. "Am I late?"

"Yes, and this time I shall never forgive you."

Hana walked over, threw her arms around Beth and gave her a long, deep kiss. All was forgiven.

Later in bed, as they lay naked in each other's arms, Beth said, "Why do you insist on being late and driving me crazy?" Then, "I wish we could be together like this forever."

"Death is forever," said Hana. "I'm in no hurry for that."

"I've put some money into your bank account."

"They get freaked out whenever I go to the bank. They can't believe it's me, that I exist."

Beth laughed. "They never recognize me. I'm the richest woman in New York and they don't recognize me…not that going unrecognized is altogether a bad thing."

Hana grabbed the TV remote and started flipping through the channels as Beth cuddled her.

"Beth, do you have to be back home at any particular time?"

"Nope. I left a note saying I was playing cards with a friend. My old man is too busy with a dozen things to notice my absence."

"Wade Sellars is a handsome man."

"I suppose. I married him so people wouldn't think I was dyke."

They both laughed.

"Why would people think that?"

"Because they often think that of single people, especially rich ones."

"Would it bother you to say to the world, 'I am Beth Rogers Stainton. I am a lesbian and proud of it'?"

Beth cringed. "I've thought of that a few hundred times…and, yes, it would be hard for me to handle. That's why I go down on my girlfriend in hotel rooms and don't tell my husband about it." She added, "In many ways, I envy you."

"Why?"

"Because you enjoy being alone. I can't do that; it terrifies me. I need to be at parties, being charming, having people admire me. When we first met, I fell in love with you right away. I adore women; I always have. I hate it that you and I have to be apart for so much of the time. I'm surrounded by people, but you're not there, and that makes me deeply unhappy."

"I pity you. I've never suffered like that," Hana said as she flipped through the channels.

"Loneliness has followed me my whole life. My parents died when I was a child, so suddenly there were bank accounts and trust funds and lawyers and whatnot. They said, 'You're not a pretty girl, but don't worry; you're so rich that you'll have an easy time finding a husband.' Of course, even back then I knew I didn't like men that way."

"Did they really say that to you? You're beautiful. You know that, right?"

"I suppose. I've had all the beautiful treatments that money can buy. I *did* start out as a homely kid, though. I was born with bad DNA."

"You're beautiful and you know it."

"Do you know who was beautiful? Joan Crawford. Her beauty got her men and fame. Her men loved her even when she wasn't very lovable. My money got me men who pretended to love me. But I'm not a fool—I knew they didn't love me, and I've never really tried to love any man. Loving you is the easiest thing I have ever done. Do you know that you're the only person I have ever truly loved?"

"Too bad for you."

"And do you know that I haven't had a happy day since we met?"

Hana frowned. "Didn't you just say you loved me?"

"Yes! And that's exactly why I'm so unhappy! Don't you understand?" She began fondling the other woman's breasts. "As intimate as we are…right now…as I'm touching you here…I don't feel you belong to me at all, or that I'm really connecting with you in any way that means anything."

"I'm starting to feel very connected to you right now…and very horny, too. Maybe we should stop talking and start making love."

So they did…and Beth once again felt inexpressible gratitude for Hana. When their loving was over, Beth, breathless and drenched in perspiration, clung to her paramour and said, "Hana, I adore you. Please don't ever hurt me or make me suffer."

"I thought I just made you very happy."

Beth choked back a sob. "That was sex. I need more than that. Don't you know how it is for me when you go away and leave me to survive on my own?"

"I always come back to you."

"How can I *know* that you'll always come back? Why must you leave in the first place? Do you know that I've loved you for close to a decade, and in that time, we've mostly been apart. How long have we been together physically? Several days here, a few weeks there—maybe three months. I need more than that."

Hana turned on the TV and resumed her channel surfing. "You expect too much from me. I'm not that interesting. You'd just get bored."

"Nonsense."

Hana stared at the TV screen. "My sweet, needy Beth. Just as you can't stand being alone, many times Hana *needs* to go off and be by her moody little self."

Beth snatched away the TV clicker and turned off the set. "Do you remember my suicide attempt the first time you went away? I said to myself, 'I'm never going to do *that* again!' Still, I suffered horribly each time you left, although I said to myself, 'I will find a way to cope till she comes back to me.' But last spring, after you left me again, I tried to kill myself once more. Nobody knew, of course, although I was hospitalized for a week. But that's when I thought, 'I need someone by my side, a partner of some sort, a person who will save me from myself.' So I married Wade Sellars."

Hana looked at her with big, empathic eyes. "You say such things and I feel so sorry for you. Maybe you would be better off if I went away forever."

Beth closed her eyes and whimpered. A tear trickled down her cheek. "You still don't understand. I cannot possibly imagine life without you, and I know that if I keep carrying on like this, clinging to you with all my strength, you *will* leave me forever. I married Wade Sellars because he is unlike other men. He won't let me push him around or bend to my will. I must be an actress, playing the part of his missus, his obedient little wife—he is my boss. As long as I play the part of the dutiful little wife, he will stay with me…because he is indigent. Did you know that? Wade Sellars, the man who used to run Broadway and Hollywood, now has nothing." She paused. "He is also very grateful to me for creating a multimillion-dollar trust fund for his daughter."

"How generous of you."

Beth grinned. "Not so generous. It's not an irrevocable trust; I can change it." She looked at Hana for a very long moment and wiped another tear from her cheek. "You must come to Florida with me. Wade will play golf all day, so we'll have plenty of time to be alone. That house is so huge that they'll never find us."

"You'd hate for people to know about us, but wouldn't they talk if they saw us together?"

Beth shook her head. "For Thanksgiving? There

would be a number of people. Nobody would talk."

Hana shrugged. "Maybe." She switched on the TV and said, "Cary Grant was a wonderful actor. If I had been around back then, I would have worked with him."

Beth lay back and admired Hana's beautiful face—big eyes, long thin nose, slightly pointed chin, full lips. Her body was slim, breasts firm. The woman's hair was dark and shiny, her skin soft, her smell down there mild and feminine. Beth could not imagine a finer sex partner and was infinitely delighted to be accepted by such a divine creature.

"Hana?"

"Hmm?"

"Have you been seeing Stephen?"

"Yes."

"I think he wants to marry Summer."

Hana smiled. "Oh? You'd like that, wouldn't you?"

"Well, he doesn't mean anything to you, does he?"

"He *does* mean something to me. I like him a lot."

Scowling, Beth bounced out of bed and pointed her finger at Hana. "Whore!"

Hana rolled onto her back and grinned at Beth. "Better put something on before you catch cold. You should also sign up for aerobics classes. Your tummy is getting flaccid."

Beth spun around and marched off to the bathroom. Hana turned up the sound and lost herself in the TV show. When Beth came back out, she got dressed and stood before Hana. "Why do you say and do those things to torture me?"

"How do *I* torture *you*?" Hana asked, staring at

Beth's stomach as if it were the TV screen. You have a husband who adores you even if you don't have much use for him. Plus, you have more money than you could spend in a dozen lifetimes. You have so much fun lording over people, saying to them, 'I have enough money and power to ruin you if you displease me.' But you cannot bully Hana."

Beth sat on the edge of the bed. "Do you know how awful it is to have so much money?"

Hana tsked. "Poor little rich girl. You pity yourself, asking, 'How can I know that people accept me for *myself*? Maybe they're after my money.' You say that you feel traumatized by your money and status. Well, we all have your traumas to cope with. Your worst trauma is the you have always had too much— *far* too much. You have no idea of how it is to have nothing, and I know far too much how it feels to go without."

"It was a challenge that you overcame. You've laughed about it. It was fun for you."

"There was no fun. I came from a poor Polish family. There was war, famine, death." She paused. "But we've just had a beautiful experience together. Why spoil it with this awful talk? I'm very sleepy. Goodnight."

"Hana, will you spend Thanksgiving with us in Florida?"

"Maybe."

"Promise me you will."

"I'll promise to think about it."

Hana fell asleep. Beth patted her bare bottom and left the suite.

11

Rikia sat on her bed and asked Summer, "What is the deal with Thanksgiving, anyway? It's just a couple of days away, and I'm trying to think of why I should be giving thanks, and to whom."

"Well," said Summer, "you already know the story of the Pilgrims and Natives. If that doesn't do it for you, try thanking the Creator."

"Also, whose idea was it to have this holiday on the fourth Thursday in November? It really complicates my business. We should have Thanksgiving in the summer so at least I could have a long weekend in the Hamptons. But a long weekend in the fall does me no good at all. Shit."

"Why don't you use Thanksgiving as an excuse to get together with your family?"

Rikia hooted. "My family! My father's new wife is little more than a dewy dollop of womanhood who's just had another baby. Having me around would make him way too uncomfortable. My mother is about to call it quits with her latest hubby—seems she caught him feeling up her best friend. I envy you; four days in Florida, flying down in your stepmommy's jet, with Daddy and Stephen there to dote on you the whole time. Will they both be there?"

"I'm looking forward to it."

"I still can't believe Stephen hated *Hair*. Who hates *Hair*?"

Summer laughed. "He slept through most of it. I'm still singing those tunes to myself."

They paused. Then Rikia said, "I'm lonely for Hank."

"You're wearing his pajama shirt."

She nodded. "It's to remind me of what douches all men are."

"I would hardly call Hank a douche. He just needs to figure out who he wants to be when he grows up."

"I don't mean Hank. He's Mister Right. I mean Noel, my art director, who's Mister Right Now. He's gone back to his wife because his shrink thinks I'm too bossy for him. Just as well. Noel never really was my type."

"Then why were you doing it with him?"

"Because he's the best art director in Manhattan. All the other magazines wanted him, you know."

"Is he staying on at *In*?"

"Damn straight. We'll still be friends, sort of. I'll try not to hold it against him that he's a douche. Plus, if he gets that itch his wife can't scratch, he knows where to find me. I've got him so uptight and neurotic from guilt that he won't leave the magazine till he burns out or drops dead."

Summer frowned. "Is *In* the only thing you give a shit about?"

Rikia lit a cigarette. "I'll tell you something. When I was a kid at the New England School for Girls, all those chicks idolized me because I was always on, always putting on a little show. The boys liked me because I put out for them. But while I spread my legs for them, I knew they would move on to someone else if they met a chick who was a better lay than I was. After I graduated, all the girls had said 'Rikia is gonna be a star!' and I believed them. I got my nose fixed and said, 'Watch out, Broadway! Here I come!' So I went out on auditions and it was *humiliating*. Summer, do you know what auditioning is? You stand there all alone on a big dark stage singing your ass off and hearing someone invisible in the audience say, 'Thank you. We'll call you if we need you.' He may say that *right in the middle of your fucking song!* Even if they ultimately hire you and you have a decent part for a while, it probably won't last for very long and you'll be back on that big dark stage, sing alone and hearing, 'Thank you very much.' The fact that you were just in a show doesn't mean jackshit to them. But then I became a flunky at *In* and knew I would have to make coffee and kiss asses for a little while before I got a promotion and some other poor girl would have to take my job. All the while at the magazine, I studied it and thought, 'This rag would be so much better if we did less of this and more of that.' I figured out fast that my bosses didn't know what the hell they were doing, so my diplomatically and tactfully tendered suggestions went over *very* well. Before I came along, they were saying, '*In* magazine is the laughingstock of New York publishing. Why is that?' After they began implementing my changes, the magazine started getting a reputation as the thing to read if you were a hip urban female—or aspired to become one. It became clear that I should run the magazine, so I got the promotion and became editor-in-chief. I looked at my job and thought, 'I will have this gig for as long as I want it.' Unlike Broadway shows or men who ball you once and leave you forever. I know there will be more Noels, and maybe even a few more Hanks. I'm O.K. with that."

Summer thought for a moment. "But wasn't Hank the great love of your life?"

Rikia chortled. "Summer, be serious. Do you think Hank was the only man I've nearly slit my wrists over? I loved him and Noel, but in different ways."

"But you said, 'I want to marry Hank.'"

Rikia nodded. "Yeah, and I meant it at the time. Know what? I'll be twenty-nine soon, which is an awful age if you're a woman. If you're twenty-nine and still unmarried, people look at you like you're *such* a loser. But I'm different, because I'm the Boss Lady at *In*, and at twenty-nine I'm the youngest editor-in-chief in New York. So I *don't* cry myself to sleep at night just because Hank is gone forever."

"Maybe he'll come back to you."

"No chance. He's shacking up right now with an older woman—a *much* older woman. Ever heard of Stella Christenson?"

"No."

"Well, she's rich. Nowhere near as rich as Beth, but still pretty wealthy just the same." She shook her head. "These women with money. They buy themselves younger faces and bodies, they get younger boyfriends. I saw a picture of Hank the other day. He was wearing a Versace jacket and he was escorting Stella to this children's-charity event at the Plaza or Waldorf."

"What does he want with her, anyway?"

"She invests in Broadway shows. He wants her to become a big backer and say to the producers, 'Give

Hank the lead.""

"Do you feel badly about you and him?"

Rikia shook her head. "I haven't felt really badly about a man since Bill."

"Who's Bill?"

"Only the most exciting man who's ever lived. I was twenty and when he said, 'We will love forever,' I said, 'Yes! Yes! Yes!' When he left me, I swallowed a bunch of pills. But I survived both Bill and those pills. After he split, there I was, alone and horny, so I rode one dick after another. That was my way of saying, 'Look at me, Bill! Maybe you didn't want me, but all these other men do!' But none of those relationships went anywhere or meant anything, because those men weren't Bill. Those relationships can last several months, maybe even a year. The problem was, I was carrying around so much love for Bill, and that was really getting in the way. Those boyfriends just sort of came and went, and eventually I started hooking up with people who I thought would be good for the magazine, and much of the time there is no sex involved. Right now, there's a huge ad agency on Madison Avenue that buys full-page ads for its clients. The president of the agency, Morris Jarrett, lives on Park Avenue. He has a delightful wife, two cute kids…and he's as queer as a three-dollar bill. Last year, he fell in love with Grant Tedman, a *GQ* model I know, and I've become part of their 'I'm as straight as the next guy' charade. Sometimes I go out with both of them, and naturally Morris's wife thinks it's a business night out. I even went to his suite on Park Avenue on Christmas Eve with Grant as *my* date. Morris's wife and I sat and made friendly chitchat in the living room while Morris and Grant got *very* friendly in the bathroom. Then there's this designer and his wife—he's a fag, she's a dyke. He has his dude, she has her chick. Sometimes they invite me along to make it a fivesome, and it weirds people out—who is with whom? The designer and his wife have had me over to their home many times and introduced me to some fascinating people. Yes, I love *In*. It's been good to me and I've been good to it. I can control it much better than I can control some guy's dick that's gone flaccid, and I've had *that* happen way too many times. When he just lies there with his limp dick and he's looking at you, like, 'C'mon, bitch! Be a goddamn woman and turn me on, get me hard!' So he can't get it up and he seems to think it's *my* fault. Once in a while, another Hank comes along and I convince myself that a great love *can* happen to me again, but it never does, and when the man leaves I don't break down and cry because I somehow expected the breakup would happen."

"I'm sorry for you, Rikia." Summer got up and started for the door.

"Sit your ass down. I didn't ask you over to piss and moan about my sex life or how much I miss Hank. I'm as resilient as the next chick; besides, I have a feeling that big things are going to happen to me next year. So, when Noel said to me, 'I'm going back to my wife,' I just thought, 'Well, I'm going to be eating alone tonight,' so I popped open a frozen dinner and started reading the galleys of Colton Thomas's new novel."

"Is it as good as most of his others?"

"Oh, much better. Less literary, more commercial storytelling. His last few have been remarkably eloquent but nothing much happened in them, so only the critics liked them. They sold very poorly, but this new one? It's going to sell millions and probably become a Hollywood movie. I figure that if Noel hadn't dumped me, I wouldn't have read these Colton galleys."

"So what's the plan? Bid for the serial rights?"

"I fucking wish. I understand *Playboy* has offered fifty thousand just for two excerpts. My thinking is, we can't get his book, but we can get *him*. Follow me?"

Summer sighed. "Rikia, it's late and I'm tired. No, I don't follow you. Please explain it to me."

"I know everyone worth knowing. I can introduce you to Colton Thomas and you can offer yourself to him."

"Rikia!"

"You need to lose your cherry sometime. Might as well be to a famous novelist."

"A little late for that," Summer muttered.

Rikia's jaw dropped. "You mean you did it? With Stephen? How come you waited till now to tell me? Was he magnificent? Talk, girlfriend!"

Summer shrugged. "It was awful. Not him. Me. It."

Rikia nodded. "The first time usually is for the woman. She bleeds like hell and it hurts, but he shoots a gallon, even if he's thirteen and he's with the town pump in a dark alley. Well, I'm glad you're no longer a virgin, but it's too bad you gave it up to Stephen."

"Yeah, I definitely think I should have waited."

"Absolutely. I could have hooked you up with a man. Noel, for instance."

"Oh, please."

Rikia threw up her arms. "What? Just think about it: Never do it for the first time with someone you actually care about. As I said, your first time is usually awful and the guy might say, 'Yuck! I don't want to see you anymore!' Did Stephen seem totally disgusted by the whole experience?"

Summer shook her head. "He keeps saying he loves me and wants to marry me."

Rikia glowered at her. "Then why are we sitting here weeping over your ruptured hymen? Well, congrats on getting laid—but let's get back to Colton Thomas. My sources tell me that he's hard up for cash and is willing to go on a big book tour."

"I thought he was rich. I met him years ago when my father was making a movie based on a Thomas novel. The guy had a Manhattan townhouse. He's written at least a dozen bestsellers…he must be rolling in it."

Rikia smiled. "Once upon a time, your father was 'rolling in it,' too. Maybe Colton's luck ran out, too. He's on his fourth marriage; he pays alimony to his three exes. His new missus just made him a daddy for the first time. Imagine! At his age, becoming a father! But, again, for the past while his books have sold poorly. When you live in a Beverly Hills mansion and have a fleet of cars and a dozen servants, you can't have a string of unpopular books and expect to keep your goodies. He also hasn't had a movie deal in over a decade, and that's where the big money is. But his new novel is different—or maybe I should say it's the same kind of thing his audience has always wanted, the tough-guy persona, the fast-paced storylines. He's said he's through writing *belles lettres* for the critics and wants to be an old-fashioned storyteller the way he was years ago. He told *The New Yorker* that he doesn't give a shit if the artsy-fartsy types call him a sellout; he wants to write bestsellers again and be number one and have Hollywood make movies based on his novels."

"What's all this got to do with me?"

"I want you to do a story on him."

"What? Why me?"

"Because you know him."

"I met him when I was a little kid. Do I contact him now and say, 'Hi! It's me! I want to do a story on you!'?"

"Well, your last name will get his attention. I'll fly you out to Los Angeles and we'll take it from there. I'm sure he'll be delighted to have Summer Sellars interview him for *In* magazine."

Summer yawned. "Rikia, I'm tired and I want to go to bed."

"O.K., go have a wonderful Thanksgiving. While you're lying in the Florida sun, making hot sexy love to Stephen, try to think up a good email to send to Colton Thomas. Be sure to mention your father's name a few times, and don't be shy about letting Colton know that Daddy is married to Beth Rogers Stainton…"

clxx

12

Wade stood waiting at the airport when Beth's Learjet landed. He watched as Summer exited the aircraft and took the steps with care, Stephen at her elbow. She did not see him yet, and he enjoyed watching her just being herself. 'A rare beauty,' he thought, 'and I fathered her. More woman now, less girl. I hope Stephen knows just how special she is.' Then she spotted him, and ran up to him, calling out, "Daddy! Daddy! I'm *so* happy to see you!"

He smiled and hugged her, pleased that he called her Daddy and wondering why, so much of the time, she thought it acceptable to call him Wade.

"Information your greeting party and chauffeur," Wade said as he got Summer, Stephen and their luggage settled into the convertible.

"How many guests this year?" Stephen asked.

"I'd say eight or nine. But I lose count because Beth has these *lunches* for thirty or forty people every day. See, I go out to gold at nine in the morning and when I get back in the afternoon, many of the lunch guests are still there. Then, at about seven, the cocktail guests arrive. But Beth has decided that Thanksgiving dinner itself this year will be a cozy little affair of maybe two dozen folks. This is

Thanksgiving, right? Let's thank the sun god for smiling down on us today. You both look in need of a tan."

The sunny weather continued throughout the weekend. Poker and backgammon games happened poolside; hot and cold buffets arrived on tables pushed by servants. Wade and Summer were inseparable—they sat together, walked on the beach and swam.

When Summer changed into her tennis whites and played Stephen, Wade watched with the deepest admiration how lithe, agile and powerful his daughter had become—and what a relentless competitor she seemed to be, swatting the ball this way and that, laughing as Stephen practically fell on his ass as he tried to return her service. How, Wade asked himself, had she learned to play tennis so well? Then he closed his eyes in shame as he recalled all those tennis tournaments he had missed because of his other "obligations." She had won a dozen or more trophies and sent them to him in New York; he'd put them in storage with so many other trivial items. Did he even know where he'd put the claim tickets?

Good Lord, how little of himself he had actually given her. How much of her childhood he had missed, and how much of her own adolescence she had missed. Now she was entering the very best years of her life and he was forced to miss *them*, too. He was married now...but this was one dud he could not simply bring down the curtain on.

As he watched his daughter on the tennis court, he felt seized with panic at the realization that he considered his marriage a dud. Yet Mister and Missus Sellars were the envy of virtually all who knew them.

Beth smiled at him from across the dinner table every night and slipped her arm through his whenever they appeared together in public. He still had intercourse with her twice or thrice per week. He grimaced again. Yes! That was the problem! *He* did *her*; they didn't do each other. Beth did her wifely duty as if it were some sort of marital chore. Maybe it was his fault; she probably felt unwanted because he spent so much of his time enjoying outside-the-home hobbies. Even *he* knew he spent very little time with her. He happily played golf till noon each day and cards in the afternoon. (He knew of a dozen places to play poker for money, and often cleaned out other men less skilled than himself.) He always managed to get back to Beth in time for a cocktail, and every night they seemed to be at some dinner party.

'Well,' he thought, 'nothing's gonna change unless I make those changes happen. Right after Summer leaves I'm gonna whisk Beth off to the bedroom and show her what good lovin' is all about. Won't kill me to spend a few afternoons with the old lady. Of course, I won't be spending them *exclusively* with her. No, I'll just be hanging out with those friends of hers, having lunch and watching them play backgammon. I'll play golf in the morning, but no more poker all afternoon. I've already won over ten thousand dollars playing cards and opened a bank account, the first one I've had in a while. Ten thousand is chump change, but it's *mine*, money I've earned or won. But I need to pay more attention to Beth in the sack. Well, after the houseguests leave this weekend, I'm gonna make my old lady the most oversexed broad around.'

He felt better right away. It helped to evaluate things once in a while and decide upon the best course of action. For quite a while he had wondered what was wrong with his marriage, and then decided that *he* was the problem, so *he* could also become the solution. He concluded that he needed to be a better husband, or at least a more attentive one. Wherever they went—and they went pretty much everywhere—they went to parties and sipped cocktails and made small talk because that's what Beth seemed to want and Wade knew it when he hooked up with her. He was supposed to supply the romance and pose for pictures with Beth so that they could be talked about in private. *Whatvere became of Wade Sellars, the man who owned Broadway and then tried to take on Hollywood? Oh, don't worry about him. He's married to Beth Rogers Stainton, who's the richest woman on Earth.*

Well, starting Sunday, Wade Sellars would be the most romantic husband around.

But for now, he simply stood around admiring his daughter. He watched her skin turn chocolate bronze; he loved seeing her magnificent breasts and bottom bounce in her bikini (Beth seemed proud of looking as white as an albino). Summer's long blonde hair swung in the breeze; Beth drowned hers in hairspray to keep it in place. Summer dressed in provocative denims; Beth arrayed herself in old-lady whites. Beth was a very pretty woman, but Summer was a knockout.

Summer was blessed with a certain immaculate sparkle that thrilled her father. He loved how she took a genuine interest in all things. All-consuming interest in *In* magazine; moderate interest in Stephen. "Polite" interest in Beth's whispered nuggets about scandals and seductions among her Manhattan society friends. Those names must have meant little or nothing to Summer, but she nodded and smiled and frowned in all the right places and at all the right times.

What was Wade to make of Stephen? He had difficulty figuring out the younger man. Stephen was always present, smiling, showing the world his big white teeth. Wade could tell they were first cousins— they were so much alike in so many ways, with their fine manners and perfect clothes. Whoever said there were no American aristocrats? And wasn't Stephen the kind of man Wade wanted for Summer? Wade loved and adored and was fascinated by show business but didn't *respect* it or the people in it, and he certainly didn't want *his* daughter marrying a showbiz man. Long before he met Beth, Wade decided he wanted the best life for Summer that money could buy. That was why he'd sent her to the New England School for Girls. His business manager had said, "That's where she'll meet rich, charming girls and be introduced to their brothers. That's why those fancy schools exist."

Wade smirked. So far as he could tell, all *his* kid had gotten from that school were an armload of tennis trophies and a job at a magazine. Of all the genteel young ladies there, she had to get chummy with that fuckin' Rikia, the toughest, hardest kid in all of New England, a chick who'd probably banged every boy in Connecticut and Massachusetts before graduating. He stared some more at Summer and told himself that everything would work out well for her in life. He believed Beth when she said, "Summer will play the 'career girl' part for a while, then get bored with it and marry Stephen."

He suddenly felt sad but didn't know why. Wasn't

his daughter growing up to become the person he wanted her to be? Did he want her to become a younger version of Beth? Well, would that be so bad? What if she had been more like him—taking her moderate performing talent more seriously and living the life of a Broadway actor? What then? Even if she made it—which she probably would, because she was gorgeous enough to hold any audience's attention— her time at the top would end a few years later, leaving her full of loneliness and despair. If a man had money, he had a few options. But a woman got old, and age did her in. Even a screen legend like Hana— did she now have a life worth living? Still doing aerobics every day; maybe that was the thing keeping her from jumping off a bridge. Also, most Broadway and Hollywood stars weren't lucky enough to be born dumb like Hana, content to spend their lives walking and bouncing around in a leotard. The brittle, fragile ones bled from rejection as if slashed with a knife; they spent their nights dreamless from booze and pills, then sat in their Beverly Hills mansions and watched daytime TV. No, Wade decided, Summer should just stay the course. All the things she *really* needed to know, she'd learned at the girls' school. He had supplied the rest. A place like this to spend Thanksgiving in—down and back in a Learjet, tennis and a tan in November, gourmet food and countless admirers. Whatever she wanted.

Wade grinned. Hadn't he gotten it for her? She walked off the tennis court with Stephen, having beaten him in straight sets. That was his girl—any and every man's superior. But he had to respect Stephen. Losing graciously was a difficult skill, but Beth's cousin had mastered it. Wade chuckled at how

Stephen, after being run ragged by Summer for close to an hour, leapt over the net to hug and congratulate her as two dozen spectators applauded. But mostly Wade liked Stephen's big sincere smile and fine manners at the many social gatherings the young man attended with Summer.

'Maybe,' Wade said to himself, 'things will turn out all right for her. Maybe I did the right thing, flying her down here for the holiday weekend. If my luck holds out, they'll fly down here for the Christmas holidays and will be engaged. Beth would love that! But maybe that's too soon. What's the rush? Summer won't be twenty-one till next July. Take it nice and slow.'

But then he thought, 'Why take it nice and slow? What's she got to gain by doing it that way? Chicks don't need to play the field; they're happy to get one guy and settle down for life. Summer isn't one of those ugly, angry feminists. When I see those broads on TV, I gotta laugh out loud and think, *If you bought yourself some hot clothes and got a handsome man, you wouldn't care about this feminist shit*. Just lonely, horny, frustrated women—that's all they are. Well, *my* kid will never have those problems.'

He got up early on Sunday and had breakfast with Summer. Neither said much; they enjoyed each other's company just fine without conversation. Wade read the sports page while Summer read galleys.

"Galleys," he muttered. "Good?"

"Great. Remember Colton Thomas?"

"Sure do. Adapted one of his novels to the big screen. Made myself a few million."

"Do you remember taking me to his home in Manhattan?"

He nodded. "Yeah, a brownstone near East

Sixtieth."

"Rikia wants me to do an article on him. What do you remember about him?"

Wade smirked. "I remember he was pretty full of himself. He had just won the Pulitzer Prize for fiction. I said, 'Congratulations on the Pulitzer.' He shrugged and said, 'Who cares? I want the Nobel.' He had written only half a dozen novels when he said that, so he would have to double that number before the Nobel folks would take him seriously, but he was determined to do it. But then he got divorced a few times and got into some barroom brawls and lost some of his 'I'm gonna be the greatest writer ever' fire." Then, "I know that, from a commercial standpoint, he's gone out of fashion lately, but I didn't think he would be desperate enough to sit down for an interview in that rag you work for."

Summer scowled. "Wade! Have you ever *read* it?"

He nodded. "As soon as I found out you were going to work there, I read it from cover to cover. As I say, it's not for Colton Thomas. Do you remember years ago when newspapers everywhere carried a story about how he manhandled sharks when his fishing boat capsized? The sharks came by and he punched them to keep them away."

"Really?" Summer asked with a nervous little laugh.

"Sure...and he's fought bulls in Spain. He knocked out a heavyweight boxer in a tavern. His plane crashed and he walked a mile for help despite having three cracked ribs. He can outdrink and out-fuck any man. He could knock out Mike Tyson in two minutes."

Summer just giggled, and Wade said, "My point is,

that's the kind of publicity he craves. Half the fun of reading a Colton Thomas novel is knowing about the crazy-fearless man who wrote those words. The truth is, over the years he has punched out many men in bars, although I don't think any of them was a professional boxer. His fishing companions swear that he did fight off the sharks, and everyone says he fought that bull, but it was one of the wimpier bulls. *That's* the kind of publicity that complements the legend of Colton Thomas, so I'm not sure what he thinks he has to gain by consenting to an interview with *In* magazine."

"Well, we'll have to wait and see."

"What did he say when you submitted your request."

"We haven't asked him yet."

Wade chuckled. "Hmm. Were you thinking of sending him an email mentioning that you're my daughter and he and I are old acquaintances…?"

She shrugged. "It had crossed my mind."

He shook his head. "Bad idea. Best thing for you to do when contacting him is *not* saying that you're related to me in any way."

"Why?"

"Because he doesn't like me. As I said, when we knew each other, he was, you know, 'Nobel! Nobel! I want that Nobel!' He was taking himself *very* seriously, and assumed that I would adapt his novel to the screen essentially intact. Well, I didn't. I was an ambitious young producer who wanted a big commercial hit—I didn't give a *shit* about the integrity of the movie based on his novel. At my insistence, we deleted some key scenes and characters so that we didn't have a movie that ran for five or six hours."

"But you made him a pile of money, right?"

"Nope. I made myself and the studio a pile of money. We paid Colton a flat fee—two hundred thousand dollars; chump change, really—and when we released the picture, he started jumping up and down, yelling, 'That was not my story! You cut it down to nothing!' Like all other artists, he's very temperamental and volatile. He can't stand to have anyone fuck with his work."

"How old is he now?"

"Oh, probably close to sixty. But from what I hear, he's still partying and getting it on with chicks who've just come of age." Wade shook his head. "I don't think there's anything worse than an aging horny guy. It's like a forty-year-old woman who's riding the dicks of college boys."

"So how should I contact Colton Thomas about doing a story on him?"

"Don't bother. Find someone else."

After that, they had very few chances to talk. Their servants came in with lunch, and for the rest of the day the house was full of people. Some of the younger men surrounded Summer and flirted with her as Stephen stood inches away. Wade noticed how those guys breathed into her face and ogled her beautiful blonde breasts. He also noticed how Stephen laughed and shook his head, as if saying, *Go ahead and check her out, boys. She's going home with* me *when this thing's over.* Wade had enjoyed his time with Summer down here but it wasn't enough. She and Stephen would fly back to New York, and soon after that the rest of these folks would disappear. He would be alone with Beth tonight, and tomorrow the luncheons would happen all over again. After that, there would be more parties…and still more…and then Christmas. He knew that Beth wanted to fly out to southern California for a backgammon tournament, and he felt O.K. about going out there and staying with her friends and playing golf in the sun—but he sure as hell didn't want to make that an entire way of life. Maybe after southern California they could go back to Manhattan, even though Wade mainly just played cards and goofed off in New York. The Apple was his home, to the extent that he had one, and each day on the street he saw people he knew. He had the easiest time convincing himself that his life had meaning and purpose, and he genuinely enjoyed the TV stars, famous musicians and culture vultures he encountered there. He would make a point of spending as much time there as possible. Tonight he'd boff Beth, make her satisfied and grateful, then suggest that they stay put for a few weeks at the Amsterdam after getting back from California.

He drove Summer and Stephen and watched them bound up into the Learjet. Then he walked back to the car and said to himself, "They're such a beautiful young couple. When, or how, or why, did I get so old? Damn, I'm only fifty-two; is that so old? I'm still in my prime, still a handsome man—no fat, full head of hair, a big white smile. Women still check me out. Of course, they're all Beth's friends, in their forties, but still…some of the younger ones pay me plenty of attention, too. I smile, I'm nice, but I keep my hands to myself, not that I wouldn't jumping the bones of a few of them…like Ericka, the daughter of Beth's banker friend, who started playing golf so she spend more time around me. Ericka and me…I'd love to jump her bones, but I won't. I made a deal with myself when I married Beth: If I married Beth and her payouts to Summer were big enough, I would be completely monogamous. Besides, Beth was still a very desirable woman, even if she was getting a little soft in the tummy at times, and I can get it up for her whenever necessary. Hey, I know a hundred men who'd be happy to bang her till she screamed, and lately I've been banging her, what, twice per week? Well, that was bad and wrong. Beth couldn't just ask if she wanted more; she wasn't Claire Tinsall, who'd just come up and say, 'Fuck me, baby.' But not Beth, and very soon she was going to discover that she had the horniest and most attentive husband around.'

Back at the house, everyone had gone, and Wade took a bottle of champagne and two glasses and headed upstairs to surprise Beth.

He found her on her *chaise longue*, writing in her leather-bound date planner. She looked up at him and said, "Champagne? Why?"

He pointed at her book. "Just us tonight, O.K.?"

She shrugged. "There are a half-dozen parties in town—"

"Just us tonight." He set down the bottle and glasses, then leaned over and kissed her. "We can have our own party right here."

"Wade, it's too early."

"Never too early for love." He placed his hand over her breast. "Let's get on that nice big bed and make hot love to each other like a husband and wife were meant to do. We can fuck under the moon and stars."

She pushed him away. "Wade! Who do you think you're talking to? One of those trashy chorus girls on

Times Square?"

He sighed. "Beth…that's just part of foreplay. I didn't mean to offend you."

"Well, you *did* offend me." She turned away. He picked up the bottle and glasses and walked off.

"Wade, don't be angry," she said. "It's just that I'm not interested in *that* right now."

"I hear ya." He raised the bottle as if toasting her. "I think I'll take this back to my bedroom and pleasure myself for a while. I promised myself I would get laid tonight, and I always try to keep my promises." He left her bedroom.

Beth stayed still for the longest time after Wade left. She shook her head and told herself that she had handled it all wrong. She should have submitted sexually to Wade. Why didn't she? Because she was tired and sleep from a full day of smiling till her cheeks hurt as she played the part of Beth Rogers Stainton Sellars, the billionaire lady everyone envied. What nobody knew was that Beth, wife of handsome, fascinating Wade Sellars, was crabby and morose because her lesbian lover hadn't shown up for the weekend. Hadn't Hana practically promised to fly down for Thanksgiving? Beth *so* wanted her to join them. She wanted Hana to see Stephen and Summer here together—playing tennis, swimming, dancing— and for Hana to know that Stephen and Summer were young and belonged together. Several days before the weekend, Hana had said "maybe," and that if maybe had turned out to be yes, she would be at the airport by four. So Beth had held the plane till four-thirty.

She had put on a happy face when she saw Summer and Stephen arrive together. She felt delighted that they bonded so well. At least *something* had gone right for her that weekend. It gratified her that Stephen really seemed to care for Summer; so tragic that Hana hadn't been there to see it! Why hadn't the bitch come? After all, everyone in Hana's New York scene had left town; what was there for her to do there all by herself?

Stephen, too, had thought about Hana. He thought about her throughout the weekend, and he sat thinking about her as the Learjet cruised towards LaGuardia Airport. He remembered that he had scarcely spoken to Summer during their flight. But she had buried herself in some galleys and barely looked up, and after putting away her reading material she just stared out the window. He wondered for a moment what she was thinking about, then started thinking about Hana some more.

Summer stared out the window, thinking of Stephen. She also thought of the galleys she had just read and resolved to contact Colton Thomas on her own as assistant editor of *In* magazine. She decided not to tell Rikia that Wade would have no involvement in their project. She looked over and studied Stephen's tanned, pretty-boy face for a few moments as he stared out *his* window. He had been *such* a darling during the weekend, always willing to play tennis or go swimming. That little flicker of something she had felt for him turned to nothing after their disastrous first night together, but she thought they could rekindle it. But she could never enter his red bedroom again. *Never.*

The car Stephen had ordered sat waiting on the airfield. They stored their luggage into its trunk, and Stephen helped the doorman with Summer's luggage at her building.

She smiled and said, "I've really enjoyed these past few days together."

He smiled back. "It's been great fun."

"It's not that late, you know. Want to come in and see my apartment?"

"Wish I could, but I need to get ready for tomorrow. Business, you know. But I promise to call you."

He got back into the car, and Summer watched him disappear. She shrugged, thinking: *I just offered him a chance to get laid, and he said no.*

Stephen had no desire to screw Summer. Hana was the woman he loved. He had his whole evening free and wished to spend every moment with her. But she had never given him her telephone number, so he couldn't call her. He threw a vicious punch at the air and decided he'd had enough of her hard-to-get bullshit. He'd go over to her apartment right now, pound on her door until she opened it and explain to her: *If you want me to act like a man, start treating me like one!*

He got a taxi to Hana's building, paid the driver and bounded up to the doorman.

"Good evening, Mister Rogers. Who are you here to see?"

Who the *fuck* do you think I'm here to see? "The usual person."

"I'm sorry, but Miz Hana left on Friday morning."

"Left?"

"Yessir. She had three suitcases."

"Where? How? Why? Did she move—"

"No, sir, she certainly didn't move. She'll be back when she's ready to return. You know how she is—just up and leaves whenever the spirit moves her. She told the driver to take her to Kennedy Airport."

"I was away myself," Stephen murmured in the dreamy, 'I can't believe this is happening' voice of someone who's just learned that the love of his life has been killed. He disliked the compassionate—pitying?—look on the doorman's face. "I was in Florida, getting a tan…Hana wouldn't give me her telephone number…"

13

Hana sat in the front seat of the jet, smoothing out her skirt. After calling every airline, she had bought a ticket for United's late-morning flight to London after they promised her that she would have the entire aisle all to herself.

She straightened her big opaque sunglasses on the bridge of her nose. So far, none of the flight attendants seemed to know who she was. How young those women were! Some of them were scarcely more than toddlers when she retired from acting. But technology had changed, and 24-hour TV stations bought up her movies and broadcast them so often, and at such varied times, that even flight attendants had likely seen some of them. She watched as they giggled and whispered together, prepared hors d'oeuvres *and cocktails. She stole glances at them as they went up and down the aisles, looking after their passengers, always smiling, delighted to be up there 30,000 feet above the world and its problems. Had* she *ever been so young and happy? No. Certainly not. Being a giggling young thing was not possible when one grew up in the village of Gorsek.*

Martina Maria Hanavosky was raised on a farm in Gorsek, in Russia. Her childhood there was uneventful and, much of the time, mind-numbingly boring. She had no dreams, no imagination, no fantasies of how wonderful life could be. Her greatest ambition was given was to her by her mother. 'Marry a local boy whose family is better off than we are.'

She attended the state school, and at age nine she met Sister Suzette, who was tall and slim and beautiful, with a big smile and creamy skin. Sister Suzette had aspired to become a ballerina, and made it clear that she would be happy to teach ballet to those who cared to learn.

Martina asked for lessons, partly because Sister Suzette fascinated her, so therefore she took up the nun on her offer and practiced with singleminded determination.

One day, the nun said, "Martina, I believe you have the potential to become a first-rate ballerina, so I am going to see about getting you a ballet scholarship if your family approves."

Her mother and father considered it a grand opportunity for their daughter; although they knew nothing about ballet, they heard the world *scholarship* and immediately surmised that it was the best thing that had ever happened to Martina. Accepting the scholarship would mean leaving town and seeing Sister Suzette much less often.

So she won the scholarship and for the next several years her life was about ballet and the one day each week when she got to see Sister Suzette. Martina danced as Sister Suzette sat in the audience. Martina's parents sat there, too, utterly confused by the ballet and what it meant; her father fell asleep many times and had to be jabbed and poked awake by his wife. Eventually, the parents stopped coming.

When Martina became ready for her first solo, she learned that she must choose a name for herself.

Sister Suzette said, 'How about *Hana*?' During their post-performance embrace, the nun whispered, 'Congratulations, *Hana*,' and from that moment on the young woman became Hana and ceased to think of herself by any other name.

'My family is very affluent,' the nun told Hana's parents. 'My uncle lives in London in a big fine house. We can send your daughter to live with them so she can have a world-class education in ballet—the same one they wanted for me. Do I have your permission to help her in this manner?'

They both nodded, completely overwhelmed by this beautiful young nun and the plans she was making for their humble daughter.

But Hana said no. "I won't go. I won't be apart from you."

"You will miss me at first," said the nun. "But then you will become immersed in your own life. In ballet, there is little left here for you. In London, you will learn so much more. Isn't that what you want?"

Hana threw herself into Sister Suzette's arms. "No! I want you! I love you!"

The nun pried the young woman's body from her own. "I love you, too."

"You do? Then let me kiss your lips and touch your body—" Hana placed her hand over the nun's breast.

The nun pulled the hand from her breast. "No. You must never touch me like that. It is wrong."

"How can love be wrong?"

"Love is wrong when it is physical and between two females."

Hana pouted. "How can it be wrong when it feels so right? I want you, and only you, and I want us to be to be touching and kissing." Then, "Sister, I know nothing about making love, and I say nothing to the other girls here, but I know at night as I lay in my cubicle, I can hear them sneaking into each other's bed…I know what they're doing. They ask me, but I say no. I want only you. I have daydreams of you and me, we are both naked and—"

The nun held up a hand. "Say no more. It is wrong. It will never happen. At your age, I had the same feelings for other girls and I acted on them because there were no boys around."

So Hana, realizing that her love affair with the nun would never happen, went to ballet school in London and rarely thought of her family after that.

She was scared to death of going to California, but her agent, Jeremiah, had already signed the contract with the studio. She went anyway, and when she and Jeremiah met up in Beverly Hills, he discovered that she was having a hot and steamy fling with Lindsay Haymer.

"Hana!" he said. "This won't do! Lindsay is a married mother of three. This sort of publicity…I don't need to explain it to you, do I?"

"It's nobody's damn business."

"Oh, but it is. Please use some discretion."

"After this picture opens in America, I will become a major worldwide star. The press here say I am the most exciting in the world of international cinema. You'll be making lots of money from me, so don't give me a hard time. I'm saving lots, too— Lindsay pays for everything."

Jeremiah was hardly surprised that the love affair

between Hana and Lindsay soon ended. But it amazed him how women in general seemed to lust for her. Hana didn't impress him as being at all butch—or especially pretty—and he wondered if lesbians could recognize their own just on sight. But Hana shunned the movie-industry lesbians who flirted with her.

Hana's next co-star, Myles Byroni, was dashing and handsome, thrice divorced and shacking up with a *GQ* model. Once she discovered that Myles had a live-in boyfriend, Hana decided she wanted a big blond male body in her bed.

They began filming, and within two weeks Myles moved out of his apartment and broke up with his boyfriend. He fell desperately in love with Hana, and when she ad-libbed at length in several key scenes, he played along with her as if he were little more than a supporting actor. Their film received great notices and she became a major star. Her "romance" with Myles also became a hot item in every movie magazine.

For a few months she delighted having him in her life. She had him over to her virtually bare house, where they barbecued steaks and ate them with their fingers. Myles joked that dinner at her place was always a "picnic," but at other times he chastised her for her poor table manners—stop chewing with your mouth open, he told her, and stop slurping your wine and soup. But she mostly ignored him, and after a while he shut up about it.

Myles loved the excitement and glamor of Hollywood—the big parties, the beautifully dressed men and women, the klieg lights at premieres and the wide-eyed, beaming faces of the nobodies who'd turned out to stand behind the ropes and ogle the somebodies. But Hana stayed away from those galas. Terrified of the crowds, cynical about the nasty small talk that always happened at big parties. She worried that those people would mock her weird accent and see her for the immigrant peasant she was. So her affair with Myles went stale, and when we went off to do his next picture and fell in love with his leading lady, Hana just shrugged and said good riddance.

She exploited her newfound freedom. The movie business was full of luscious young women who practically wept with gratitude at the opportunity to enter the great Hana's home. In public, and especially on the movie set, Hana ignored the girl, so any "I made it with Hana" stories the starlet might tell later went disbelieved. Every so often a man came along who captured her imagination for a time, and she would have him over to ravish her in her bedroom and barbecue steaks in her backyard. The fan magazines always learned of such liaisons early on and ran drooling stories about Hana and her lovers, but by the time each story was available for consumption, the paramours had ended their tryst.

Hana signed on to make a movie with Kel Christiansen. His blond hair and hazel eyes turned her on, and he was at his peak professionally. He cooked steaks in her backyard, and during their three months of acting together onscreen, their romance grew hotter.

During their last week of filming, Hana began to tire of Kel. The conclusion of a project usually did that to her—end the picture, end the relationship. But for the first time, she found herself unable simply to walk away. Female lovers were different, at least for her—she could make the rules and dismiss them as soon as they bored her. They lacked the power to hurt her, and when she said goodbye they seemed, if anything, grateful for how much of herself she had shared with them. Men, too, sat at her side and begged for scraps of affection.

Kel, though, was different. He made her visit him at his Beverly Hills palace and both of them stripped naked poolside. He taught her to swim as his servants went about their business of keeping his home tidy. He tried to teach her tennis but she got too frustrated and bored. For the twentieth time, she mopped sweat off her face and arms. Then she threw down her racket and marched off the court.

They had almost completed filming their picture. In several weeks she would start the next one. She could have Kel as her leading man, even though the studio had already cast someone else, an actor much less expensive than Kel. No matter; if Hana said, 'I want Kel,' the studio would replace the cheaper actor with Kel Christiansen.

Kel cared very little. As long as he got star billing and big paychecks, he stayed happy.

As soon as they completed filming their picture, the two went for a drive.

"I'm pregnant," she told him.

He nearly lost control of the car. "Wow! That's terrific! We'll drive to Mexico right now and get married…Then we'll come back and tell everyone the great news! Your guy Jeremiah can handle the situation for us…"

She laughed, and he said, "We can sell both our houses and get one gigantic estate. I have a couple of alimonies to pay, but so what? I still make seven figures per year, and combined with your fee, we can live the way Hearst did. We can be an old-fashioned Hollywood couple, throwing lavish parties and being the envy of the whole world…"

"Turn back now," she said.

"Why?"

"Just do as I say. If you try to take me to Mexico, I'll accuse you of kidnapping."

He did as told, and they stayed silent all the way back to her house. Marry him and have his child! Sell her house, buy one with him and spend her life throwing parties for Hollywood freeloaders! What nonsense. She could never do things his way—welcoming people into her home so they could eat *her* food, drink *her* liquor and do nothing for her in return. Only a fool would do such a thing.

Jeremiah called. 'I've booked you an appointment with an abortionist. Are you sure that's what you want?' She said yes, and the following week he called again. 'Kel's in the hospital. He tried to commit suicide.' But Hana still refused to answer the actor's telephone calls.

She spent thousands of dollars trying to locate Sister Suzette. The private eye could only shrug. 'I've tried everything I can think of, but it's as if she's never existed.' Hana said, 'Fuck it all. My only concern now is my career.'

Despite her stinginess, Hana was much less wealthy than she should have been. She told Jeremiah, 'I've done all the work but you're the rich one. Why is that?'

'Because I've made my money work for me. I've invested it in the markets and watched it quadruple any number of times. How many times have I said,

"Hana, pull your money out of those stupid savings accounts and invest with me"?' He wanted to add, but did not, 'You never know when your public is going to lose interest in you and stop buying tickets to your pictures.'

Her next three or four pictures flopped, but her public's interest in Hana intensified. She watched no TV, did not own a radio or computer and remained largely oblivious to her movies' minuscule earnings. When entertainment journalists asked Jeremiah if his client was in good spirits, he hinted at her retirement and the showbiz press repeated it.

'I want to be the highest-paid woman in Hollywood,' she said to Jeremiah. 'Tell the honchos at Galaxy that I will agree to a three-picture deal as long as I get more money than all the other women.'

Jeremiah nodded and went off to negotiate with the honcho, bluffing and lying and threatening and promising. Hana did ballet exercises and waited for Jeremiah to come to her with good news.

He joined her for dinner and they ate steaks in her backyard. She gnawed away at the succulent meat like a famished animal. Jeremiah watched gravy dribble down her beautiful chin.

'Hana,' he said, 'do you know of the novel *My Warrior*?' He sighed, knowing that she never read books. He suspected she might be illiterate. 'It's a major bestseller and the Galaxy honcho thinks he can get Tom Cruise to play the title character.'

'Tell me more.'

'They want you to play his lover.'

She shrugged. 'And this would be good for Hana?'

'It would be great.'

'And the money?'

'Not so much. They have only so much money for actors, and Cruise would get most of it.'

She stopped eating but did not wipe her chin. 'I thought your job was to get me the most money of any woman.'

'Hana,' he told her, 'you pay little attention to the movie *business*, so you don't know that your last few movies have failed badly. The fan magazines have people shouting, *Who is Hana? Where does she come from? Why does she love so many men? Does she love women, too?* They are interested in the lend of Hana but not in your movies. This new movie with Cruise? They will pay you a quarter of the amount you want, and a small percentage of ticket sales. If the movie grosses tens of millions of dollars, your earnings will be adequate.'

She said nothing. She wiped her face and pushed away her plate.

Jeremiah said, 'That's what there is. We have no options left.'

'If I accept this insulting offer, then the world will say, "Hana is fading." But if I retire, nobody will say unkind things.'

'You are far too young to retire.'

'Not *real* retirement; *fake* retirement. After a year of no Hana, Hollywood will want me back and pay me my price.'

'In the meantime, how will you survive? You have bills to pay and not very much money saved up.'

Hana got up. 'I am going for a walk.'

'Want some company?'

'No, you wait here till I get back.'

He did as told. He sat on the sofa and wondered

why Hana spoke and behaved as she did. When she returned, he looked up at her and said, 'So, what's the plan?'

'Have you ever heard of Teddi Jo White?'

He nodded. "She's an oil millionaire down in Louisiana."

"Yes. She's also a total lesbian. She has made it clear that she wants to eat my pussy. She will pay half a million dollars for the pleasure of going down on me for one night. I have gotten this information from Juanita Kindler, whose job is to know every dyke and queer in America worth knowing. I shall tell Juanita to tell Teddi that I will sit on her face at her convenience."

Teddi Jo White…the obese, sweaty lesbo. Ugh. But the bitch had marched into Hana's home and tossed a tote bag of greenbacks at Hana's feet. 'Count it if you want,' she'd drawled. Hana shook her head and they got down to business. Teddi Jo knew how to give head; Hana had screamed so loudly that Teddi had to stop and say, 'Shut up, will ya?' Afterwards, Teddi said, 'Money well spent. I have some rich friends who'd like to do you, if you're interested.' And she was *interested…*

As her retirement continued, her legend thrived. Her "comeback" offers grew until, three years into her retirement, she got a call from Jeremiah, who said that Galaxy wanted her for a starring role, five million dollars plus ten percent of the gross.

'No,' she said. By then she had met Beth Rogers Stainton, "the richest woman in New York," and the two had fallen in love. Besides, Hana felt too anxious about returning to films. What if it failed and her comeback became a joke? Always best to walk away while you're still on top, and let the world remember you as young and beautiful. Beth considered herself the luckiest woman alive to be spending so much time with the legendary Hana. In the last few years, Hana had managed to save over a million dollars without working a single day. Beth had her own private jet, an oversized yacht, a few fancy homes and a homosexual hubby who let her do her own thing. Beth was a bit stingier than the other ladies who'd courted Hana; Beth had this "prove you love me for who I am, not what I have" thing that some rich folks were into. But Beth was pretty and obscenely rich and would remain in Hana's life for as long as Hana wanted her there. So she rejected all movie offers, secure in the belief that she controlled Beth and would do so for a very long time. Everything had been going fine and dandy until Beth's gay husband was killed and Beth said, 'We need an escort. Let's get Stephen.'

Stephen…Hana didn't like the idea from the outset. Why did they need a male escort, anyway? And why Stephen, who was *so* young…and Hana was *so* old. But then they started spending all that time together, and she felt young and carefree and wonderful and decided it was O.K. to have him in her life.

As they rode in the car, Jeremiah kept on about the studio's latest offer: Five million dollars, two weeks' work and a thousand-dollar per diem. *She nearly laughed as she shook her head. What was the point of appearing in another movie? She had never thought of herself as much of an actor, nor had she believed in her potential as a dancer. She'd done the ballet thing because of her attraction to Sister Suzette, and continued them because they helped her to stay in shape. Hardly religious—she was nowhere in sight when the church bells rang—she nevertheless got on her knees sometimes in the darkness and said, at her bedside, 'Why don't You stop me when You see me making an ass of myself?'*

She entered the big, grand hotel, pleased that people shot her only the briefest glance before concluding she was a nobody and moving on. She felt grateful that Jeremiah was with her. She knew her future was with Beth. Her relationship with Stephen had become too complicated and difficult—time to say goodbye. After having her facelift, she had spent the night with Stephen and learned that she really wasn't a lesbian. In his arms she had convulsed, again and again, as he drove his big stiff cock inside her. Each time they were together, she craved him more and more and began to dread her nights with Beth. And when she prayed, she began thanking Him for bringing Stephen into her life…

cc

14

Summer sat in Rikia's office, nursing a tall cup of takeout coffee at frowning at her boss. Rikia, up and down for most of her life, was at a particularly low ebb, and not just because it happened to be Monday. 'The beginning of the week always sucks,' she had said myriad times. 'But a rainy Monday in February? That makes me question whether life is worth living.'

'Look at it this way,' Summer had told her. 'February is the shortest month, and once we get into March, we can pretend it's already spring.'

"I still envy you," Rikia was saying. "Christmas in Florida."

"It was the same old crowd. What do you buy for people like my stepmother, a woman who has everything she could possibly want?"

"So what *did* you buy her?"

Summer smirked. "Some place settings she could wrap up and give to someone else."

"Hmm." Then, "How's it going with Stephen?"

"Well, not long ago, he called and said, 'I'm flying out to a conference in California for the Securities Professionals' Association.' I'm not sure that such an organization exists. I think Hana was out there at about the same time, so maybe that's why he made the trip."

"*My* sources say Hana flew out to Los Angeles to see her friend Juanita Kindler."

Summer shrugged. She had little time to wonder about Stephen or Hana or Juanita Kindler. Colton Thomas would be arriving in town in a few days to attend a party, as the guest of honor, that his publisher was throwing. As Summer sat drinking takeout coffee, Rikia snarled at the bad behavior of a woman named Louise Ritamen who had failed to return her telephone calls.

"I've called five times in the past three days." Rikia glowered. "I've even spoken to the secretary of Levin himself."

"Who's Levin?"

"Larry Levin. The boss of the whole publishing company. I told them, '*In* has not received an invitation to the Colton Thomas party; is it in the mail?' Well, she gets a bit huffy with me and says, 'Well, Miz Saddy, it's not what we would call a press party, although some media people will certainly be there. It's really a "welcome to New York" party for Mr. Thomas, although we know that the mayor and some major celebrities will be there.' Rikia glowered some more. "I got the impression that we're just not good enough for them. She said she would give my message to Levin. Big fuckin' deal."

"Well, we still have a few days left. Maybe that invitation will happen," said Summer.

On the day of the party, Summer sat in Rikia's office and said, "It'll probably be a boring party anyway."

Rikia snarled. "Is it raining?"

"Snowing."

"Good. I hope the bad weather makes everyone

say, 'Let's not to go to the Colton Thomas party.' Or people get wet on their way to the party and catch cold and have a perfectly shitty time." Then, "You know what, Summer? Everyone I have ever met who has worked with your father says, 'Oh, Wade Sellars? He's a wonderful man—I adore him!' Everyone, that is, except Colton Thomas!"

Summer shrugged. "Maybe they were too much *like* each other to like each other. Or Colton Thomas was just being himself. Rikia, I did my best to make a good first impression. I sent him an email in November, making sure I did not in any way mention that I was related to Wade Sellars, because that would have turned Colton right off. So I just signed it S. Sellars, but maybe he figured out that because Sellars is an uncommon last name, I must be related to you-know-who. I followed that up with another email a couple of weeks later. *Nada.* So I contacted Allen Jays, his flack in Los Angeles, who said, 'I can give you the address of his beach house in Malibu.' Well, I didn't even know that Colton Thomas *had* a Malibu beach house. I sent him a Christmas card with a little 'Hope to see you over the holidays' scribbled on it. Not long after that, I sent him a shamelessly brownnosing letter saying, 'I have read the galleys of your latest novel and it will be a major bestseller.'" Then, "Rikia, be serious. When my father adapted his novel to the big screen and that movie got a bunch of Oscar nominations, Colton refused to go to the ceremony. He was, like, 'I'm a serious writer, I'm not interested in the Oscars, they're a bunch of bullshit.'"

Rikia nodded. "Still and all, he *is* Colton Thomas and he does need publicity, and I'm sure if we had been invited to that party, we could have talked him into consenting to an *In* story…especially after he'd had a few cocktails."

Summer smiled. "Let's do it."

"You mean crash that party?"

"Damn straight."

"I wish. Can't do it. Too big a deal. Security people everywhere."

"Give it a try. We'll dress up, hire a limo, act like we belong."

Rikia cackled. "Hire a limo? Do you think it'll work?"

"Well, it'll be a big party where some folks won't show up because of the weather. If we show up in style, maybe they'll be grateful to have two well-dressed ladies to compensate for all the well-dressed ladies who've stayed home because of the weather."

Rikia nodded. "Let's get busy."

The party happened in a medium-sized ballroom. When Rikia and Summer arrived, they could see that the inclement weather had prevented very few people from attending the function. Guests spilled out of the ballroom and out into the hallway and splintered off into many tipsy cliques. The guest list lay on a table, largely discarded by the security personnel, who preferred to mingle with the famous people and duck over to the bar for free drinks and *hors d'oeuvres*.

Rikia and Summer muscled their way into the ballroom. There they saw some famous authors, a handful of TV and movie stars, some high-profile media people and the inevitable freeloaders.

At the bar, they spotted Colton Thomas right away. He was much handsomer than his book-jacket photo. He had a full head of dark hair, steely gray eyes and a muscular build.

"He looks like the protagonist in one of his own tough-guy novels," Rikia said to Summer.

"He looks ready to fight," replied Summer. "You go up and say hi. I'll wave from here."

"He's too handsome."

"So is a black panther. But you don't just go up to it and say, 'Nice kitty.' Rikia, you can't just go up to a man like him and ask to consent to a story for a magazine like *In*. He might get offended and punch you out."

"I think he knows better than to punch out a woman, Summer. Let's go say hi." Rikia grabbed her and pulled her over to the end of the bar where Colton Thomas stood holding court.

"Excuse me," he said as he saw the two women come nearer. "My cousins from Canada have just arrived, and I must go give them a hug. They've hitchhiked all the way here." He marched up to Rikia and Summer and took them aside. "Thanks for being you. I don't know you, but you've just rescued me from having my ass kissed by that group of losers."

Rikia stared up at him with the terrified fascination that Summer had seen in her face whenever Rikia looked at Wade Sellars. Summer said, "Well, I'm glad we were able to help you—"

"And now you can help *us*," Rikia said.

The big man frowned. "Not sure I like the sound of that."

"I'm Rikia Saddy, editor-in-chief of *In* magazine, and this is Summer Sellars, my assistant editor."

Colton Thomas frowned some more. "Wait a minute. Are you the woman who keeps sending me emails and Christmas cards?"

She nodded, feeling her face go very hot.

He laughed. "So you're. S. Sellars. For some weird reason, I thought S. Sellars was some twerpy little queen. Well, pleased to meet you, S. Sellars. I'm glad you're a beautiful woman and not a twerpy homo, but it's a big *no* on your story request. I'm already committed to doing too many of those things." Then he pointed a finger at her and said through gritted teeth, "Say, are you related to that asshole Wade Sellars?"

"Don't call my father names!"

"He fucked up one of my best books!"

"He won an Oscar for it!"

"Big fuckin' deal!"

Rikia rolled her eyes. "Summer—"

"It's all right," Colton Thomas said. "I like a broad with balls." He added, "Let's start all over again. Hi, I'm Colton Thomas." He shook their hands.

"Pleased to meet you. I'm Summer Sellars."

"Likewise. I'm Rikia Saddy."

He threw his arms around their shoulders. "Now that we've kissed and made up, let's go do some serious drinking. Where to?"

"Elaine's," said Rikia. "That's a pretty popular spot for writers."

Colton shook his head. "That bunch back at the bar said *they* were going to Elaine's. Pick somewhere else."

"You pick the place," said Rikia.

"The Smiling Buddha. It's the only place for the kind of drinking orgy I have in mind." He again put his arms around the women's shoulders and led them away.

Just then a woman ran up to them, pulling a strand of hair out of her face. "Mr. Thomas! Where are you going?"

"To get shitfaced."

"No! Not yet! Wolf Radnitz hasn't arrived yet—"

He reached out and gave her shoulder a brotherly little pat. "Chill, flack lady. You've done a great job. The booze is flowing and everyone is happy. I've been here for two hours, talking—but mostly listening—to every doofus in this room. The deal was that I would attend this thing and say hi and make nice-nice. But the agreement said nothing about how long I would have to endure these festivities. By the way, have you met my cousins from Canada?"

"I know you. You're Louise Ritamen. I'm Rikia Saddy. I tried to connect with Colton but some people wouldn't let it happen."

"Well," said the woman, "it looks like you've made that connection."

"No thanks to you," said Rikia. "What I want right now is an in-depth interview with Colton for *In*. We would put him on our cover. It would work out great for all involved."

"No," she said. "He's already set to do interviews with all the major weeklies and monthlies."

"Our coverage would be different," said Rikia.

"Yes," said Summer. "We'd do—"

"You'll do nothing. We don't want him in your rag," said Louise. "So stop bugging him with your requests."

Colton Thomas, who had been observing the back-and-forth with a big smirk, suddenly snarled. "Hold on a minute. Louise, are you my publicist or my mother?"

Louise threw up her hands. "I meant no disrespect, Mr. Thomas. It's just that Miz Saddy here can be too persistent. I'm trying to make it clear to these ladies that you're all booked up with interviews as far as publicity goes. Apparently Rikia and Summer are unwilling to accept the fact that our publicity plan excludes their magazine. What you do in your personal life with these two women is none of my business…but you can't let them interview you for an *In* story. The big, general-interest magazines are doing stories on you and they would hate it if Rikia got you, too."

He stared down at her. Killers' eyes could not grow colder. "Look here, sweetie. Let's get something straight right from Jump Street. You can book my appointments, send me out to answer interviewers' inane questions and I'll even roll over and beg at your command….but don't ever tell me what I *can't* do." He put his arm around Summer's shoulders. "I've known this little girl since she was a baby. Her daddy and I are as tight as a cat's asshole. He made an Oscar-winning picture out of one of my novels, and you're telling me I can't appear in Summer's magazine?"

Louise looked at Rikia with big sad eyes. "At least make it a small one, O.K.? I have this *agreement* with the other magazines that *not everyone* gets access to him. Understand?"

"Which part of what I just said did *you* fail to 'understand'? They can follow me into the head and watch me drop a deuce if that's what they want. But right now, we're gonna go get loaded." He led the women out of the ballroom.

Summer touched her face. Even her eyeballs hurt. She opened her eyes with the greatest care, then realized that she was still sitting in her easy chair. She put her hand on her stomach and discovered that she was still dressed. She stood up, but the floor began to slant like a carnival funhouse. She fell back into her chair and checked her watch. Seven in the morning! She had slept for only two hours!

She got to her feet again and pulled at her clothes. By and by she managed to strip down to her brassiere and underpants. As she tried to pull down the Murphy bed, her stomach roiled, so she raced over to the bathroom and vomited into the toilet. Presently she got the bed down and flopped down onto it. The events of the night before appeared in her mind's eye like the most vivid dream. She remembered the kind words Colton Thomas had for her father…the three of them departing the hotel as the beleaguered publicity lady threw up her arms in exasperation. His delight at their having rented a limousine. ("Party crashers with their own limo? Fantastic!") Then their entrance at the Smilin' Buddha…the Buddha, a huge beaming bald man greeting the writer with how-ya-doin' back slaps, sitting with them at the best table in the joint. But nobody spoke of food. Here it was Wild Turkey and nothing else. When Colton Thomas said, 'Nobody can be my friend unless they drink Wild Turkey,' Rikia and Summer hesitated for a moment, then blurted, 'We're in!'

Summer found her first sip much like cough medicine, but the second one went down much better. Her sips got bigger and soon the relaxing warmth of alcohol washed over her. Every wiseass remark Rikia, Colton or the Buddha made caused Summer to throw back her head and howl in hilarity. Some sportswriters who had known her father sat down with them; all the while, Colton kept everyone's glass full. He said, 'It's midnight! Let's go to Twenty-one for a nightcap!' So they did, and stayed until closing time, then piled back into the limousine and headed out to Bea's. At four in the morning, they staggered out, managed to climb back into the car— she could remember that, and felt amazed how the bunch of them had gotten their shit together enough to enter the limousine without their chauffeur's assistance. She wondered what she and Rikia were giggling about as they stumbled out of Bea's lobby. She could remember very, very little of what they said or did during the ride back to her apartment otherwise whether she needed anyone's help in getting back into her suite.

She made it back into the bathroom and took a couple of Tylenol 3s, then crawled into bed. When she closed her eyes, the room began to spin as if she were at an amusement-park ride. She opened them and made herself stare at a spot on the wall. The Tylenol tablets kicked in and she fell into a half-dream in which a man stood over her, his eyes blazing with lust. He spread her legs and began to unzip his pants. He was about to fuck her, but she felt no fear because she wanted it to happen. Who was he? She didn't know…his face was a blur. It was Wade. But then he kissed her lips and she knew this man was Colton Thomas. His eyes were beautiful and shining, but they kept changing color! As she reached out to hold him, she woke up. Sometimes, she thought, dreams were *so* much better than real life.

Still comfortably buzzed from codeine, Summer went back to sleep, hoping to dream of a handsome, horny man with dazzling eyes. Instead she dreamed of nothing at all and woke up to the sound of her ringing telephone. "Summer? It's Rikia."

"I don't feel so good. What time is it?"

"Close to noon. I am severely hung over."

"I think I'm going to die. Maybe I should go to a hospital."

"You're not going to die for several decades. Just drink some milk."

"Yuck. It would make me barf."

"Drink some milk and eat some bread. That will absorb whatever liquor is left in your stomach. Do that and call me back. We have to get our plan together."

"Plans for what?"

"Colton Thomas."

Summer groaned.

"Don't make that noise. Last night you said you adored him."

"We were drinking. *I* said things. *You* said things. People say regrettable things when they're drinking."

"Well, that's not going to happen tonight."

"What's not going to happen?" Summer asked.

"We're not going to drink when we go out with him. We'll say, 'Colt, we're drinking iced tea tonight, but you can drink all you want.' If we're going to do an *In* story on him, we'll need to stay sober. We're not going to get into a drinking match with him."

"Did we do that last night?"

"Well, we tried."

"Rikia, I think I'm going to vomit."

"Like I said, eat some bread and drink some milk. Let me throw on some clothes and I'll go see you. We can figure out what we're going to do with this Colton Thomas story."

Summer drank half a glass of milk and watched Rikia make coffee. Both women smiled. "Now, Summer, we've got to get serious and get busy. You need to make that call to Colton."

"Why?"

"Because, while I'm going to ride his dick tonight, I doubt he'll remember my name afterwards. But you're different. Like he said, 'Her daddy and I are as tight as a cat's—'"

"Yeah. I don't really think he meant it. Colton Thomas, like everyone else, sometimes says things he doesn't mean."

Rikia sipped some coffee and grimaced. "This instant shit is awful. Why don't you get a coffee maker?"

Summer shrugged. "It's cheap and convenient. Good enough for me."

"But not good enough for him."

"Who?"

"Any man who spends the night. In the morning, he'll say, 'Hey, wench, serve me some decent java.'"

"And I'll say, 'McDonald's is two blocks away. Make sure mine is double-double. And while you're at it, get me an Egg Muffin.'"

"Hank would never go for that. He ate granola and other healthful shit. Totally impossible to please for very long."

"Do you miss him?"

"Not really. When his new show opened, I almost sent him a telegram. But then I thought, 'Fuck it. We're over.' I'm glad his show is a hit, because his private life can't be much easy or fun since he's moved in with his rich older girlfriend. Besides, whenever I'm with Colton I know that he's a man and Hank is a boy."

Summer frowned. "'I'm going to ride Colton's dick tonight; he's a man and Hank is a boy.' Isn't that what you said? Colton is married and has a baby son, so why are you going to have sex with him?"

"Why? Because his wife and kid are in California and he and I are here. Besides, I'm not trying to break up his family, just jump his bones."

"And *why* do you want to jump his bones?"

"Because he's famous and handsome and *so* talented. It's the talent that turns me on. So many people can look good but there's nothing in their heads. You're horny for him, too."

"Am I?"

"Yes you are. When he was kissing us last night, you kissed back as much as I did."

"Did I?"

"Yes you did. I think you were kind of new to having a man's tongue down your throat, but you closed your eyes and leaned into it."

"Imagine," Summer murmured. "Colton Thomas Frenched me and I don't even remember it."

"That's because you were fucked up on Wild Turkey. Do you recall what happened on the drive home?"

"No, and I'm not sure I want to know…but I suppose you're going to tell me anyway."

"He felt you up. Don't you remember? He

213

slipped his hand inside your blouse and said, 'Nothing there. Too bad. But the rest of you is great.'"

Summer buried her face in her hands. "I'm glad I don't remember that." Then, "If a hundred men meet me, ninety-nine will say I'm the most beautiful woman they've ever met...but all of them will complain about my breasts."

"Colt felt me up, too. He kissed my tits and said, 'You'll never drown.'"

"While Colton was having his way with us, what was the driver doing?"

"Driving the car, I guess. Colton put up the partition, so the driver couldn't see what was happening. I don't imagine there was anything happening in the backseat that would have surprised the driver in the least—that guy has probably driven around Manhattan while a rape was happening back there."

Summer kept her eyes closed. "I'm starting to remember some of it....like how he put in hand in there and started feeling me up and I *liked* it. Why would I react that way?"

"Because you were a drunk, horny young woman who wanted to be felt up. Anyway, don't get uptight about it. It was just a joke, all in fun."

They stayed silent for a few moments. Then Summer said, "I want to fall in love. That's what I want more than anything."

"So you're not in love with Stephen, I guess."

"Nope."

Rikia sighed. "I want to fall in love, too. I want to fall in love with someone who loves me back. Don't know how to do that. If I ever figure it out, I'll tell you how I did it."

Summer nodded. "Yeah, that's it: To love and be loved. That's what it's all about. Being kissed and felt up without being loved? That's empty."

"You know, Summer, whenever people get high on booze, pot or whatever, the things they say and do are usually very honest. They say, 'Oh, I didn't mean what I did. The booze made me do it.' No, you made yourself do it; the booze just loosened you up enough to do it. So, when we went out drinking with Colton Thomas and he kissed us and felt us up, we wanted it as much as he did."

"No. I mean, I admire and respect him because of his success in a brutal business where ten thousand people fail for every person who succeeds." She added, "So I try to contact him for *In* but he's uninterested. They have a party for him but don't invite us because they're not interested in us or our magazine. So we hire a limo and crash the party. We end up in the back seat with him. What does he think of us? We must think we're a couple of sluts. We're no sluts. I hate it that he thinks—"

Rikia waved her off. "Stop fretting. He was so stoned last night that he probably remembers *nada* about groping us. Now, it's getting close to noon. Call the man."

"What?"

"You heard it. Please do this…for me. Set up a date for tonight for the three of us. If, halfway through, you decide to go home, say you feel sick and take a taxi back here. But I want to be with him some more. As the cliché goes, 'I've never met anyone quite like him.' He's such a tough-looking dude, but when he smiles at you, oh, man…"

"You mean you want to jump his bones,

knowing that nothing good could come of it—"

"*I* could 'come of it,' and certainly would. Him, too."

"Rikia, be serious. He has a wife and child, you know."

"Well, what of it? Maybe he screws around; maybe his wife does, too. She's out there in Malibu; maybe she gets lonely and screws her famous friends. Now call Colton."

"No."

"Why not?"

"Because," she said, "a man should call a woman."

Rikia rolled her eyes. "Your parents should have named you Gidget. Summer, this is *business*. A very famous writer has just published a new novel, and we have access to him. We also run a magazine and have some great ideas on how to cover him for our magazine. That's our top priority right now. So if you won't call him, *I* will." She picked up Summer's bedside telephone and dialed Colton's hotel. "I know that we'll have to pair him up with that monster Anya Semko so she can get a sense of his style…Hello? I'd like to speak to Colton Thomas, please."

"Why put Anya Semko on this?"

"Because this is the biggest story *In* has ever had, and Anya is the best writer we've ever had…Oh, hello? This is Summer Sellars calling….Summer like the month…"

"*Rikia!*"

"Hi, Colton! No, this isn't Summer, it's Rikia Saddy. Summer is sitting right here. We're both fine, thanks for asking. Well, a little hung over, maybe, but we would love to see you. Who? *Robertson Hughley?*

Are you serious? Oh, we'd love it! Seven would be fine. See you then." Rikia looked up at Summer and smiled. "Robertson Hughley is going to be having drinks with Colton Thomas this afternoon, and *we* are going to have dinner with them. Colton is sending his limo to pick us up."

"So he was happy to hear from you."

"Actually, no. He sounded cold and distant. But after a few drinkie-poos tonight, he'll say, 'Call me Colty.' I wonder how it will be, riding the dick of an astronaut."

"Well, I guess you'll find out tonight. At least he's divorced."

"You take Hughley. I want Thomas."

"Why are you rejecting Robertson? He's a national hero, an American superstar. He made the covers of *Time* and *Newsweek* in the same month."

"I'm not 'rejecting' him. I am not a superstar groupie. I've never boffed a star, much less a superstar. Hank got into *Butterfly* after our breakup, and he's still no star. They rarely mention him in the notices. I would be horny for Colt even if he were some unemployed bookkeeper. He's just got that *Je ne sais quoi*. He's so virile...nobody's fool. Still, at times he seems to have that inner little boy who just wants a hug. Have you noticed that?"

"No. I made friends with Wild Turkey and it plucked my eyes out. But tonight I'll keep looking for Colton's inner little boy."

15

Rikia and Summer sashayed into the Plaza as if they were two teenagers out on the loose together. In the lobby, Summer froze.

"What's the deal?" asked Rikia.

"This place. We practically lived here."

"That was then, this is now. Colton Thomas, Robertson Hughley—remember? Let's *go*." Rikia grabbed her arm and pulled her along into the elevator.

Robertson Hughley opened the door, introduced himself and let them in. "Colton's on the phone. All I can offer you to drink is Wild Turkey. Want some?"

Rikia said yea but Summer said any as the younger woman looked around the suite, scarcely able to believe that this was the very same one Wade Sellars had kept throughout the year. She smiled at the sight of that cherrywood table near the window. She caressed it for a moment, almost expecting it to speak to her. How many times had she sat a couple of feet from her father, watching him do deals? Sometimes all the telephones would ring at once, all of those callers wanting something from—or to do something for—the man she called Daddy. She turned away and shuddered, feeling freaked out because now those phones rang for Colton Thomas, who entered the room, saying, "Fuck them all. Let them ring. I'm taking the day off." Then he walked over and shook her hand. "Hello, beautiful girl. Have you recovered from last night?"

"Uh, yeah." She blushed, disappointed in herself for failing to say something clever and charming.

Colton went over and shook Rikia's hand. "Let's go to Twenty-one."

At the restaurant, he remained mostly sober. When he noticed that Summer had scarcely touched the bourbon he had ordered for her, he asked for the wine list. "White wine? Isn't that what you fancy ladies drink?"

"I thought you said we were going easy on the booze tonight," Rikia told him.

He shrugged. "I changed my mind." Then, "I'm going to take you over to Doubleday's and buy you each a copy of my new novel. If you're nice to me, I may even sign them for you. My publisher says I'm guaranteed a long stay on the bestseller lists. I've written better novels, but this one is commercial as all hell. The other ones? I wrote my best, and my best is always pretty damn good. But potential readers were intimidated by my eloquence and refused to buy those books. But this time I've dumbed it down so that the common folk out there, the masses, can understand every word of it." He turned to Robertson Hughley. "So you're up in Westhampton now, huh? Why?"

"Mother Nature invited me. Manhattan had been freaking me out for the longest time."

"My father used to say, 'At night, look up at the stars and pick one you like because after you die, that's where you're going to live,'" Summer told them.

Robertson smiled. "That was a good idea your father had—promising you a fun afterlife so you wouldn't go through this life being afraid of death."

The two men got into an intense discussion about what would happen to Earth in the decades ahead and the possibility of moving to other planets—"or the *necessity* of doing so once the population here reaches ten or twelve billion"—Robertson said. Rikia got bored and tried to get the conversation onto a more personal level, but presently failed and sat back. She shot a livid glance at Summer when the big-eyed young blonde asked Robertson to expand on something he'd said about interstellar communication.

"Do you gamble?" Summer blurted at Colton.

The man raised an eyebrow. "Why do you ask?"

"Because you remind me of someone."

"Who? A boyfriend?"

"Her father!" exclaimed Rikia.

Colton laughed. "I'm trying to chat you up and turn you on, and what do you tell me? That I remind you of your father! Well, I'm about Wade's age, so I guess I deserve that."

When they left 21, the sky was clear and the breeze gentle. Colton said, "The weather's great. Let's walk the ladies home. You're roomies, right?"

"Same building, different suites," said Rikia.

Colton dismissed his car and they all walked to Doubleday's. The staff there jumped to greet him as if he were Frank Sinatra. He bought hardcover books for Rikia and Summer, signed them, then reluctantly signed a half-dozen other copies for the store. "Let's split," he muttered to the others.

They walked as couples: Colton and Rikia in

front and Robertson and Summer directly behind them. Colton and Rikia held hands; Summer didn't like it. She believed that married men should hold hands only with their wives, and nobody was going to tell her otherwise. She had half a mind to tell Rikia to knock it off. Then she felt Robertson tap her on the shoulder.

"I asked you a question."

"Oh, I'm sorry. I guess I got distracted by the noise of the taxi."

He smiled. "Don't get weirded out by those two up front. He's married...and you don't look to be the kind for one-nighters."

"What makes you think I'm 'weirded out'?"

"Just the way you've been staring at them. They're holding hands."

She sighed. "I was just spacing out. I do that sometimes—just get lost in my own thoughts."

"Colton and I have never learned much about women, dating and relationships. I have a dozen interests that keep me busy, and he has a new wife and baby. Do you know something? This is his first baby. He's pushing sixty, this is his fourth marriage and now, for the first time, he's a daddy. So I hope your little girlfriend up there isn't getting any ideas about him and her—"

"No, Rikia knows how it is."

"Does she?"

"What's that supposed to mean?"

"It means that I know who you are and what you are. I also know who and what Rikia is. Colton always ends up with the Rikias. He's even been married to a few Rikias. Want to know why? Because he never goes out looking for women; he hangs back and lets

222

them come to him. He's just plain lazy. Besides, I don't think he's capable of falling in love with any woman. The only people who matter to him, the ones who are real and worth loving, are the characters in his novels. So far as he's concerned, when it comes to the real world and real women, he just chooses among those who make themselves available to him. But now that he has a wife and child, he's going to stay married to her for the rest of his life."

"Tell me about her."

"Gorgeous. Curly red hair, big blue eyes. She had a little movie-acting career going for a while. Couldn't act for shit, didn't really get anywhere professionally. But she sure looked hot. I guess she knew she would never become a movie star, so when she met Colton, she figured he could give her a better life than she could ever get for herself, so she married him and bore his child."

"What's his wife's name? Maybe I've seen her in something—"

"Summer," he said, "let me give you some good advice: Leave him to the Rikias of this world. If you got involved with him, nothing good would come of it."

Just then, Colton called out, "Hey, Robertson, you still want me to go out to the beach tomorrow?"

"Yeah, sure. I've got steaks in the freezer."

"Should we invite these girls along?"

"We accept!" Rikia shouted.

At their apartment building, Rikia said, "Want to come up for a nightcap? I've got booze."

"Better not," said Colton. "We want to get an early start. I love the beach in bad weather—*especially* in bad weather. It's deserted; I have it all to myself. In

Malibu I've done some of my best writing sitting on the beach, all alone, under gray skies with a blustery wind."

Sunday was cold, and the weather man was expecting rain, but they went to the beach at ten in the morning in heavy clothing and old jackets. Summer thought Colton looked happy for the first time.

The rain started, and soon fell hard, but the house was warm and dry and the men kept the fireplace loaded and crackling. As she sat at the fire, Summer closed her eyes and pretended that the four of them were the only people left on Earth.

"A perfect house for a couple in love," said Rikia, winking at Colton. "Don't you think so, Colty?"

He winced. "Rikia, you can call me a motherfucker, dickhead or asshole—but *never* call me 'Colty.'"

The limousine arrived at ten-thirty to take them back to Manhattan. Robertson stayed behind; before leaving, Colton went behind the bar and took out a bottle of Chivas Regal. "To keep me warm on the road," he said.

Rikia looped her arm through Colton's as they walked down the path towards the car. Robertson said to Summer, "Looks like they're going to be an item for a little while. Rikia says you and she are going on his book tour with him. Your magazine story is going to be something like 'On the Road with Colton Thomas.' He'll hate the tour. He'll get drunk too often. He's really very shy. I've known him for half a dozen years, so I don't know what his private demons are. Women adore him and men say, 'I want to be Colton Thomas when I grow up.' He seems to feel the need to prove himself every minute; maybe that's what the drinking is all about. Maybe after every book he thinks, 'I've said everything I have to say, but I have to keep writing books. What will I say next?' This tour could be bad for his mental health. Your job will be to say to him, 'Lighten up—it's not as bad as all that.'"

Summer smiled and nodded as Colton and Rikia got into the car. Robertson stuck out his hand and said, "It's been perfectly delightful meeting you, Miz Sellars."

She shook his hand and smiled. "Oh, the pleasure has been all mine, Mister Hughley."

"I think," he said, "that you're a very special young lady and some wonderful things are going to happen to you in life."

"Thank you," she replied.

"And I want to be here for you as a friend."

"I'd like that."

They both smiled as she climbed into the car. Colton had opened the bottle of liquor and took a drink. He passed it over to Rikia, who took a gulp and cringed. Then she passed it over to Summer, who snarled as she raised it to her lips. Colton reached over and grabbed the bottle from her. "Everyone's gotta stay sober. I have a busy day tomorrow—radio, TV, other things. Boston, Philly and Washington first, then the rest of Uncle Sam's Yoo-Ess-Ay."

"I guess we should stay away from your radio and TV appearances," Rikia said. "Your little flack lady would go *ballistic* if she saw Summer and me hanging out with you."

Colton frowned. "Why would it bother her? What business is it of hers if you're there?"

"Colton," Rikia asked, "have you ever been on a book tour?"

He grunted. "Absolutely not."

"Well, they can get pretty, uh, different."

"When the car pulled in front of Summer's building, Colton walked the two women to their front door, kissed each on the cheek and started back towards the car. Rikia looked at Summer with what Summer could describe only as wide-eyed panic, then Rikia pushed Summer through the doorway and bolted off to rejoin Colton in the car. Summer went into her suite, stripped and crawled into bed. She lay in the darkness, wondering if Rikia was going to spend the night with Colton in the suite that Summer and Wade used to call home.

She decided not to concern herself with things that were none of her business. If Rikia wanted to have a thing with Colton, well, what of it? Summer lay sprawled out in bed, trying to sleep but unable to do so. She fluffed her pillow and made herself as comfortable as possible. She sneered and whistled a couple of times. Everything was just too damn quiet.

Then her telephone rang. She jumped out of bed and plucked it out of its cradle. "Hello?"

"Hope you were still awake."

"Huh? Who is this?"

He laughed. "How soon they forget. It's me. Colton."

"Oh, O.K. So, what's up? Besides us, I mean."

Another laugh. "I was just thinking that *Les Mis* has been a Broadway smash for years and I still haven't seen it. How about you, Rikia and I catching it tomorrow evening?"

"I haven't seen it. Maybe she has."

"If she has, I'm sure she'll be willing to sit through it again just to spend the evening with us."

Presently their conversation ended and they hung up. Summer smiled at the thought that Rikia wasn't with Colton. *Why isn't Rikia with him? And why am I so happy that she isn't? Because I want him all for myself!* There, she'd said, if only to herself. She lay in shock, naked under the covers, scarcely able to believe what she had just acknowledged. But it was entirely true—she had fallen in love with a man older than her father…a married man with an infant child. A man who clearly felt something for her as well.

Otherwise, why had he called her rather than Rikia about that Broadway play? Could, and did, Colton actually feel something for her? But hadn't Robertson said, "Colton is lazy—he just hangs back and waits for the women to come to him"? Well, hadn't Rikia pretty much gone up to him and said, "Take me—I'm yours"? Was one of them going to get him, and if so, who? Suppose his wife suddenly wanted a divorce or died or something, and for whatever reason he became available and wanted to marry Summer. She would say "Yes!" and move into his Malibu beach house. She would be his muse and answer his emails…

IT WAS RIDICULOUS! TOTALLY RIDICULOUS! ·

She rolled over and went to sleep, dreaming about Colton Thomas and her ridiculous life with him.

16

She slept poorly, but when her alarm went off, she sprang out of bed, eager for her day to begin. She stood under the shower, singing pretty songs and thinking about Colton Thomas. She admonished herself for a moment that being in love with a much older married man was nothing to sing out. But she kept on crooning because she felt beyond happy. She was *ecstatic!*

But Colton *was* married, a fact she pondered as she put on her brassiere and panties. Where was her conscience? She knew how much her mother had suffered while her father jumped the bones of one woman after another. The thing was, Summer was not about to go to bed with Colton Thomas. She simple loved the idea of having such deep feelings for a man…who wasn't named Wade Sellars. To get so much pleasure from a man's company, to bask in his admiration…could that really be so wrong?

"What the *fuck*, Summer?" Rikia had practically screamed when asked about the three of them going to see that play. "What do you mean *we're* going to see *Les Miserables*? I would much rather see *The Lion King*. Anyway, why did he call *you* instead of *me*?"

"What does it matter? He's invited us both. Do

you want to go or not?"

"Yes...but only for tonight. After that, it's only him and me."

"What about the 'Life on the Road with Colton Thomas' thing for *In*?"

"Oh, that's still on, but you're off."

"Why?"

"Because I said so. Anyway, once your work was done, Anya Semko would rewrite every word you'd written, so it shouldn't matter that much to you. My plan is, Colton and I will go on the road without you. If he asks about you, I'll just say, 'Oh, I had to put her on another story.' I'll introduce him to Anya and say, 'She's going to my special assistant on this story.' Colton believes that a woman's main job in life is to look good and turn men on. Anya's the ugliest bitch in town, so he'll be relieved that she won't be joining us on the road."

Summer said, "Rikia, please let me try to write the story. I've really been looking forward to this. Just let me go on the road with you and do this project. I promise I won't get in the way."

"Sweetie, you're already in the way. Effective immediately, you're off the story. The three of us will go to the show tonight. Try not to hate me too much."

The three of them sat in the darkness of the theatre. Colton said he really respected stage actors because they were so highly disciplined and it took brains, brawn and balls to get up there in front of a live performance and deliver a compelling performance. "You know what they do I movies? They do as many

230

takes as necessary to get it right. Remember Marlon Brando in *The Godfather*? He arrived on the set totally unprepared, so Coppola just kept doing takes and Brando kept blowing them. Finally they got enough acceptable footage and released the movie. So everyone is saying, 'Brando is simply magnificent.' He won the Oscar but refused it. But this? Legitimate theatre? It's totally different. Utterly professional."

After the show, they went backstage and met the cast. Also there was the veteran actor William Daniels, who joined them at Sardi's. Colton said, "Bill, if I ever write anything for Broadway—which I will not—I'll write it for you." They talked about plays and musicals from decades past, and Summer came up with facts and anecdotes that made Colton gape. "How do you know all that? It's well before your time." She nodded. "Yes…but from age eight, I saw practically every show on Broadway and sat in this restaurant, listening to stories about Broadway over the years. You see, my father had custody of me and didn't know what else to do with me, so he simply took me to work most days."

She looked at the others and realized that Rikia knew less than zero about Broadway history. "Rikia here was one of my best friends in high school. She was quite a star. Many of us thought she could have made it on the Broadway stage."

Rikia smiled and nodded, and before their evening was done she started talking to William Daniels about doing an *In* story on him.

When Colton said goodnight to the women outside their building, Rikia did not invite him up. "We'll be alone together much of the time during the road tour. We'll both be lonely then. If anything is going to happen between us, it'll happen then."

Summer got into the office and Rikia said, "I left a short story on your desk. Read it and get back to me. It's sort of an O. Henry-esque thing about this big-nosed chick who gets her *schnoz* done to make her boyfriend happy, but he ends up leaving her for a chick with a big nose. Funny story, and it came in over the transom."

"What's a transom?"

Rikia gave her an indulgent little smile. "That means it's unsolicited—we didn't ask her to send it, but she did so anyway—and she doesn't have an agent, either. So she mailed it to us on the off chance that we'd read it and maybe even publish it. The manuscript is in pretty sad shape, so I guess that Mallory Debbits, its author, doesn't know enough to print a fresh copy once the current one looks old and wrinkled.

Summer picked up the story, called "Rhinoplasty," and read it. She found much of it funny, but did it deserve to be published in a national magazine like *In*? What the hell, Summer thought, why not give Mallory a break? She put the manuscript back into its envelope and headed over to Rikia's office.

"Pretty good." She tossed the envelope onto Rikia's desk.

Rikia smirked. "I agree. Anya's got the biggest nose since Barbra Streisand, so if she thinks it's acceptable, we'll use 'Rhinoplasty' in one of our summer issues. Yeah, that sounds like a plan—use a piece of short fiction by an unknown writer in the same issue as our story on Colton Thomas. I need to get some terrific shots of Colton on tour." She sneered. "Dammit, if only Hank wasn't still doing *Butterfly*..."

"Would you want Hank *and* Colton on the road with you?"

"Yes—if only because any other photographer of Hank's quality would be *way* too expensive." She snapped her fingers. "I know—I'll call Cooper Wherry. He's young and doesn't yet know how talented he is. I'm sure I can cut a deal with him."

"Has Colton said it's O.K. to take pictures on the road?"

"I haven't asked him, and I'm not going to. It doesn't matter, anyway, because by the time we're on the road we'll have a hot romance going. Last night in the theatre he kept playing footsies with me. In the restaurant, he started up with kneesies."

Summer stood up. "On that note, I'll go back to my office."

"Sit your ass down. The coffee lady is due."

Just then the telephone rang. "Maybe that's Colton," Rikia said as she picked up the receiver. "Hello? What? Margie, you're kidding! Talk to me, babe. I want to hear this. Come right up." She said to Summer, "Stay here. You're going to hear some wonderful gossip. Margie says Louise is freaking out over something. I've tried to call Colton twice already today, but no answer."

Margie Sherryton, a pretty, vivacious young woman who headed *In*'s public-relations department, entered the office and plopped down in the chair Rikia pointed at. "So, what's Louise freaking out over?" Rikia asked with an unctuous smile.

"She asked me if you had heard from Colton Thomas. She's just beside herself. She called Colton at seven in the morning because he had an eight o'clock appearance on *Good Morning, America*. Then she went to the Plaza to collect him and he was still asleep. Seems he thought his appearance was for the *following* Thursday. She sat in the lobby, practically having a panic attack, and at ten to eight he moseyed on down, not a care in the world. She had a car, so they *did* make his gig. After the show, he hung out and talked to the producers and hosts, so Louise ducked into the ladies' room to powder her nose. But when she returned, Colton was gone. Someone said he had wandered into the newsroom. There was an awful commotion. She kept looking around, and she spotted him on his way to the elevator. He got on but the doors closed in her face. She doesn't panic because she's thinking, 'He knows he has an interview at ten, so maybe he's gone back to the Plaza.' So in the Plaza's lobby she meets with the *Playboy* writer who's supposed to do the interview, but the guy is drinking Manhattans, and Louise is worried he'll be too drunk to talk if Colton *does* show up. Louise was sort of under the impression that you were with him last night and might know his whereabouts better than others."

Rikia smiled. "Tell Louise I did not have sexual relations with Colton Thomas last night at the Plaza or anywhere else."

Presently Margie departed and Rikia winked at Summer. "Louise has had hot pants for Colton for quite some time now. She will go to group therapy tonight and they will tell her, 'If he rejects you, it simply means that you two were not meant to be.'"

Rikia shrugged. "Because I've done that group-therapy thing. I've also spent way too much money on fifty-five-minute sessions with private shrinks who've said, 'Try to accept those things that are beyond your control.' Yeah, right. Like a headstrong bitch such as myself will ever take that kind of advice."

Several moments passed. Then Summer said, "Rikia, what's the deal with all you women wanting to go to bed with Colton? It's like a competition, as if you were high school boys betting on which one will get to lay the head cheer—"

Margie barged in and blurted, "Turn on your TV! Big quake in California!"

Presently everyone sat huddled around the TV set as the newscaster went on about the Los Angeles-area earthquake: 6.8 on the Richter scale, epicenter just north of L.A.

The local coverage switched to LaGuardia International Airport, where vast numbers of people felt desperate to fly out to check on their loved ones in the Golden State.

Margie shrieked. "There's Colton!"

The reporter hurried up to the writer and said, "Colton Thomas, why are you rushing off to Los Angeles right now?"

Colton frowned. "Because my wife and child are there."

Rikia stood up and turned off the TV. "Back to work, people." Everyone left the office. When only Rikia and Summer remained, Rikia let out a huge sigh. "I can't believe it. I honestly can't. My love is doomed to failure. Well, since I have no dinner date for tonight, want to go Bea's with me?"

Summer shook her head. "I better get to work tonight on some stories in progress." She half-ran back to her office and stared at the wall for the longest time. Colton was gone. She had shared some of her nights with him and let her imagination run wild about him and herself.

The following week, Rikia said, "I guess he didn't need our help. His new novel is getting great reviews and climbing up all the bestseller lists that matter. I guess he can do all the TV and radio he wants from the Coast. But at least he could have contacted me and said thanks for the effort."

Summer resolved never to think about Colton Thomas again. She believed that their sudden separation was God's way of saying, "You're no good for each other; stay away." She had little interest in religion—her experience had been that churches and broadcast ministries' main messages had been mostly, 'Send us your money and you'll go to heaven'—but each time she looked at the sun or the moon or the stars or saw a baby, she knew that *someone* or *something* had to be responsible for all that vastness and beauty. She decided that God was the wise old white man her father had told her about, the one who knew who was naughty and nice and praised or punished His children accordingly.

She made many excuses to avoid having dinner with Rikia. Summer and Stephen ate out most nights at one dreary place after another. People in her circle kept talking about the imminent backgammon tournament in Gstaad. Beth had already booked her ticket; Stephen couldn't go because of work commitment, but he envied Wade because Wade had no real "work" to be committed to, and Gstaad was just too gorgeous at that time of year.

Stephen said goodnight and headed home without inviting himself up for a nightcap. Summer smiled, thinking that if Wade and Beth were going to Gstaad, they would have to go through New York first, and she would get to see her father. She wanted—and needed—that more than anything: A nice long lunch with him, a heart-to-heart talk during which she could tell him all about her confusion and ambivalence concerning Colton Thomas. He would know what to tell her; he always did.

But when she called Florida, the butler told her that Wade and Beth had already flown to Gstaad. She hung up and nearly wept. How could he have flown into New York without contacting her? Had something tragic happened to him. in a panic, she dialed his hotel in Gstaad and he answered, deep-voiced and exuberant.

"Are you all right? How is everything?" she blurted.

"Couldn't be better. You sound worried, sweetie. What's that all about?"

"I knew you were flying to Gstaad and that you'd come through New York, so I looked forward to hooking up with you. When I called Florida, they said you were already in Switzerland. I didn't know what to think…"

"O.K., here's the deal. We flew up to New York and were there just long enough to refuel. We couldn't even get off the plane. We'll be coming back soon, and I promise to spend a few days with you. By the way, this call is costing you s fortune. Better hang up now."

"Wade! I don't care about the fuckin' phone

bill!"

He laughed. "Well, *I* do. Talk to you soon, sweetie." Click.

That evening she accepted a dinner invitation from Rikia. "We'll be a foursome—this guy I know is bringing one of his pals. Try to order the cheapest thing on the menu because both of these guys are drowning in debt.

Summer decided that her date was the ugliest man alive. He was tall and skinny, with a snout for a nose and flyabout sandy hair. He talked about his muscles that refused to grow and his new hobby of long-distance running. He bragged about his difficult job on Madison Avenue and shared gossip with Rikia's date, who worked at the same behemoth advertising agency. Neither man seemed to have any idea as to how to relate to a woman, so they simply sat there and related to each other. Rikia and Summer rolled their eyes at each other, acknowledging that these two were, as Wade Sellars would say, "Born losers." Full of anxiety, the two ad guys talked shop as a way of saying to these ladies, *We're surviving on Madison Avenue! Don't you think that's terrific?* Instead, the women thought, *You guys are ugly and boring. If you* owned *Madison Avenue, you still wouldn't get to jump our bones.* At ten-thirty one of the guys asked for the check. Outside, Summer's date said, "I know it's freezing, but I haven't had my exercise for the day, so let's walk."

They did just that. Rikia invited everyone up for a nightcap, but Summer declined. "I'm beat," she said.

Her date said, "I'll walk you up to your door."

Summer said, "That isn't necessary."

"Show me the way."

238

At her door, she said, "Thanks for a lovely evening."

He said, "What about us?"

She shrugged. "There is no 'us.'"

"Oh, but there could be."

"I seriously doubt it."

He grabbed her and forced his tongue down her throat so fast that she scarcely knew what was happening. He squeezed her breasts and she thrust her knee in the direction of his groin. He let out a horrible squeal and doubled over. He looked up at her, his face contorted in pain, and said, "You cockteasing fucking cunt! I'm going to beat your ass!" He started to lunge for her, but instead grabbed his wounded privates and whimpered. Summer, more angry than frightened and more than a bit amused, gave him a hard shove down the hallway, then opened her door, slipped inside and locked it. Needing some comfort, she ran a bath and burned some incense. Then her telephone rang.

"Summer, is Eugene still there?" asked Rikia.

"Who's Eugene?"

"Your date. Mine's Seymour. He's in the john right now, but soon he's going to be in my bed, so I have to talk fast. I was just checking my messages, and guess who called this evening: Colton Thomas!"

"Colton Thomas!"

"Seems he's back in New York. He's staying at the Plaza, of course. You should call him now."

"Call him yourself."

"Can't," she said. "I'm kind of busy right now entertaining a gentleman friend. Just call Colton and tell him I'm out of the office and am unavailable to speak to him but would love to arrange a get-together for us. You can invite yourself along, if you want."

"No, Rikia—"

"Gotta go. Later."

Click.

Summer sat on her bed and stared at the wall. She debated for the longest time about calling Colton Thomas, then snatched up her telephone, dialed his number and heard his gruff recorded greeting. She hung up without leaving a message and went to sleep.

"Summer! Wake up! I need to talk, but Seymour is in the can again."

Summer rubbed sand from her eyes. "Rikia? What time is it?"

"Not quite seven. Seymour is going to jump my bones in a few minutes. Did you talk to Colton?"

"I left a message."

"Well, that's good enough. Talk later. 'Bye."

At just before noon, Rikia called Summer into her office. "I've spoken to Colton. The three of us are going to see *Cats* tonight."

"I see."

"No need to thank me."

"Rikia, if you're O.K. with my *not* going—"

"He said, 'Last time, *I* picked the show, so now it's *your* turn.' I picked *Cats*. He said, 'Yeah, I can sit through that. Invite Summer along.' I said, 'Good idea. Everyone knows you're married, so it might look bad if it's just the two of us. With Summer along, it would look like we're all just friends.' So that's where it stands now. I think I want to seduce him tonight, so let's get him very drunk, and then you can leave him to me…"

They arrived at the Plaza at about six. Louise Ritamen was there, as was a skinny young man from *Time* magazine. Louise blanched when she saw Rikia and Summer enter the suite. Colton stood holding a glass of Wild Turkey as he introduced those who hadn't already met. Rikia and Summer sat in a corner while Colton served them each a Wild Turkey and water that they just stared at. The reporter asked questions and Colton answered him while shooting looks at the wall clock.

"How many more questions? I have plans for this evening?"

"We have plenty to cover, Mister Thomas," said the skinny young reporter.

"Colton," said Louise, "this gentleman is from *Time*. A major magazine. We'll keep going till he's satisfied he has enough material, then the photographer will be here to do *his* thing—"

Colton shook his head. "Bullshit." To the reporter, he said, "Sorry, guy, but I have tickets to the theatre. Looks like we'll have to do this later—"

Louise jumped up. *"Colton!"* she screamed, flicking a teardrop from her cheek. "Do you have *any* idea how much *trouble* I went to in order to get this *Time* session? If you end it now, my bosses will say, 'Louise, it's all *your* fault! Can't you do *anything* right?' I mean—"

"Shut up," Colton muttered. To the reporter, he said, "O.K., guy, let's talk." To Rikia, he said, "The tickets are in my name. You and Summer go see *Cats* without me. I don't mind; I didn't want to see that fuckin' show anyway. When it's over, come back here.

My car is out front; it's all yours." He went to the bar, dumped two shots of booze into his glass and said to the reporter, "Let's do it."

In the car, Summer asked Rikia, "If you like Colton so much, why did you go to bed with Seymour?"

Rikia shrugged. "Why not? He was there and I was horny."

"Oh, well, that's certainly a good reason."

They returned to the Plaza just as Louise got ready to leave. Colton greeted them with a kiss on the forehead and insisted that everyone except Louise—who was halfway out the door—have a nightcap.

"I really shouldn't drink," said the reporter. "I'm famished. I missed dinner. My wife is heating some food for me at home."

"You should have said something, fella. They have *primo* room service here, you know. We could have ordered up something. I completely forgot about making sure everyone was fed. That poor flack lady—Louise?—she must have been starved, too. I can be *such* an asshole, you know. Where do you live?"

"Near SoHo," said the reporter.

"Take my car. Go home. Chow down. Send the car back here so that Rikia and Summer can use it to go home."

"Summer," said Rikia, like one actor giving a cue to another, "I really love that article you're working on."

Summer nodded and got up. "I want to work on it some more tonight. Why don't I share the car? We can both go home now."

The reporter left and Summer stayed. Colton

said, "Rikia, my glass is empty. I'll have a Wild Turkey over ice, and pour Summer a soda."

Rikia did as told. Colton drank his down and licked his lips. He looked down at the documents on the table. "That's tomorrow's schedule from the flack lady."

"Better read it," said Summer, "so you'll know what's going on."

"Oh, I *know* what's going on: New York, Boston, Philly...TV and radio...answering the same old questions."

"Are you going away?" Rikia asked.

He shrugged. "Just a couple of days, then back here for a week...then out into the Midwest for a few days and back here for a week. Soon I'll be in Los Angeles."

"What time are you leaving tomorrow?"

"Open the paperwork and tell me."

Rikia did so. "Says here you don't leave till noon. The car will come by and take you to LaGuardia. But wait—you have a nine-o'clock breakfast meeting with someone named Zach Donaldson."

Colton nodded. "He's an old friend from one of the London papers. He's doing a story on me for limey consumption." He stood up and yawned. "I better get my beauty sleep so I'll have my shit together for Zach in the morning." He started for his bedroom.

"Summer," said Rikia, "your story—"

"I gotta go. I can take a taxi."

Colton turned around. "No. You'll both go home in my car. I'm going to get undressed. When I say 'Enter!' you both come in and kiss me goodnight. Then we'll have a drinkie-poo."

He went into the bedroom. Summer stood staring at Rikia, shrugging. Rikia, fists on hips, glowered. "I need to find out when he's going off to the Midwest, because I'm going with him. I can't go to Philly and Washington because it's too late to make arrangements for that. Besides, he'll probably have some of the *Time* people with him." Her eyes darted towards his bedroom, and she said, "Look, get out *now*."

Summer frowned. "You mean just leave?"

"Yeah. Scram. I'll make your apologies."

"Rikia, that's just too rude."

"He doesn't want you around. He's just being polite. He wants you out of here as much as I do."

"Does he really? People are so weird."

"Just leave. I'll go in there when he calls, and he'll forget all about you. Trust me on this."

Suddenly they heard Colton's big deep voice. "Girls, Daddy's ready for his goodnight kiss."

"He wants us both," Summer whispered.

Rikia nodded and they both went in.

Colton lay on top of his bed in a silk paisley robe. Summer felt immensely relieved to see him clothed; it would be just like him to be nude, if only to see their reactions. He said, "Rikia, go get the bottle of Wild Turkey and three glasses. Summer, I want you in on this one. I want you to toast me and my incomparable genius."

"And your humility," she retorted.

He guffawed. She did as told and presently the two women sat on the bed with him. He poured them each a shot and himself a double. He rumpled Rikia's hair and said, "Now we drink to the famous writer who is about to go out into the world and sell himself like a two-dollar whore. See and talk to a real, live literary whore. Yell at him, spit on him, degrade him all you like—just make sure you buy his book." He tossed back his glass of booze. Rikia did likewise and smiled up at him.

He winked and refilled their glasses. Then he looked down at Summer as she took small sips. She felt her cheeks burn but told herself that the liquor wasn't bad if she drank it slowly. Not bad at all...in fact, pretty good. She turned to look up at Colton, upon whose head Rikia now rested her head. Summer wondered how she could leave the room without ruining the mood for these two. Colton ran his hand through Rikia's hair and said, "You're too beautiful."

Rikia and Colton looked into each other's eyes. Summer wished she could find the strength to get *out* of there.

"You've got to help me," Colton said to Rikia.

"Help you," Rikia murmured.

"I'm in love with Summer. Help me."

Summer stared straight ahead, unable to believe what she had just heard. Then she muttered, "Gotta go," and scrambled from the bed to the bathroom. She locked herself inside and rested her forehead against the cool porcelain of the bathtub, thinking: *Did I hear him right? Did he tell Rikia that he was in love with* me*?"* She made a big noisy deal of her time in the bathroom, flushing the toilet and splashing water around in the sink. When she came back out, Colton was sitting up, staring at her.

"Where's Rikia?"

"Gone home."

"Maybe I should go, too."

"No. Come to me." He held out his hand and

she inched her way over to him. "Don't be uptight," he said. "Be flattered. I don't go around falling in love with girls whose fathers are older than I am. I can have any number of girls—it's always been that way for me. I guess it's because I've been famous for most of my adult life and many women are star-fuckers. Yeah, I can get all the brainless cuties I want—I even marry them sometimes. In case you're wondering, no, I'm not desperately in love with my wife. However, she did give me a child, and I really wanted to become a father. That's the thing about me—as I've gone through life, I've gotten most of the goodies I wanted, even if I really didn't deserve them. If I left her, she'd get custody of our kid, and I don't want *that* to happen, so I'm going to stay with her." He sighed. "It's a crazy thing—I want you, and there's not a damn thing I can do about it. Rikia would be mine for the taking, and I tried to want her, but it didn't happen. I've been thinking about you all the time. I didn't have to come back to New York, you know. My book is selling great, and Hollywood is already trying to figure out some way to adapt it to the screen, but I came back here just to see you." He pulled her in and put the gentlest kiss on her lips. "Nothing will ever happen between us, Summer, until you say yes…"

Summer swallowed hard. "Colton, I *do* care for you…more than you'll ever know…but you have a wife and child."

"My wife and child…have nothing to do with anything. They have nothing to do with you and me."

She shook her head. "I couldn't be with you for just one week, or just one night…or just right now."

He smiled. "All we have is 'just right now.'

That's what life is. That's what love is, too."

Summer stared at him for a few moments. "Do you love me, Colton?"

"I don't know what 'love' is. It's the biggest, most provocative four-letter word in town. I've used it casually enough times to know that I should use it only when I really think it's appropriate."

"I'd feel awful, having a sexual relationship with another woman's husband," Summer said. "I knew that when my parents were married, my father never stopped screwing around. I remember thinking, 'That's terrible1 I would never do that.' I think it's wrong that we're here right now, having this conversation." Then, "Oh, Colton, I must sound like the world's biggest fool…"

He cupped her face in his hands and said, "No, Summer, you're the most wonderful person I've ever met. But you must go now." He led her into the next room and helped her into her overcoat. "Goodnight."

A tear trickled down her cheek. "Colton, please don't go. Stay here with me."

"It's just for a little while. It's a good thing—we need time apart, to think, to get our heads straight." He opened the door and watched her walk towards the elevator.

She felt—what? Fear and delight. She told herself that anything that felt so right couldn't be completely wrong. She loved the idea that Colton now lived in Wade's suite, and that her affair with Colton—if it happened—would occur in Wade's Plaza bed.

Summer sat back in the limousine and thought about something Colton had said: *I'm going away for a few days. It'll be good for us. It'll give us a chance to think.* She squirmed in her seat. What was there for them to think about? What was there for *him* to ponder? Did he mean, despite all his lovey-dovey talk, that he might change his mind about them? Then she frowned in the darkness of the limousine as she remembered, a few moments earlier, her body pressed to his...he didn't have an erection! Was that her fault? Had she failed to turn him on? What was her *problem?*

17

She slept poorly that night. In some ways she felt more tortured than when Wade said to her, "Summer, I'm married." *That* night, she had simply stared out the window, feeling nothing, as if the cops had come to her and said, "Your father died today." Throughout her latest, largely sleepless night, Summer had smoked an entire pack of Pall Malls and repeated to herself, *It'll just be for a few days. It will be good for us. It will give us time to think.* His words refused to go away. She didn't want to play games with him, or with anyone else. If she and he had something, anything, worth pursuing, it would be difficult enough for them because of his marriage—playing games with each other would be beyond stupid. She wanted a relationship with him in which she could speak her mind and tell him how she felt. But did *he* want that with *her?* She didn't know.

At about nine o'clock she traipsed into the office, dreading a confrontation with Rikia. Instead, her boss smiled and waved her into the big office.

"Sit down, have some coffee and talk to me."

"Rikia, about last night—"

"Forget about last night. I do admit that I felt like

slashing my wrists, but instead I went to see my shrink without an appointment. I waited outside his door until he showed up to unlock it. He was, like, 'Rikia, I have a full day—patients have been waiting for a month to see me today.' But I forced him to give me twenty minutes. So he relented and I ran it all down for him and burst into tears a dozen times. He was, like, 'Colton Thomas is not in love with you or Summer. A man his age who's such a womanizer is just trying to prove to himself that he's still virile and masculine. That he would choose Summer tells me that he's trying to get even with her father over something.'"

"Hmm," Summer murmured. "I'm glad I've never gotten involved with a headshrinker."

"But didn't you have one at that rehab place in Switzerland?"

"Yes, but it wasn't the same thing. He would just give me encouragement about walking again and returning to America and seeing my father again. Anyway, I couldn't see myself spilling my guts to some man in a suit."

"My shrink has helped me many times. He's made me understand that even though I've had a nose job and most people think I look good, my inner ugly girl is still bugging the shit out of me. He thinks your awful motorcycle crash had something to do with your father. You got on that bike because you were opposed to your father's sexual thing with that French actress."

"I can't believe you told your shrink about me!"

"Well, why not? I'm supposed to tell him about myself and the people in my life. So naturally your name came up. He spoke of your Electra complex.

He said that you will never fall in love with Stephen for the simple reason that he's young and handsome."

Summer buried her face in her hands. "Rikia…"

"Don't worry—we don't always talk about *you*. Lots of times we talk about *me*. He thinks I have a superstar complex, only I don't have the tools to achieve superstardom. Because of my nose job, I'm a real cute chick, but I lack world-class beauty. I can sing pretty well, but I'm no Barbra Streisand—I'm not even a Celine Dion. So I assert my greatness through *In* magazine. *In* is a superstar, and *I* am *In*, so I am a superstar. But enough about me." She reached into a drawer and took out a small black gadget. "Know what this is?"

Summer shrugged. "A hand-held voice recorder."

"Yes…and you're going to take it with you on the road with Colton Thomas. Record all of your impressions and interviews and give it to Anya when you're done; she can write the story based on your verbal notes. Pretend this little machine is your diary. Tell it everything."

"Rikia—"

"Oh, I don't mean, 'Colton Thomas jumped my bones last night,' if such a thing happens. That's for my ears only. But talk about your impressions of him and the people he meets. This won't be boring— Colton Thomas isn't just a man. He's a legend in his own time and blah, blah, blah."

Summer smirked. "I've lived with a legend. They're only human. Anyway, I think you've spent too much time with your shrink. Maybe you should just try to figure out stuff without running to him every time life throws you a curveball."

Rikia ignored her. "Take this voice recorder, and

when you return it, maybe we'll learn more about the real Colton Thomas...and also figure out who Summer Sellars is."

She tried talking into the machine about Colton—her impressions of him here and there, his strength and tenderness—but when she played it back, she thought she sounded like a cheerleader gushing over some cute boy's ass.

She spent a boring, endless day at *In*, thinking of Colton most of the time. What if he didn't contact her again? Or if he called to say, "I've changed my mind—no story on me"? She closed her office at four-thirty and walked home, thinking that maybe she should write the story on her computer, then read it back into Rikia's voice recorder. That way, she would be able to see each word as she wrote it and, ideally, keep her emotions out of it. As she walked home, she wished she could pick up her telephone and call Daddy. He would know just what to tell her...

At home she dialed Stephen.

"What a nice surprise," he said. "Usually I have to call you."

"Stephen, I have a problem. I've been writing like a fiend all day and it's occurred to me that I don't understand the man's point of view. Think you can help me with that? Want to grab some dinner and talk about it?"

"Wish I could, but I have a dinner commitment with a rich, boring client. How about if you pop over here and we have a drink and talk?"

"No," she said. "I've been cooped up in an office all day and now I'm cooped up writing in this puny apartment."

He laughed. "You sound so serious and professional! Then let's go someplace convenient for both of us. How about the Cheshire Cat? We can drink and talk there."

So they did. Stephen chuckled when Summer ordered a Wild Turkey over ice. She always cringed at the liquor's taste but it reminded her of Colton.

"So," Stephen said, "what's happening with America's most beautiful woman writer?"

"It's this short story I'm working on. I'm saying to myself, 'You've got everything from the woman's point of view! Where's the man's point of view?'"

Stephen nodded. "What's the story about?"

"There's this young woman, see, who's in love with an older man. He's married."

"Does he have a dozen grandchildren?"

"No, but he has a much younger wife and they have a baby son."

"How old is this dude?"

"Pushing sixty."

"Then make him a granddaddy. His grandkids sort of remind him how old he is and how little time he has left."

She waved him off. "That stuff doesn't matter. What does matter is the relationship between the older man and the younger woman."

Summer took a big swallow of booze. "I dunno."

"Then make her about thirty-two. A man his age rarely marries anyone younger than that."

"Why can't she be in her twenties?"

"Because your readers will think, 'What a pedophile! What a pervert!' If the man is well into

253

middle age and he falls in love with a woman even though he's married, the other woman must be just that—a *woman*, not a girl."

Summer sighed. "Well, whatever her age, what if she gets involved with him but starts feeling very guilty about their relationship because he's a family man…and she refuses to be casual about things and treat him like some guy she hooked up for one night. But the thing you need to understand about her is that she is mad about him and doesn't want to break up his marriage but she does really want to have a relationship with him…"

"Why are you asking me about this? Sounds like it's something you'll have to work out for yourself."

"My heroine says to him, 'I need you to tell me you love me.'"

Stephen groaned.

"What?"

"Summer, even the dumbest girl in town knows better to say, 'Tell me that you love me, dammit!'"

"Is that a bad idea?"

"The worst. It's the quickest way to scare him off."

"Well, maybe my heroine *is* the dumbest girl in town. She says to him, 'I can't settle for less than love,' and she says it just before he goes off on this really important business trip. She says, 'I will miss you for the next few days,' and he says, 'It'll be O.K.; it'll give us a chance to think.'"

"Bravo!"

"Huh?"

"You've got a potentially *great* story. That should be your last line, followed by an ellipsis. You'd be letting your reader provide the ending she wanted—

does he come back to her or does he stay away?"

"If you were the reader, what would you think?"

"I would say, 'Better start looking for a new squeeze, sweetheart.' Women would probably say, 'He'll come back, sweetie! Don't you worry!'" He paid the check and helped her on with her coat. "'Time apart is good for us.' Famous last words."

"You think?"

"I'm afraid so."

18

The next evening she went out on a date with Clay Nedforth, a boring but handsome acquaintance of Stephen. Clay had called her several times and asked her out, and each time she refused. But then she grew so lonely that she let him take her out to a nightclub where a group of his friends were expecting him. There, she sipped white wine, allowed herself to be groped on the dance floor and even tried to participate in their shouted conversation. By eleven, she felt stupefied by exhaustion and hoped nobody would notice as she covered her mouth to hide her yawns. Relief came at midnight, when somebody suggested that they head out to Joni's to play backgammon. Summer said she didn't know Joni and couldn't play backgammon. She said to Clay, "I can take a taxi home. The rest of you should to Joni's." Clay replied, "Whatever."

Summer went home and flopped into bed. She slept until eight, when her alarm went off. She checked her cell phone messages: Anya Semko wanted to know when she could hear what Summer had recorded; Colton Thomas said he was in Washington and wanted her to call him. She did so right away.

"I was up till midnight and I just woke up. I

needed a good long sleep," she told him.

"Nice for you. I'll be back in New York on Friday. How about dinner?"

"Yes, yes, yes!"

"In the meantime, if anything comes up, I've got your cell number and you've got mine. See you then." Click.

Summer spent hours composing a professional, journalistic account of the cocktail party for Colton Thomas: His attitude, the others in attendance, and the profound discomfort he surely felt because he was Colton Thomas and everyone else wasn't.

She presented it to Rikia, who nodded. "Acceptable." Then, "Something wrong? You look unhappy."

Summer shook her head. "Rikia, I don't know what to do. I'm freaked out."

"About what?"

"Colton is coming back soon, and I want to get it on with him...but suppose it doesn't happen?"

"A man like him will get very aroused by your beautiful blonde body."

Summer paused. "When he held me that night at the Plaza, he wasn't wearing anything underneath his robe—"

"And he didn't have a boner?"

"Exactly."

Rikia frowned. "Yeah, I forgot: He's in his late fifties and likes his booze, a very bad combination if you want to get it up and get it on. I guess you'll just have to help him rise to the occasion."

"How?"

"Fellatio."

"Blow job?"

Rikia nodded. "That's what I said."

Summer sneered. "Not sure I could do that. I'd gag."

"Just pretend it's a Popsicle—"

"But it's not. It's gross—an ugly pink blue-veiny thing—"

"*I* think a cock is very beautiful. Don't make such an issue of it. I've been told I give the best hummers in all of Manhattan, and I can assure you that a man like Colton Thomas has received thousands of then. You get down on your knees and he'll guide you along…"

"But what happens if he ejaculates?"

Rikia shrugged. "You cop the load."

Summer made a gagging sound.

"Please," said Rikia, "don't pretend that oral sex is unknown to you. When you're in bed with someone you really care about, you pleasure each other in every way possible."

"What if I get uptight when I'm in bed with him?"

"Well, when are you going to see him again?"

"For dinner tomorrow."

"Before you see him, get a vitamin shot."

"Really? Why?"

"Just do it." She scribbled a name on a slip of paper. "Dr. Al Simonyi gives vitamin shots. He did them for Hank and me. I'm sure Hank is still getting them because he needs to get boners for his new girlfriend, who's actually kind of and old woman."

"I don't see how a vitamin shot is going to make me into some kind of great lover."

Rikia blew out a big sigh. "All I know is, when I started getting the shots, everything turned into a big acid trip—and I mean that in a good way. I had so much energy, I could pull double shifts at *In* and then go home and boff Hank till dawn. My orgasms lasted for an hour. I was terrific in bed without being too bossy. Hank used to bitch that I acted in the sack like the director of a porn video—'Move this way, turn here; when you eat my cunt, lick harder.' Furthermore, many men will perform cunnilingus and then look up at the woman as if she should be full of gratitude because he was willing to wet her down. Anyway, after the vitamin shot my sex live improved so much that I think *you* should check it out."

"Why did you stop taking them?"

"Oversimplified, because they were too damn expensive and Hank left me, so I decided I didn't need all that energy. The closest thing I have to a boyfriend right now is Noel, and he's not worth the trouble and expense of those shots."

"Anything else?"

"Yeah, ask Noel to get you some amyl nitrite. I think it's illegal, but it goes great with sex. The gays love it because it gives them a heart attack and loosens up their sphincters for anal intercourse."

"Whatever happened to good old-fashioned sex without vitamin shots and amyl nitrite?"

"You had that with Stephen. You didn't like it."

Summer left the office at five and hurried home to take a long bubble bath. Then she sat in her brassiere and panties, smoking Pall Malls and sipping Wild Turkey from the bottle she'd bought in case Colton came over.

He called at nine and said, "Summer, I had

trouble getting out of D.C. because of bad weather—nothing was departing or arriving. So I said, 'To hell with this nonsense' and took a train but *that* got all fucked up, too—"

She busted out laughing.

"So here I am, at the Plaza, *way* too tired to go anywhere. Why don't you come here and we'll order in? My car is outside your building."

"So you *knew* I wanted to see you."

He chuckled. "I had a hunch."

Colton stood waiting at his door when Summer emerged from the elevator and came running down the hallway. She threw herself into his arms and he put a gentle kiss on her lips. "Beautiful girl," he murmured. "I've ordered steaks for us."

He was full of complaints about his tour. "I hated every moment of it. I'm not a professional actor or performer, so why the fuck am I appearing on TV? The professional performs go on those shows and they're so poised; then I go on and it's like I'm some brute from the zoo who should be on a leash. The *Times* says my book is number three, just behind Danielle Steel and Stephen King, and I guess I should be very grateful for that. But I also know that I've earned every sale I've gotten."

They ate dinner and then cuddled on the sofa as they watched the TV news. Colton drank Wild Turkey and grinned at the sight of Summer sipping a glass of bourbon and water. He said, "Want to go to the beach?"

"Robertson Hughley's place?"

"Yeah. We can use his bed. He sleeps most nights out on the beach. He'll curl up on the sofa if necessary."

"When?"

"Tomorrow."

She beamed. "Let's do it."

They stood up and embraced. He kissed her and she kissed him back. He reached underneath her clothing and ran his finger along her underpants and brassiere. She remembered Rikia's advice—*Put your hands on him! Show him he's sexy!*—so she maneuvered her hands around his waist, to his front...

He backed off. "It's late and I'm tired. We'll have the whole weekend together." He helped her with her coat and said, "You haven't mentioned it once this evening."

"What's that?"

"Love." He smiled. "Do you love me?"

She giggled. "Of course! Of course!"

They hugged and kissed. "Colton," she said, "do *you* love *me*?"

He nodded. "I think so."

The next morning she went to see the doctor to get the vitamin shot. She knew that Colton had pulled away from her because he was impotent. When she called Rikia and said, "He couldn't get it up," Rikia replied, "Then go get that shot."

"Rikia, is sex all that crucial? I mean, could it be that Colton loves me but just can't get a woody?"

"Boners are funny things, Summer. Many guys have come to me with the stiffest Johnsons I've ever seen, but one we get into bed their cocks go limp and we have a *hell* of a time pumping them back up."

"Rikia!"

"Summer! We're talking about a man who's

schtupped vast numbers of broads all over the world. He's also pushing sixty and more than just a tiny bit jaded. You must turn him on. Your creamy young blonde body isn't going to turn the trick, so *you've* got to do it."

At the clinic, Summer filled out a card, received a paper gown and went down the hallway. She gave a blood sample and presently a middle-aged man came into the room.

"Hi. I'm Doctor Alvin Simonyi."

He had discolored teeth and needed a haircut. Summer wondered how such a disheveled-looking man could run such an immaculate facility. "So, Miz Sellars, what's our problem today?"

"Well, there's this man—"

He shook his head. "Sorry—no abortions or contraceptives here."

"Nothing like that. This man is wonderful and all the women adore him…"

"I hear you. He's dumped you and you're feeling miserable. I'll be right back." He went away.

Presently he returned with a syringe. "This will help. You young things, you're so much in love with love. You become obsessed with a man, you stalk him. This is not a new thing in the world."

He shot her up. "Promise Uncle Alvin that you won't call him ever again…son of a bitch like him doesn't deserve a beautiful girl like you."

The injection kicked in right away. She had marvelous feeling all over; she wanted to masturbate, because that's where she felt best of all.

The good doctor smiled. "Feeling good?" He reached over and tweaked one of her nipples. She smiled back, having forgotten that she was naked. His tweak wasn't the gesture of some drooling old perv; it was the kind gesture of nice Uncle Alvin.

He smiled. "You'll be fine. I can see that you're already responding to the treatment. If you want some more, make an appointment and come back. As long as you receive the injections, you'll be able to work all day and make love all night." He tweaked her breast again and left the room.

She tweaked her nipples and stared at her turgid nipples. The fire down below got hotter, so she masturbated till she practically screamed. Her arm got sore, so she dressed herself with her other one and went to the receptionist. She wiped sweat from her hot, red face as she wrote a check and promised to come back for shots. She walked down Park Avenue and bought Colton a cornflower-blue necktie. Then she picked up a belt Rikia had admired once or twice; she wrote on the gift card, *Thanks for Uncle Alvin!* She hurried home and packed her suitcase, and when the chauffeur rang her buzzer at three, she danced out of her building and into the waiting car.

She could hardly wait to see Colton, and looked forward to seeing Robertson, too. They both were terrific! She was terrific! Life was just way too wonderful!

19

Colton said, "I love the tie! I'll wear it on TV. Want a drink?"

She shook her head and smiled. "I'm high on life—and high on you." When they arrived at the beach house, she threw herself into Robertson Hughley's arms and said, "I feel like I've just come home."

He pointed at his oversized sofa facing the fireplace. "You two sit and enjoy the fire. I'll cook the steaks."

They did as told until the steaks and vegetables started sizzling and Colton got up to help Colton.

At ten, Robertson stood up and said, "Well, it's time for me to go out there and sleep."

"Brrr," said Summer. "You'll catch a cold."

"Oh, I'm not going to spend the whole night out there," he said. "I have a cot behind the kitchen that I often use. You two use the bedroom."

After Robertson left, Summer and Colton sat for the longest time on the sofa, watching the fire and listening to the crashing of the waves. Summer loved the peace and quiet of being away from Manhattan and its nonstop insanity.

"Bedtime," she murmured, taking him by the hand. Their bedroom had a large bed, a dresser and not much else. She undressed and said, "Here I am."

He turned off the light and took off his clothes.

She could see his muscular buttocks, his broad shoulders and tight stomach. *At his age*, she said to herself, *still looking that good even though he smokes like a chimney and drinks like a fish. Good DNA, I guess.*

"What I want," he told her in the darkness, "is to make you happy."

He lay on top of her and smothered her with kisses. Then he kissed her breasts and went lower, to her stomach, and lower still. She thrashed and arched her back, unable to believe the sensations rocketing through her, wanting them never to end.

After what seemed a glorious eternity he crawled up to her and gathered her breasts in his hands. "Did I make you happy?"

"But *I* wanted to make *you* happy."

"Did I make you happy?"

"Yes…oh yes…but we didn't do it…"

"I wanted to make you happy. Now let's just hold each other."

She lay there in his arms, thinking that something was wrong but not sure what. She wanted to pleasure him in the same way he had just done her, so she planet kisses on his body, lower and lower. But he had no big throbbing member like the thing Stephen had forced upon her. Instead, a harmless little penis lay napping between the big man's legs. How, she wondered, could a six-footer like him be so pathetically underendowed? Such a virile man who'd ravished so many women! Or *had* he? Were his legendary tales of carnal fun with the world's great beauties as fictitious as his written words?

"Summer," he said, as if hearing her thoughts, "all I want is to make you happy." She stroked his penis until it hardened. Then she mounted and rode him until he shuddered and his manhood once again became flaccid.

He said, "Thank you, Summer."

She said, "Thank *you*, Colton."

"You know, that was my first time in a decade…"

"I'm glad it was special." Then, "Are you crying?"

He wiped his face. "The tears are for me because I've just had a wonderful experience with a beautiful girl…and the tears are for you because all you're getting is what's left of Colton Thomas. Not that my stuff was any bigger years ago, but at least it was dependable. For the past decade it's been strippers, porn movies, vibrators—whatever I could find. Nothing worked…unless now, with you."

Summer frowned. "But Colton—you have a baby."

"Let me tell you about my sex life. For all these years, women have hooked up with me even though they knew I wasn't hung like Johnny Wadd. But I was Colton Thomas, a man who could satisfy and gratify them in a hundred other ways. But lately I've gotten to thinking about my life and work; who would inherit it, who would give a shit about it and me once I was dead? I really was alone in life. My two brothers were killed in Vietnam and our sister had no children. So I said to myself, 'Colt, you've got to have a kid.' At first I thought about adopting one, but then decided it wouldn't really be *mine*. So I started asked the women I knew how they would feel about having my baby, but all of them either had kids from earlier relationships or they just flat-out hated kids. So there was just nobody around who was appropriate. Around this time, I'd say a couple of years ago, at a party in Malibu I met Jennifer Randall, a little starlet type who was now pushing thirty. She had nearly given up on screen acting. So I'm at this party, and she recognizes me right away and gets *very* friendly. We get to talking; she says, 'I'm from Canada, and I'm an actor but all I've gotten lately is a TV commercial here and there. They tell me I need to do something about my accent.' I asked her how she felt about kids and she said, 'Oh, I love kids! There's this cinematographer I know who wants a baby and I thought of marrying him and having his baby because I'm getting older, and if I'm going to have a family, now is the time.'

"Well, we dated for a few months and I told her about my impotency. She said, 'That's O.K.; we can go to a doctor and see about artificial insemination.' It took several months, but it worked. She bore me a son. So, there it is."

Summer nodded. "You must be deeply in love with her."

"I am *profoundly grateful* to her. I've never been in love with her and never will be. One of my pleasures in life is hanging out with smart people, and I've already forgotten more than she's ever learned. But I give her the freedom to, uh, fulfill her own wants and needs—so long as she's discreet about it. She has a *GQ* boyfriend who comes by to bang her, you see, and she's a terrific mother to our son. Plus, she really gets off on being Missus Colton Thomas, wife of the man they call King Shit of American Fiction. We get invited to parties, we're introduced to everybody worth meeting, and we have that house in Malibu. We have a viable marriage, I suppose. I tell myself that, just a few years ago, she was a good-looking, untalented Canadian woman pushing thirty, nowhere on her way to no place…until she met me. She's given me an heir and I've given her a new life."

"Colton, you had sex with me just now. You proved to both of us that you could do it, so doesn't that mean that you and Jennifer could have a sex life—"

He shook his head. "We've tried and tried and tried. My wife, had she been so inclined, could have been Los Angeles' most popular high-priced call girl. She's gorgeous, sweet-natured and a very imaginative, resourceful sex partner. But even she failed to get me hard. Tonight you succeeded, and I will always remember you for this."

"We can do this again and again—"

He sighed. "Summer, I can't get a divorce. Jennifer would never go for it, and she would get custody of our son. I want him to have absolutely, positively everything, which is why I'm doing this tour and promoting my work. Right now, I have more than enough money to live comfortably for the rest of my life—but that isn't good enough. I want to leave a fortune to my son." He pointed at the bottle. "Shall we have a tiny?"

Summer shook her head. "I'm fine, thanks."

"I think you know that I love you," he told her. "I've never loved any woman like this, or at least have never been so open and honest with her. You and Jennifer, that is. I *needed* to talk straight to her, but I wanted to talk this way to you. Most of the time, I've been a real asshole with women. They would say, 'Your cock is limp! What's your problem?' and I would say, '*You're* my problem. You don't turn me on. If you were sexier and you turned me on, my dick would be thirteen inches long and stiff as steel.' Look,

Summer, I don't know how long you'll stay interested in me and my puny *putz*, but as long as we're together, I'll be open and honest with you and I will belong to you."

She took him into her arms. "Colton, I love you too…and I will be there for you whenever you want me or need me."

They lay together for a while, and then he fell asleep. Restless, she got up and stretched. She looked down at his sleeping form, telling herself that she loved him no matter the size of his manhood. She went into the living room and saw that the fire had nearly died. Summer placed some logs and wads of newspaper into the fireplace and soon it roared to life. She flopped down onto the huge sofa and closed her eyes, feeling warm and loved.

"You're up."

She smiled at the sound of Robertson's deep, resonant voice. "Couldn't sleep. He's drunk. He finished all the booze and passed out."

"Want some leftovers? You didn't have much dinner."

She shook her head. "I feel marvelous. I have everything I need right now."

He paused. "Summer, I don't know what he's told you about his marriage or child—"

"I can't have him. I'm O.K. with that."

"Are you in love with him?"

"Mmmm."

He sat and faced her. "I've seen women fall in love with him, and they all say, 'I'll enjoy him for as long as I can.' But when he says, 'Goodbye, sweetie, time to move on,' they've come close to throwing themselves off a bridge."

"Robertson, how well do you know Colton?"

He shrugged. "How well does anyone know him? How well does he know himself? We met a half-dozen years ago. His novel at the time concerned space travel, so he contacted me because he wanted to get the details right. Well, of course I was very flattered that Colton Thomas wanted me to help him, so we hung out together and I answered his questions and even edited some of his manuscript. He was getting a divorce, so we became roomies. He said, 'If you need a date on Saturday night, I'll fix you up with one of my sloppy seconds.' Classy guy, right? Well, his space novel was a big hit, and he's been a true friend to me. He's a fascinating man—no wonder he's held the public's interest for all these years."

"Hey, guy…"

They both turned around as Colton entered the room. "You tryin' to make time with my best girl?"

"Are you thirsty?" Robertson retorted. "I'm all out of Wild Turkey. Got some bourbon in the bar."

"I thought you might run out," said Colton, "so I had my driver put a case in the kitchen. I'll go get some."

He disappeared, and Summer and Robertson failed to hear the two bad guys enter the room. Summer turned and felt a big clammy hand on her mouth. She felt the cool steel of a blade at her throat and saw a flashlight pointed in Robertson's face. "If you want the bitch to live," muttered the man holding the flashlight, "tell us where the money is."

"No money or jewelry," replied Robertson. "It's all at home."

"Fuckin' liar. You beach people always bring good shit out here. Now give it up." The man must have been six-six and weighed nearly three hundred

"She's got nothin'," said the robber holding the knife at Summer's throat. "No rings, no Rolex, no nothin'. Shit."

"Empty your pockets," said the other guy to Robertson, who dumped a small wad of bills, some change and keys onto the coffee table.

"Get the fuck out my face with that bullshit," said the big robber. "Maybe I oughta take you into the bedroom and ask you pretty-please to turn over your valuables."

Presently Summer stood alone in the living room with the smaller man who held the knife. Where, she wondered, was Colton? The only way he would know about this trouble was if she screamed, and then this little bad guy might slash her throat.

He reached out and yanked open her robe. Staring at her nude body, he wiped his mouth. "Looks like you and him were gonna get *busy*."

She closed her eyes and tried not to scream as she felt him jiggling her breasts. Then she heard him say, "Lookee what I got down here. Hung pretty good for a little dude, huh?" Then, "My pal in the other room? He's a man of business—he comes in, does what he gots to do, then leaves. Me, I'm a man of business *and* pleasure. So you and me is gonna gets to know each other just a little bit better. Now turn around!"

"No…" She burst into tears.

"Maybe you want it all lovey-dovey. I s'pose I could put you on that nice big sofa and pretend that I was sweet on you, but then I would have to put my knife down and you could snatch it up and kill me with it. So I don't think we're gonna play that particular game. You're gonna take it from behind."

"Please," she said, whimpering. "Just take what you want and get out."

He laughed. "What you think I'm doin' right now, bitch? Just takin' what I want. Open your eyes."

She did as told, and he thrust his penis into her face. "This here's my friend Johnson. Give him a little kiss and say hi." The smell of his privates repulsed her so much that she scrambled away and headed for he front door. The little man reached out, grabbed a handful of her hair and backhanded her across the face so hard that her ears rang. "Get on your knees, bitch. I'm going to shove my cock so far up your ass that you won't be able to walk for a month."

He leaned closer to her, and she screamed. He flinched and said, "Tryin' to wake the neighbors? Nobody's home. We already checked. And don't think the cops are gonna drive by and save your ass. They're too busy having coffee and donuts at Winchell's."

Summer, out of the corner of her eye, saw Colton's shadow in the doorway. She thrashed and growled, doing her best to antagonize the robber while Colton came to the rescue. The little man tried to stick his penis into her and pawed at her hair until Colton, standing unseen behind him, brought down the empty bottle on his head. After a small cry and groan, the bad guy fell backwards and lay prostrate.

Colton helped her slipped into her robe. "Take this bottle. If he wakes up, whack him. If he doesn't go down immediately, whack him again."

She nodded. "There's another one in the bedroom. He's huge. Be careful."

Colton went halfway up the stairs and waited.

Summer could hear punches and groans and curses and guessed that Robertson was getting pummeled. The big man emerged, saw Colton, then looked past him and saw his accomplice out cold on the floor. The big man said to Colton, "The other guy's half dead in there, but I'm gonna fuckin' waste you."

The two men grappled for the longest time, and the bad guy began punching Colton in the stomach. Colton doubled over, and Summer grabbed the knife, which she'd put on the sofa. She ran across the room brandishing the weapon and screamed, "Bastard! I'll kill you!"

The big man looked at her and laughed. "Gonna fuck me up, little girl?" He bounded away from Colton and stood a few feet from Summer. "You're a pretty little girl. Wish I had time to get to know you better." Then the two heard Colton struggle to his feet. "Look, cunt," said the robber, "I'm here to do business. You're not supposed to be here. Too fuckin' bad for you." He lunged at her so fast that she had no time to react. He snatched the knife out of her hand, grabbed her by her hair and dragged her over to Colton.

"Motherfucker," he said, "this is one night you're gonna remember for a long time." He came at Colton, who crouched like a panther and then sprang, slamming his forearm into the robber's throat. With a little groan the huge man went down.

Presently Robertson emerged with a black eye and swollen jaw. "He really kicked my ass. Afraid I can't fight so great anymore."

"Don't worry about it," said Colton. "Now we got to get these two jokers bound and gagged. They're both addicts—I can tell just by looking at them. They came here to steal money to buy crack or meth or whatever. We need to dump them somewhere."

"Why not just call the cops?" asked Robertson.

"Because," Colton told him, "then the media will have some fun with it. 'Colton Thomas and Summer Sellars get held up at knifepoint in Robertson Hughley's beach house'? Well, fuck *that* shit."

Robertson looked down at the huge bad guy and said, "You cracked him pretty good."

Colton said, "I think maybe I killed him."

"No, he seems to be breathing a little bit."

"Then we better get his sorry ass to the hospital right away. Robertson, you drive Summer back to Manhattan. You"—he pointed at her—"get dressed *tout de suite*." She nodded and hurried off.

"And what are *you* gonna do?" Robertson wanted to know.

"I'm going to call an ambulance. When they get here, and the cops will be here, too, I will just tell them what happened: That you lent me your beach house, and while I was in the kitchen these two surprised me."

"Then why don't *I* stay here and give them the same story?"

"Because you're five-nine and there's no way in hell you could have taken out a guy his size. I even have the scarred knuckles to prove I did it."

Summer came back with her overnight bag. Her face was ashen and she hugged Colton as Robertson went out to start his car.

"I heard what you said to Robertson. What if they wake up and start giving their own versions of what happened?"

"Who cares? Nobody will take their word against

mine." He walked her to the door, and she said, "Oh, Colton."

"What?"

"I thought we were going to have a whole weekend together, safe and sound."

He laughed. "Well, you have to admit one thing: Life around me is never boring."

20

Summer and Robertson remained silent during the drive back to Manhattan, neither of them having the slightest idea of what to say to the other. The night had become a dark gray by the time they reached Summer's building. The car's heater was on too high but she shivered, cringing at the ugliness of early-morning New York City. She could scarcely believe that her eagerly anticipated weekend on the beach with Colton had ended the way it did.

"I wish the doorman was there," she said. "The building looks abandoned without him."

"You're feeling low," Robertson said, "because of sleep deprivation. Go inside and have a nice long snooze. You'll feel better."

"I have some crappy instant coffee, if you'd like some."

"Thanks, but I'm needed elsewhere. The cops out by the beach are polite, but they ask questions. I'm sure Colton would feel much better with me around." He kissed her cheek and she got out of the car.

Back in her apartment, she opened a can of Pepsi and lit a Pall Mall. She wanted to call Rikia but decided to wait till later. She also wanted to go outside and walk for miles, to sing and dance and say hi to everyone she met, to scatter happiness to all of humankind. Instead, she picked up her cell phone and called Wade.

"Where the hell have you been?"

She laughed. "Never mind that. How was Switzerland?"

"Beth came in second. She flew straight back to Florida, but I went to New York to visit you. Obviously, you weren't there. When Beth called and said, 'How is Summer?' I said, 'Oh, fine, we had a nice visit.' I didn't want her to think I was a jackass, flying in to see you when you weren't there."

"Smart thinking."

"Anyway, here's the gig. We're going to be down here till Easter, and we insist that you and Stephen fly down for Beth's last big party of the season. Also, I have a great surprise for you."

"Yummy! I love great surprises!"

"I'll tell you what it is: the Cannes Film Festival."

"Cannes!"

"Yes. Remember when you were recovering in Switzerland and we talked about going to Cannes some day? Well, there's a backgammon tournament in Monte Carlo at around the same time, so I had an easy time persuading Beth to go. We'll stay at the Carlton—you're twenty-one now, so you can go into the casino and I can teach you to break the bank. We can go to all the Cannes movies, say hi to my old friends and have ourselves a hell of a fine time."

"Let's do it! When?"

"It starts in May, so I'm thinking around the fifth. We can stay there for most of the month. Beth can come back to New York if she gets bored with Europe, and I can watch as many movies as I want. You can, too—if Stephen will let you. I think I should teach you backgammon; I've never played better and

278

have won lots of money at it."

"The main thing is, are you happy?"

"Well, I'm gambling and winning, so my answer is yes."

"If you're happy, I'm happy for you."

"Are you happy with Stephen?"

"He's a very nice gentleman."

"But are you happy with him?"

"It's complicated," Summer said.

"Is there anyone else?"

"As a matter of fact, yes." Then, "Wade, I've met a man…I think he could be the one…I *know* he could be the one…"

"And…?"

"He's married."

"Tell me more." Wade's voice sounded deep and harsh.

"Does that bother you?"

"I hate it. When I screwed around, I screwed around with trash, and I knew they were trash, even if they were good-looking and famous. But you? You're twenty-one and have every advantage imaginable, plus you have the love of a man like Stephen…"

"His love isn't worth much if I don't love him back."

"You tellin' me that you, Summer Sellars, the girl who has everything and could have just about any man she wants, has decided that the only man she wants is a married one? I suppose he has kids, too."

"He has one."

"Will his wife grant him a divorce?"

"I don't think he wants one."

"Let me guess: the love of your life is an ad guy in his thirties. He's married to some chick he met a decade ago and he has her stashed in the suburbs…"

"No, it's nothing like that."

"Have you gone to bed with him?"

Oh, no, she wasn't going to get into *that*. "You're sounding like such a prude."

"I'm just trying to have a frank conversation with my daughter."

Presently they hung up, and Summer decided to call Colton, but then Wade called her back. "Hey, I'm sorry I ragged on you that way. You know that all I want is what's best for you, right?"

"Of course I do."

"Do you love me?"

"Always."

"I know you do."

Colton called her some hours later. "I've sent my car to your building. Come to me."

"Right away. Are you O.K.?"

"No. But I will be as soon as you get here."

The Manhattan traffic was especially heavy and Summer tapped her toe in supreme impatience as the big car crept towards the Plaza. Once she reached the hotel she sprinted down the hallway to his suite.

"You look tired," she said as he took her into his arms.

"I'll live," he replied with a big smile. He sat on the sofa and sipped Wild Turkey as he ran it down for her. "The big guy is in a coma. Nobody will be filing any charges. He had a long rap sheet—"

"Surprise!"

"And they're still checking out his accomplice."

She shook her head. "I still don't know how you took him on. You'd had so much booze."

He shrugged. "I've had some practice fighting.

280

Also, I've taken lessons from Chuck Norris and Steven Seagal."

"I'll bet you've never lost a fight."

He gave her a big smile. "See these teeth? They're not all real. I've lost a few in barroom fights, but I've got this killer instinct that allows me to win fights. Sometimes it worries me that I fight so hard, because I know I could kill my opponent. Norris and Seagal said, 'A man's fists and elbows can be lethal weapons if he knows how to use them right.'"

Summer stayed the night with him and once again, through patience and persistence, managed to harden him for intercourse. "Thank you for that," he said, tears of gratitude streaming down his face.

The next day reporters banged on his door, and he let them all in. The story of his heroics at Robertson Hughley's beach house was in media all over. Colton Thomas, in beating up some bad guys, had lived his own myth. By noon, the police had learned that the smaller bad guy was wanted for homicide and rape in Chicago. Now Colton's incident had acquired national significance. The cops and reporters shouted at themselves and each other, and the telephones rang often and loudly.

Louise Ritamen, ecstatic, managed the news media and ordered up coffee for everyone. Summer had left the suite just before the craziness began; Colton called her at *In* and said, "The cops and reporters have overrun my suite. The FBI is saying, 'You may have to fly to Washington to give testimony.' It's about that little guy—his name is Mort Hendrix and he's wanted in Chicago—plus his accomplice has a wife and two kids, and she's thinking, 'That guy who beat up my old man? He's a famous writer, so I'll sue him for a few million bucks.' Her lawyer has already filed the motion."

"She can't actually *do* anything to you, can she?"

"Just take up some of my time and be a big pain in my ass. I'll probably end up paying her a thousand dollars just to make her go away."

"You shouldn't have to pay her anything, considering what her husband was going to do to us."

"That's just how it works. A modest, out-of-court settlement is a bargain compared to going through the hassle of an actual lawsuit."

"That sucks."

"Yes, it does. Anyway, you better keep a low profile. That little guy who's wanted in Chicago? He's starting to talk about 'this skinny blonde who was gonna open my head with a booze bottle if I moved.' Nobody believes him, of course, but it's better for everybody if you and I don't see each other for a few days."

"That sucks, too."

"My publisher loves this shit. He says, 'Colton, did you set up this home-invasion thing as a publicity stunt? It worked great! We've had thousands of reorders! You're going to hit number one!"

"Yummy!"

"I guess so. As they say, there's no such thing as bad publicity. But I would have been happier if the increased sales had happened just because my readers wanted to check out my book instead of their morbid curiosity over my private misadventure."

They both laughed, and Summer said, "How am I going to get through the rest of today without you?"

"I'm just one punch away on your cell phone. Plus, as soon as I get done with this bullshit in

Washington, I'll fly back up and we can be together."

He went down to Washington and called her at midnight. "Looks like I might be down here for a little while. I'm going to do some promo shit for my book, so that's convenient." He added, "You get some rest, and when I get back, we'll spend the weekend together."

"But not at Robertson's beach house."

He laughed. "Hell, no. We'll kick it at the Plaza." Then, "Summer, don't tell Rikia you were at the beach house when all that bad shit went down. That broad has the biggest mouth in Manhattan."

"She sure does." When the story broke, Rikia was full of questions.

"Where were you when that happened?" she'd asked. "I thought you said you were spending the weekend with him at that beach house."

"I did, but just for the day. Colton said he had a huge amount of writing to do, so I split."

"Are you saying that nothing happened?"

"Oh, I'd say *plenty* happened."

"Not what I meant. I was asking about in the sack."

Summer shrugged. "Everything was fine."

"For real?"

"Yes."

"Was he awesome?"

"More than awesome. That's why I'm so tired. I haven't gotten much sleep. I've been too busy screwing."

That night, she got into bed but couldn't sleep. In the morning, she called Alvin Simonyi and his receptionist got her in right away.

"I can't eat or sleep. I have too much energy,"

she told him.

"When did you eat last?" he asked her.

"Can't remember."

"I'll give you a shot. You'll feel better right away."

He injected her in the right buttock. She didn't feel the euphoric rush she had expected, and she told him so.

"When you feel good," he said, "the shot makes you feel marvelous. When you feel poorly, the shot makes you feel better." He left, she got her stuff together and paid the receptionist.

On her way home, she had to admit that all of her little aches and pains had gone away, but she still didn't have that chew-through-steel feeling she craved.

Colton returned to the Plaza on Friday night. She hurried over to meet him, and felt pleased to see him looking far less fatigued and stressed out than usual. "Good news," he told her. "I'm officially number one on all the bestseller lists that mean anything, and Hollywood wants my novel."

But that night, in bed, he just couldn't get a boner. "Must be all that Wild Turkey," he said. "We'll try again tomorrow."

She said she had a dental appointment, but instead rushed over to see Doctor Simonyi. He was available, and in a good mood, so she waited with a smile in his examination room while he went out to get the needle and syringe. When he returned, he asked, "Will you promise to eat even if you aren't hungry?" She nodded as she held out her arm. Afterwards, she hugged the doctor, handed his receptionist her check with a wink, and half-ran back to the Plaza.

When she threw open the door to Colton's suite, he sat in his robe, doing a telephone interview. She plopped down on the easy chair across from him and tucked her legs under her butt. He blew her a kiss and rolled his eyes.

"Look," he said into the telephone, "are you asking me to compare myself to other writers? I'm not going to do that. I think I'm the best Colton Thomas around, but each writer does his thing his own way. Hell, writing a novel is the hardest kind of work I know."

She crawled onto his lap and began kissing his neck. She kissed his neck and pulled open his robe. He let out the tiniest groan. He swallowed hard and said, "Listen, I think we've covered everything worth talking about. I have another appointment right now—I can hear them knocking on the door—so let's hang up now." He did just that and laughed. "You just fucked up an interview with—shit, I can't remember who they wrote for!"

"Too bad for them. Not so bad for us." She unbuttoned her blouse, unhooked her brassiere and removed it. "Let's go to bed."

Afterwards, as they lay in each other's arms, Colton said, "Summer, thank you for this."

When he left town, she felt desperately lonely. Over lunch, Rikia said, "I'm in love with Oakley Donaldson. He anchors one of the local newscasts. When he goes network and hits the big time, he'll leave his wife and kids and be all mine."

"Do you want to marry him?"

"Well, why not? I'm getting damn close to thirty. Plus, Oakley is so damn smart. He's already forgotten more than most people have ever learned. He's given me two dozen books to read—'Titles every educated person needs to know.' Plus, he's turned me on to magazines like *The New Republic* and *The Nation*. We talk about politics and I'm feeling like this major Twinkie, right, because I'm realizing that I don't know *shit*. I used to read *Vogue* and *Cosmo* because they are my competition and I'm the editor-in-chief of *In*. Problem is, Oakley thinks *In* is a fucking joke, so we don't talk about my work that much. Well, our day will come. He'll make huge money and leave his family and be all mine."

"Rikia, can't you ever find an acceptable single man?"

"Nope. I guess that's what you and I have in common."

21

Colton called her every night. He told her about the TV shows he had appeared on, the monotonous interviews he had given, the occasional confrontations with interviewers. The critics had given his new novel mixed reviews; his was still number one, but he felt worried about some of the novels about to be published. 'I don't need that competition,' he said.

By the middle of the week, Summer started to feel stressed out. Colton was due back in New York within days, and said, 'I can't be without you'—but there he was, out there *without her*—and he seemed to be coping well. He had said to her once, 'My work comes first—always has, always will.' Had his time on the road, alone, caused him to question his relationship with her?

She went back to the doctor's office, got in to see him right away, and he injected her without asking the purpose of her visit. As soon as the clear fluid entered her body, she again felt that chew-through-steel rush she so desired. Summer blew him a kiss and danced out of his office.

Colton had returned on Friday night and stopped by her apartment without telling her he was back. She screamed his name and flung herself into his arms. They spoke at the same time and neither heard much of what the other said. But both knew their love would last forever…even longer.

He asked, "How long is your lease?"

"It's a sublet. Good till August. The guy says I can have it for another year; he's just as happy staying in Europe."

Colton shook his head. "Move out. We're going to get a condo—you pick it out, I'll pay for it. It's got to be by the river, with a wood-burning fireplace, a living room, bedroom and den, because I'm going to use the den as my own personal workspace."

"What about California?"

"What about it?"

"Last time I checked, you sort of lived there. Don't you have to go back there?"

"Yeah, next week we'll go there."

"You mean us?"

He sighed. "Look, I can speak only for myself, but these past few days without you have been torture. Let's be realistic: I'm closing in on sixty and you're still a child. What that means is that all we really have is now, and neither of us knows how long we'll last. But let's do our best with the time we have left. I love you and want us to be together. I have some promotional obligations to fulfill in California, Oregon and Washington, so really have to go out there. I've told my wife about you and how I feel about you. When we fly out there, we'll stay at the Beverly—two suites—and I'll tell everybody that you're doing a story on me for *In*. I'll go to Malibu and see my kid as often as I can. My wife will be a good sport about it because she's really fond of her *GQ* model."

Summer nodded and smiled, delighted that she and he were still together.

"Now, we're going to be in Manhattan for another week," he told her. "Your job, starting immediately, is to find us that condo we want. This is the cyber age, so it'll take a good rental agent about fifteen minutes to go online, find exactly what we want, and make an appointment for a showing. You go with the agent, see what's available, and narrow it down to two or three. You and I will then see those properties and decided for ourselves which one we want."

"But Colton, what about your son?"

"I'll fly out to Malibu every other weekend. That's the best I can do. The only thing I'm certain of in this life is that life without you isn't worth living."

Summer spent the next day looking at condos. When she told Rikia, the older woman threw back her head and cried with delight. "You and Colton are buying a Manhattan condo? *Fuckin' A!* Let me go with you!" Then, "It's just too delicious that an *In* editor is also the live-in squeeze of Colton Thomas. Oakley loves it that I know an American literary icon like Colton, and with you as Colton's life partner and my assistant, well, you and I will have so much juice in this city that *In* will be the arbiters of what's hip or lame in the Apple. Shit, Summer! Your condo could double as a salon in which we could meet everyone in the whole world who was worth meeting!"

Summer giggled, charmed by Rikia's exuberance, and let her friend talk uninterrupted. Summer's condo would be a fortress for herself and Colton. No parties or salons. But she felt grateful to have ballsy, outspoken Rikia at her side as they looked at apartments because Summer's underarms grew flooded with anxious sweat as the bossy real estate lady showed them first this place and then that one.

After several days, Summer, having visited every great or mediocre residential building in Manhattan, decided to narrow her choices to two properties: A U.N. Plaza suite on the fifteenth—or was it the fiftieth?—floor or a ground-floor apartment in Sutton Place with a huge terrace ten feet away from the Hudson River. Rikia drooled over the U.N. highrise but Colton said he wanted Sutton Place. They made an offer, and the lady in the office blah-blah-blah'd over the advantages of living in such a neighborhood. Colton kept nodding; he signed the documents and gave her his accountant's email address in California so she could obtain the money.

Afterwards, they went to a bar and toasted their new home. "I know this is crazy," Colton said, "but I really want this to work out well for us. I know it isn't forever—"

"Oh, but it *is* forever. *Our love is forever.*"

A few hours before her flight to California, Summer went to see Doctor Simonyi. "I'm going to Los Angeles for a week or more. Do you have a longer-lasting injection to give me?"

"Where will you be staying?"

"At the Beverly."

"Good. An associate of mine is there right now because a big music star is trying to make a comeback and needs a shot every day, so my associate sees him each day and is staying at the Beverly Hills Hotel. You can contact this doctor while you're there."

Summer took a deep breath and said, "Doctor, are these injections...you know...habit forming?"

"Why do you ask?"

"I mean, if that singer who's staying at the Beverly needs one every day—"

"That singer is an alcoholic…anorexic…he's sexually promiscuous. He needs the shots. You do, too. Tell me, before you came to see me, did you have a traumatic experience of some kind?"

She nodded. "More like three years of trauma. That was a long time ago. Things have worked out fine."

The doctor frowned. "Delayed reaction is not unusual. There are doctors who treat the head. Something happened years ago, it hurts the mind now. So why do patients say, 'It happened months ago, so it can't hurt my body now'? If you're exhausted, what's the problem with taking vitamin shots three times per week if they help you to feel better?"

She nodded at this wonderful man with his kind talk, who made time for her despite having a dozen patients in his waiting room. He smiled. "Have a nice time in Beverly Hills and be sure to call my associate. When you get back, come back for more shots…but make an appointment first. It's unfair of me to treat this as a walk-in clinic just for you."

Summer walked home in the April sunshine, feeling sorry for all those New Yorkers she passed by who weren't about to fly out to California and didn't know a man named Colton Thomas.

As her day went on she felt better than alive. Her head was full of wonderful visions and her body was as full of vigor as a twelve-year-old's. She and Colton boarded the mammoth jet airliner and held hands as it flew west. But then the flight attendant placed Easter eggs on their dessert plates.

Easter! thought Summer. Easter's coming. I'm expected in Florida but I'll be in southern California

291

instead. Better let them know what's happening. She took out her cell phone and sent her father a text:

I AM IN LOS ANGELES DOING A STORY ON COLTON THOMAS. WILL HAVE TO MISS EASTER. LOVE, YOUR 'IN' GRRL. LOL

At the hotel she checked into her own room but the bellman delivered her luggage into Colton's bungalow.

The publisher had set up a half-dozen interviews for Colton, and Summer went along with her notebook, playing the role of Chick Reporter from *In* magazine.

On Saturday, Colton insisted that Summer sit by the pool while he went to Malibu to visit his son. Within an hour, she felt so anxious and out of sorts that she knew she needed to find that doctor who was staying there at the Beverly.

She reached into her beach bag, pulled out her cell phone, dialed the hotel's switchboard and asked for Doctor Richard Yenson's room. But the operator told her that the doctor would be in Malibu until six. She smoked Pall Malls and drank Wild Turkey until she ran out of cigarettes. Then she called downstairs, ordered some more smokes and ludicrously overtipped the bellman. She kept calling the doctor and finally got through.

"Am I speaking to Doctor Yenson?"

"Who's asking?"

"Summer Selars."

"What do you want?"

"I'm a patient of Doctor Simonyi in Manhattan. He told me you would be here in case I needed your help...I need a vitamin shot."

"When did you have your last one?"

"Three days ago."

"And why do you need another one now?"

"Because I do."

He sighed. "I'll speak to Doctor Simonyi this evening and ask him about you. Call me back in the morning."

"*No!* I need the shot tonight. I need another injection immediately. I'm out here because I work for *In* magazine. I'm doing a story on Colton Thomas—"

"Colton Thomas?"

"Yes, and I really need to have my shit together—pardon my French—in order to do this story the way it deserves to be done."

"Oh, I can empathize with your predicament. I'll call Simonyi and find out which vitamins you take. Which bungalow is he in?"

"He's in Bungalow Five and I'm in Room three-thirteen."

"Oh, then you're not the young blonde who's staying with him. Everyone at the Beverly is talking about it."

"Well, I'm Colton Thomas' tender young blonde but I will be one freaked-out bitch if you don't get over here soon and shoot me up."

"I'm on my way."

Presently he stood over her and finished the injection. "Yummy," she said. "Now I feel divine. How much do I owe you?"

"This one's on me."

"How come?"

"Because any woman who can get a man like Colton Thomas deserves a freebie." Then, "Maybe he should get a shot, since *I'm* here and *he's* here."

"Not him. His elixir is Wild Turkey."

"He has the pressures of public life, of an advanced age and the challenges of satisfying a much younger lover…"

"My baby's doin' just fine without the needle," Summer drawled. She went back to her suite, opened the minibar, took out a single-serve bottle of bourbon and drank it down. Then she drank a few more, and the booze took the edge off that shot. What was in that shot? Summer asked herself. Certainly not just vitamins. She'd read an *In* story about mixing an upper with a downer…it was called a speedball. You got the best of both drugs and none of the worst.

She floated about the room, utterly indifferent to the pain of being human, when her cell phone rang.

"Summer?"

"Wade?" She burst into giggles.

"What's so funny?"

"Life, baby. Life's a goddamn laugh-riot."

"Are you feeling all right?"

"Papa, if I felt any better, I'd get busted."

"Who's with you right now?"

"There are three of us: Me, myself and I. We're waiting for Colton."

"Let me ask you a question, Summer. This Colton Thomas story is a big deal, right? So how come Rikia sent you to do it? She would have done it herself or sent that chick Anya Semko, right?"

She laughed some more and said, "Wade, are you happy?"

"What?"

"Are…you…happy? Happiness is the only thing that matters in life. Are you happy with Beth?"

"Don't worry about us. You've said you've been

taking injections. What's that all about?"

"Vitamins."

"What do they do for you?"

"They make America beautiful."

"I want to you leave Los Angeles right now."

More giggles. "Not gonna happen, baby. We're gonna be here till the work is done. Then we're going back to Manhattan and move into our new condo…"

Click.

She lay nude and spread-eagled on the bungalow's bed when Colton arrived. "Well, good evening to you, too."

"You were away for so long, I missed you."

"I told you I'd be gone all day."

"Wanna fuck?"

"Nope. I'm tired as all hell."

"Were you bouncing your baby on your knee?"

Colton smirked. "Yeah, for about fifteen minutes. Then the kid vomited and the nanny took him away. I don't think my little boy likes me very much."

"Then why go there?"

"Because I have to make it look like I'm a husband and father. Also, you've come into my life at a time when the world has just rediscovered Colton Thomas—and believe me, there have been many times when the world has done a great job of ignoring me. What I'm saying is, I have to get publicity and do interviews while I'm fashionable again. But always remember that you're the only woman in my life even if it appears to be otherwise."

"The only one?"

He nodded. "Damn straight."

She got up and said, "Too bad we can't fuck right now."

Colton said, "What are you high on?"

She shrugged. "Just vitamin shots. Got one today."

"Who gave it to you?"

"Doctor Richard Yenson, who knows Doctor Altogether Simonyi in New York."

"So there's a quack here in the hotel who's just shot you up like that guy in New York. Get Yenson in here."

Within fifteen minutes Richard Yenson stood in Colton's bungalow, pumping the writer's hand like a starstruck kid. Colton received an injection, and reacted as if he'd just been given sterile water. "What's the damage?"

The doctor named his fee.

"That's three times what Simoni charged in New York!" shouted Summer.

"This is a house call," said Yenson. "I went out of my way for you. This special service costs money."

Colton threw a wad of bills onto the bed. "Take it. Get out of here. You're nothing more than a street dealer with a medical degree."

The doctor frowned. "Aren't you grateful for that injection? Don't you feel anything?"

"Oh, I feel wired nice and tight. What was in that syringe besides methamphetamine hydrochloride?"

Yenson ducked out of the bungalow and Colton said to Summer, "I feel as horny as a teenager right now. Let's get it on." He threw her onto the bed.

The next morning, he said, "No more speed, O.K.?"

296

"I promise."

That night they ordered in room service and as soon as they were done, Colton jumped on Summer. "Don't," she said, laughing. "The waiter will come in—"

"Fuck the waiter. He's paid to look the other way. I've still got some meth in my cock, and I don't want to waste it."

They slept as the doorbell rang, and they heard nothing at all as their bedroom door opened. The incident happened so fast that Summer could scarcely figure out any of it. She opened her eyes, closed them against the turned-on lights, then opened them again as she felt Colton being pulled off her. She heard the sickening *crack!* of a man's fist crashing into another man's face, and she heard Colton's whimper. She forced herself to watch as her lover, bleeding and breathing hard, staggering about the room. She then glanced at the other man.

"Wade!"

She closed her eyes and buried her face in her hands as the beating continued. It flashed through her mind that Colton, the toughest of men, seemed unable to defend himself against Wade, whom his daughter had always regarded as far more a lover than a fighter.

She heard the sound of a man crashing into a wall and looked up to see Colton half sitting, limbs askew. "You could have killed him!" she screamed at her father. "You've knocked out his teeth!"

"Not teeth, just caps. He can buy new ones." He walked over and pulled her out of bed. His face went the darkest red as he realized she was naked. "Get dressed and we'll get out of here."

"Who the hell do you think you are? Why did you come here? What do you have against Colton?"

Wade looked in the wounded man's direction and snarled. "He's a loser."

Summer wiped tears and snot from her face. "He's not! I love him and he loves me!"

He checked his Rolex and said, "Hurry up. I've got the plane waiting."

"Why did you come here?" she repeated.

"Because," he told her, "last night I spoke to you on the telephone and you sounded totally fucked up on drugs. I was afraid that you had gotten mixed up with a bunch of druggies, so I flew out here to see what was going on. Now I regret this trip, but since I'm here, let's go board my plane and head out to Florida."

"Dream on," she said.

He checked his watch again. "I'm going to the bar and have a drink for half an hour. If you've got a lick of sense, you'll get your shit together and tell that guy to call his old lady in Malibu to drive out here and collect him. But if you're not in the bar in half an hour, I'm leaving by myself." He stormed out of the bungalow.

Summer helped Colton into the bathroom and wiped off most of the blood. "He's much tougher than I thought," he said. "I always thought he was such a pussy."

"Your teeth…"

"Like he said, they're caps, so I can buy new ones. I think he broke my jaw."

"I better go to the bar and tell him I'm staying

here with you."

Colton shook his head. "No. You let a half hour go by and he'll understand. But if you leave me to go to him right now, we're through. You need to make your choice right here, right now—him or me."

She nodded and they both walked over to the bed and sat together, watching the minutes tick by...

As he sat in the bar nursing a bourbon and water, Wade Sellars couldn't believe how much his right hand hurt. That was one reason he had avoided fistfights throughout his life—even if he won, he ached all over for the next day or so, and that felt almost as bad as a hangover.

He knew that the only reason he had beaten up Thomas so badly was that he had caught the man by surprise. If he can gone up to him and said, "All right, Thomas, you and me outside in fifteen minutes," he knew that Thomas could have taken him in two minutes. Wade knew that when he discovered Colton lying there on top of Summer that Thomas would be at his weakest and most vulnerable. He still couldn't believe how insane he'd gone at the sight of that dirty old man lying naked with his beautiful young Summer. *How* dare *that perverted old bastard stick his cock into my daughter!*

With a huge sigh, Wade dropped a fifty-dollar bill onto the bar and walked out. He checked his Rolex and saw that he had given his daughter just over ninety minutes to join him and she had not.

He drove out to the airport and tried very hard to think of nothing at all. When he reached his Learjet and the pilot asked him, "Where to? Florida?" he said,

"No, we're going to Las Vegas."

He sat in the aircraft as it made the brief flight to the big gambling city. One thing about being Mister Beth Rogers Stainton was that he would get all the no-questions-asked casino credit he wanted—his wife's spectacular wealth was well known to every pit boss in town. He had been lucky lately; he planned on betting big and winning bigger.

22

Summer woke up to the sound of rain pounding her bungalow. She loathed California when it rained. The clock radio said seven-thirty. She hated mornings when she lacked somewhere to go and something specific to do that day. She closed her eyes and murmured, 'Go back to sleep.' The rain had lasted for three days, and the mindless clatter it made as it struck her roof sometimes enraged her. At other times, she merely accepted the noise much the way she tolerated the clicking of Colton's laptop computer. She had been in California for one month but it felt like a decade. Shit, she thought. Just shit.

The nonstop rain meant she had to stay indoors. Colton lay beside her, in the deepest sleep of his life. His face had healed remarkably well; he'd gotten his new teeth, too, and slept just about ten hours each night. He worked like a fiend, spending most days at his computer, taking a handful of twenty-minute breaks during which he smiled as he mentioned the sale of the movie rights to his latest bestselling novel.

On the day that the studio made the commitment to make a film based on Colton's novel, he twirled Summer about the bungalow and bragged that, if the movie became the hit he expected, his earning would probably equal the money he'd already spent on their Manhattan condo.

"You'll make big money," Summer told him, "if they make a movie that's half as good as your novel. But they may goof it up."

He shrugged. "Well, if they get the right director and screenwriter, it'll be a hit."

"Colton, why don't you write the screenplay?"

"Because," he said, "it's beneath me."

"Why is it beneath you?"

"It just is."

She shook her head. "Don't be so arrogant. As the old saying goes, 'If you want it done right, better do it yourself.' If I were you, and I had gross participation in a movie based on a book I'd written, I'd make damn sure that they started out with the best screenplay possible, and the only way I could do that would be by writing it myself."

He nodded. "I'll look into it."

Colton got on the telephone with his agent with his new development—the author of the bestselling novel was insisting that he be permitted *personally* to write the script—and after some arguing ("He's a novelist! What the fuck does he know about screenwriting?") the studio said yea.

"We're buying a condo in Manhattan," Colton said to Tubby Samuels, his agent.

"In which building?"

"Sutton Place. My people are still dealing with theirs about mortgages and whatnot. But it's pretty much a done deal. In the months ahead, I want Summer to fly out there and get it all furnished and decorated. Meantime, I'll keep myself busy with the treatment of this movie and then the actual screenplay."

"Don't be in any hurry to get back to New York,"

said Tubby. "You need to be out here when the movie decisions are made so that you can object if necessary."

Colton said to Summer, "Think you can endure Beverly Hills life till I say, 'Go back to New York'?"

She nodded. "I'll call Rikia and quit *In*."

"Bad idea. I'm sure she can give you some work to do out here. Interview up-and-coming or down-and-out TV and movie actors."

On the telephone, Rikia said, "Terrific! You have access to *so* many people out there!" She named a dozen actors Summer had never even heard of. "While you're at it, do a story on that wonderful section of Malibu where Colton's old lady lives."

"I thought *I* was his old lady."

"You know what I mean."

Presently Summer went into meth withdrawal. Colton held her as she shivered and told her just to tough it out. She knew her bad feelings had something to do with Wade, and that her complete indifference to *In* was related to him. She felt that her job at that magazine was just a way for her to attract his attention and give them something to talk about. Now that Wade had gone, she had only Colton.

The world had rediscovered Colton Thomas, so Summer went into the Beverly's gift shop, bought up all their bestselling novels and read them at poolside. Colton's latest novel remained at number one and he spent most of each day banging out prose fiction on his laptop computer. To give her man his own creative time and space, she forced herself to sit by the pool and peruse paperbacks that often bored her senseless. She tried to ignore the fact that little or nothing happened between them in their bedroom.

After being worked over by Wade Sellars, Colton told her that pain caused his impotency; subsequently, his devotion to his work kept them sexually apart. Throughout the day, he made it clear that if she insisted on sharing the bungalow, she would have to remain silent so as not to disturb his "writer's trance"; at night, he would read to her what he had written.

She let out a big sigh as she lay in bed and listened to the Beverly Hills rain. She felt but could not say why. She had so many things that other women her age did not, including a famous millionaire lover. She reached out and touched his shoulder, but he simply rolled over with a tiny moan. Her eyes welled up with tears, and she said to herself, *He is rejecting me. What is this ego trip I'm on. I'm not trying to help him. He doesn't want me or need me. She got out of bed and dressed, making no noise at all.*

She sat in the coffee shop, having a carrot muffin and a cup of tea. Looking this way and that, she observed that every seat was occupied, and everyone in the joint was loud and garrulous, ready to do business at ten to eight in the morning. She overheard chatter about what *Variety* and *The Hollywood Reporter* had written that morning or the night before; a few people bitched about being unable to play tennis due to the damn rain. She paid her check with cash—she'd thought of merely charging her light breakfast to Colton's room but decided against it—and headed upstairs to the lobby. She ordered his car and stood just under the hotel's awning, peering up and swearing at the torrential downpour. Cars, many of them the finest and most expensive in the world, entered in one lane and exited in the other. She heard a dozen wisecracks about the glorious California weather; inevitably, someone called it "liquid sunshine." She saw Richard Yenson climb into a car with a famous British singer who had flown out to appear on American television. She asked herself, *Is Yenson shooting that singer with speed, too?* Her car arrived and she drove out to Santa Monica, where she found some cover near the beach and watched the rain come down some more.

Maybe Colton could sense her *ennui*, because as soon as she returned he pushed himself away from his laptop and invited her to have a drink with him. She did, and they drank bourbon and stared at each other. He insisted that they go to The Bistro for dinner.

People looked up and stared at Colton as he and Summer entered the restaurant. As the couple sat and ordered, famous actors and directors invited themselves over. They congratulated Colton on his success and gave him myriad pieces of advice on which actors and directors would do justice to the film version of his recent bestseller. Summer picked at her food and listened in, feeling very alone and unappreciated.

He whistled as they sauntered back to their bungalow. In bed, he did his best but soon rolled over and swore at his flaccid penis.

On Monday it rained some more. Summer tried to watch soap operas and game shows but grew bored and turned off the TV. On Tuesday, the rain got even heavier and she tried to finish the armload of bestselling paperbacks she'd bought at the bookstore. On Wednesday, she fired up her laptop and tried to write an *In* article called "Liquid Sunshine," but decided her story was crap and she deleted it from her hard drive. On Thursday, when the legendary California sunshine finally returned, she threw herself onto her man's lap as he wrote. She said, "Let's do something together."

"*You* do something. I have to work. You should sign up for tennis lessons."

"I can play tennis just fine. I don't need lessons." Then, "Colton, in case you've forgotten, I came out here to be with you, not play tennis."

"You *are* with me."

"Physically, yes, but your mind is a zillion miles away."

"That's because I'm a writer." He stared at the screen's blinking cursor as if expecting it to do the writing for him.

"You're writing a movie treatment. It's not that big a deal. You'll revise it a hundred times. Lighten up, O.K.?"

"I'm a writer working on a project. It *is* a big deal."

She sighed. "I'm so fuckin' bored."

"Then go to the shopping arcade and buy yourself a new wardrobe. Bill it to my bungalow."

"I don't want any new clothes, I just want something to do. Tell me what to do."

"I don't give a fuck what you do. Just quit bugging me."

"I'm flying back to New York," she muttered, getting off his lap.

He smirked. "Going back to Daddy, huh?"

She shook her head. "I'll go back for our sake. At least there I can go back to being Rikia's gofer and I can live like a normal person. Maybe I'll even put on

306

my shorts and headphones and go into the park and pretend I'm the Central Park Jogger. Then I won't be bugging you any longer."

He pulled her back onto his lap. "Sorry, baby, I didn't mean it. I take it all back. Look, you've never lived with a writer. We're moody bastards. We have a great thing going. You make me happy. I'm doing my best writing in years. Let me get this little project done and then we'll drive up to San Francisco for a week. I have friends there; we'll have fun. Maybe you should go for a swim right now."

"We can swim together."

"You swim now; I'll swim later."

"She nodded and got up. She changed into her bikini and swam, waiting for him. when it got dark and cool, she returned to their bungalow and discovered him still at his laptop, scarcely more than grunting whenever she spoke to him.

On Saturday the heavy rain started again. He drove out to Malibu to see his son. He told Summer that when he got back they would go to dinner, see a movie, just hang out—whatever she wanted. He called at nine or so from his wife's house, able to speak above the din of drinking and laughing. He swallowed a small alcoholic laugh or two and said, "The rain out here is turning the roads into mud. I better spend the night here. We'll talk tomorrow. Later."

She sat in the darkness of the bungalow for the longest time, wondering what had become of her relationship with him. He'd just announced, quite without apology, that he would spend the night with his ex-wife. Well, maybe this was her own damn fault; she'd driven him away with her bitchiness. But then she smiled in spite of herself. He surely wouldn't be able to screw his ex, that was for damn sure. Only Summer, like a magician, could make his cock as stiff as steel. Now he seemed mostly uninterested in sex; he'd go down on her when he felt it was the thing to do, but that was about it. So now he's called her to say he's spending the night in Malibu but will be back tomorrow, and he will...but if his dissatisfaction keeps up, there will come the time when he stays away and doesn't bother coming back—and what will she do then? Suddenly everything seemed so hopeless and desperate and awful. She knew she had to do something; she could just sit on her hands and expect things to resolve themselves—or assume Daddy would put things right. This time, *she* had to take her broken life and make it all shiny and wonderful and new again.

She sat some more, staring out the window. Then she picked up her cell phone and called Doctor Richard Yenson.

23

Stephen stood at the bar, waiting for his father. The old man, usually the most punctual of people, was now almost fifteen minutes late. The restaurant, seldom slow, now filled up nearly to capacity. He kept looking at the table being held for him; too many others were checking it out, so he decided to sit there and nurse his drink while he waited for his father.

He looked up and saw his father hurrying towards him. "Women," the older man muttered as he ordered a cocktail.

"Mom giving you a pain in the butt?"

"Always."

"What's her problem now?"

The father sighed. "We're going to Europe for the first time in a decade, and we need to get our passports renewed. That means new passport photos. So we go to see a photographer, and your mother sits there and says, 'No, that's not good enough. Do another one.' She's still there."

Stephen guffawed. But then a murmur swept through the restaurant. "Oh, it's just Claudia Knaack, recovering from her tenth facelift."

He stared as the German actress accepted hugs and best wishes from the restaurant's management and then shook hands with a number of others. Still ravishing, Claudia Knaack, unlike Hana, had never retired. When movie audiences lost interest in her and stopped going to her movies, she appeared in a Broadway musical. A competent singer and dancer, she played Las Vegas each year to sold-out crowds who went mainly to ogle the sixty-year-old woman who looked half her age.

"That body," George Rogers muttered, shaking his head. "No tummy, butt and breasts like a teenager. A miracle."

"Hana said that Claudia uses a body stocking to get that 'firmer than firm' look. She should know."

Stephen frowned. "What's that supposed to mean?"

"Just that Claudia and Hana used to be lovers."

"Says who?"

Father Rogers shrugged. "Many people who know the two ladies."

"Hana," Stephen said, "is heterosexual."

"Are you still dating her?"

"As often as possible."

"What about Summer Sellars? I understand she's been in Beverly Hills for the past while."

"I call her. We talk."

"I think it's time for you to make some decisions about which woman you want."

Stephen nodded. "I'm going to propose to Summer. All her time in California has been great for me. I've been with Hana and enjoyed every moment. I'm almost dreading the time when I have to say, 'Will you marry me, Summer?' and 'Goodbye, Hana.'"

"It doesn't have to be that way. You can have them, if you do so discreetly."

"I wish. Hana would never go for it. If I married Summer, I would have to spend the rest of my life romancing her, charming her and making her believe that she married the right man."

"She's young, very beautiful and her stepmother is filthy rich. All in all, not a bad deal." Then, "Let's have another drink. That always makes me feel better."

Stephen went home and got ready for his date with Hana. When his cell phone rang, he snatched it up and said hello. The voice in his ear said, "Stephen! I was afraid you wouldn't answer your telephone."

"No worries, Hana. I'm looking forward to seeing you tonight."

"Another time, Stephen. Something's come up…I've made a change of plans…My financial advisor from Europe…I must meet with him…"

"Oh, *that* guy. You've told me about him."

"Yes."

"Well, make it a brief 'meeting.' I can come by later."

"No, I will be too exhausted by the time our business is done."

"Dammit, Hana! Don't do this to me!"

Click.

He made himself a cocktail, drank it down and made himself another one. He thought of the other women he could call and visit, but he felt too morose now to enjoy anyone's company. Plus, he was just plain drunk and probably couldn't get it up. Shitfaced and surly, in a mood to torture himself, he sat in his favorite chair, sipped some more booze and convinced himself that Hana was a taxi ride away, sucking the cock of her friend from Europe. Or maybe it wasn't a man she was fucking. Hadn't he and his father seen Claudia Knaack that evening, and hadn't his old man said that Claudia and Hana were once lovers? Well, he thought, Hana has no lick-her license. She enjoys me too much.

Feeling profoundly sorry for himself, Stephen got up, put on his overcoat and stumbled outside. He took tiny steps towards Hana's building, assuring himself that he would stop before he got there. But some minutes later, he nodded hello to the doorman and took the elevator up to Hana's floor. Too drunk to use his better judgment and follow the advice of the inner voice that told him to forget this nonsense, he rang her doorbell again and again, his heart pounding in his throat, his mouth as dry as sandpaper. Hearing footsteps, he stopped pressing on her doorbell and swallowed hard. He watched as she opened the door an inch or so, and saw an angry eye checking him out.

"What?"

He cleared his throat. "Well, today's my birthday and I thought it might be nice if you'd ask me in for a drink."

"Shoo."

He fought back tears. "It's just that it's my birthday and I want to have a drink with you and whoever's in there with you."

"Shoo!"

"No!" He wedged his foot in the doorway.

"Go away or I'll call downstairs," she said with a red face.

"Hana," he said, "please forgive me. I'm so sorry…" He removed his foot and she slammed the door in his face.

For a minute or two he swayed in front of her door, asking himself what more he could do. Then he pounded on the door and screamed, "Open up! Just show me who's with you so I'll know you're not lying to me!"

Presently he heard the sounds of locks sliding open and doors opening the slightest bit. He began ringing Hana's doorbell again. "Let me in, dammit! Let me in!" He kicked at the door. "I'll stay here all night! I'll wait and see who's in there with you!"

He scarcely the elevator doors as they opened; he hardly felt the two men's four strong arms grip his shoulders and drag him away.

"Miz Hana called us," one of them said. "She told us you were causing some noise."

"You cunt-eating whore!" Stephen yelled in the direction of Hana's door.

Doors swung open; residents, mouths agape, stared at the tall, handsome young man who'd had the privilege of some sort of personal relationship with the glamorous, reclusive Hana.

Once they were in the elevator, the doorman and elevator man eased up on Stephen. "Seems like you've had too much to drink," said the doorman. "Best thing for you right now would be to take a taxi home and sleep it off. You and she seem to have known each other for a little while. Maybe this spat you're having will work itself out."

Back in the lobby, he tore himself away from the two men and swore under his breath as he exited the building. He looked up at Hana's window and made an obscene finger gesture at it.

Hana stood by the window and chuckled at the sight of Stephen's outstretched middle finger. Then she went to the bathroom and tapped on the door. "It's all right, Beth. You don't have to worry. He won't be coming by again."

24

Beth smiled as she lay sprawled out in the bathtub. The radio, or computer, or whatever it was, was playing '60s music, and she adored music from that decade. Well, any music sounded wonderful whenever she got to enjoy it with Hana. All food tasted good, all weather fine and dandy. She had missed Hana so much during their time apart, and when they finally reunited, Beth felt so gratified to see Hana's big smile and feel her long, warm kiss. Their time apart apparently had done them good.

She'd been terrified that evening when Hana wanted to take a rain check on her date with Stephen, and he'd shown up minutes later, drunk and practically in tears as he rang Hana's doorbell and then tried to force his way in until those guys came up and took him away. How unlike him to freak out that way! That experience convinced Hana to terminate her relationship with him, which pleased Beth and apparently caused Stephen to seek solace in the arms of his *Sports Illustrated* swimsuit models, although he still talked nonstop about wanting to get engaged to Summer.

She remembered how heartsick Stephen had

been over Summer's absence in Florida on Easter weekend. The girl had made a commitment to fly out to Beverly Hills to do a story on Colton Thomas for that goofy magazine. She had been in California for quite some time now. How long did it take to do research and interviews and write a story, anyway? Or was she doing more than that with Thomas? Ludicrous! Colton Thomas was much too old for her and he had a young family. Besides, Colton Thomas and Summer Sellars were just incompatible in every way. Wade had unenthusiastic about Summer's assignment, then he'd flown out there, stayed several days and not said much of anything about it. She would have to change her will again; now that Stephen and Hana had called it quits, Summer's marital status meant zero to Beth.

She called George Rogers and made an appointment to change her will. Then she got dressed; Wade was at one of his clubs, playing cards. Beth told him she wanted to go to a school reunion. "You stay at the club for dinner and don't worry about what time you get home. I go to this reunion every year, and each time, I learn that at least one of us has died."

Her marriage to Wade started to make her angry and frustrated. With Hana so available, Beth cringed at the sight of Wade. But her husband increasingly spent time pursuing his own interests and left Beth to hers, the most prominent of which was her relationship with Hana. The retired actress had flown down to Florida to spend Easter with Beth and Wade, and since then had made herself readily available to Beth. Like so much of the rest of the world, Beth found Hana fascinating in a dozen ways; aside from

316

her ludicrous wealth, Beth, in her soul, considered herself the commonest of women, and her eight years as Hana's lover and confidante was something she took as the most touching and wonderful of compliments.

She wanted to give Hana a thanks-for-being-you gift but knew that Hana had no use for jewelry and would wear a mink coat as if it were the cheapest of garments. So she wrote Hana a check for ten million dollars, knowing that only money—preferably mint-fresh greenbacks—would make her lover's face grow rosy with delight and gratitude. Hana, stingy like so many others who had known grinding indigence, bought Beth dimestore novelty gifs for Christmas and refused to adequately furnish her huge Manhattan apartment. "All these rooms are bare," Beth had said. "So what?" Hana had retorted. "What matters is that the apartment is now worth twice what I paid for it."

Beth took a taxi to meet up with Hana. The aging yellow car crept along, taking its own sweet time, but its passenger cared only about seeing the love of her life, feeling the woman's soft lips on her own and inhaling Hana's lovely scent. As soon as Beth arrived, Hana hugged and kissed her for several long moments. Then Beth handed her the check, saying, "Here, I've brought you a little something." Expecting a cry of gratitude, instead she watched as Hana, scarcely looking at the slip of paper with its many zeroes, merely smiled and said thank you as she slipped it into her desk drawer. "Come," she said, "I've prepared a feast for us. A seafood salad and vintage white wine."

That night they made love, and Hana carried on like a schoolgirl in her first backseat makeout session,

317

full of giggles and moans. Later, as they cuddled, Hana hummed some songs from her childhood, then abruptly stopped and jumped out of bed. "I'm going to take a shower. I know you don't like movies, so watch the news and tell me if an oil spill or civil war happens while I'm getting myself clean."

Beth switched on the TV set and watched CNN while Hana crooned and splashed around in the shower. Hana seemed very happy, which made Beth happy. Yet Beth's happiness was tinged with despair, because she knew that soon she would have to return to Wade. She got out of bed and padded over to Hana's laptop, which sat asleep on her dresser. Beth pressed a key and the machine suddenly glowed. Its screen was filled with Hana's online telephone bill; Beth's eyes bulged at the many calls appearing on the document. Why such a high number? Hana usually didn't like make or receive calls, and when she was on the phone, she stated her business as succinctly as possible. Beth grabbed a slip of paper and a pen out of her shoulder bag, scribbled down the phone numbers that concerned—they were all overseas— and put the paper back in her bag. When Hana came back out, the two women made love again, and Beth gave no thought to the telephone bill or anything else. Back home, she found the slip of paper and put it away, guessing that Hana, like so many other cheapskates, had one insane indulgence, and hers happened to be long-distance telephone calls.

The next day, Beth went to a fundraising event for a shelter that took in pregnant girls who were strung out on street drugs. She didn't like fundraisers for down-and-outers, but her appearance at such a function left everyone, including Manhattan's power elite, with the impression that she cared about saving drug-addled, knocked-up street girls from themselves. Imagine that!

She tried calling Hana but got no answer. That evening she and Wade were expected at a party where members of congress would ask for their votes and tell them funny stories about the insanity of trying to get things done in Washington.

As always, Beth had Hana on her mind. She wanted to ditch Wade and hang out with her girlfriend that day because she had to go out with Wade that evening. He always wanted her to go to the movies with him; he liked sitting there in those dark theaters, watching grindhouse trash as he ate popcorn and drank one soda after another. Beth disliked movies except those starring Hana. Wade kept after her to authorize the construction of a cinema in their Florida home. She would say yes if she knew she could get all of Hana's movies, but she doubted that such a thing would happen.

Right now she needed to think of an excuse to get away from Wade for the evening. She could no longer say, "I'm off to play backgammon because she'd taught it to him and he now liked it, so he would insist on going with her. That wouldn't do. She thought of insisting that he play golf while she did— what? It irked her that she, Elizabeth Rogers Stainton, needed to make up excuses so she could go wherever she wanted and do as she pleased. But no; she couldn't assert herself like that to Wade. He might just say, "Yeah, sure. Go do your own thing—and don't bother coming back." Yes, he would very likely say that, especially since he seemed much less worried about Summer, and his relaxed attitude was due to the billion dollars Beth had promised to give her. Well, he'd figure out at some point that Summer's billion wasn't exactly a done deal, and that made Beth smile a little bit. Wade needed to remember who in their marriage was rich and who wasn't, and he needed to be grateful that she was willing to have him around. On the other hand, he knew that she needed him in a dozen ways, especially as a husband who always looked good when she clung to his arm in public.

Feeling the desire to converse, Beth picked up her cell phone and dialed Hana, thinking her girlfriend might have an idea of what new lies Beth could tell Wade so that the two women could be alone for a while. No, she thought, Hana would be useless in such a capacity; she was just a sexy dumb cunt from Eastern Europe.

She picked up her iPad and clicked on it for a time. Checking on the society Websites, she saw an image of Hana at Heathrow Airport.

Hana had gone off to London!

Beth flung the tablet the length of the room and yelled, "Fuck!"

London!

She retrieved the slip of paper with Hana's often-called numbers and placed a person-to-person call to Pierce Anthony of Anthony and Wilkinson, the firm that handled all of Hana's business in London. After a few minutes of polite, pointless chatter, Beth said, "Pierce, the reason I'm calling is that my stepdaughter has placed some calls in London that I would like to know about—"

"Give me an hour and I'll give you what you need to know about those numbers." He got back to her and said that one of the numbers were for a house in the suburbs and another was for a psychiatrist.

"Pierce, I need to find out more, especially the psychiatrist."

"Then I'll have to call Wilf Donaldson. He's the private investigator we deal with when clients ask us to do things we're not trained for."

Beth thanked him and hung up. She felt panic as she let her mind wander into fantasies in which her beloved was fucking other people. She resolved to fly to London to check things out. Over dinner with Wade, she said, "When you go to Cannes, I think I'll fly to London and amuse myself."

"Fine with me," he said. "I'm sure you'll have a great time in London."

"Not great…but definitely fascinating."

25

Beth felt out of sorts as she sat in Pierce Anthony's office. That damned jet lag always made her feel a hundred years old.

Pierce said, "Look at those pictures. Wilf climbed a tree and took them. The scandal sheets would love to have them."

"It's not like they're having sex."

"Well, they're quite compromising just the same. The two are naked and kissing."

"Beautiful girl," murmured Beth.

"Isn't she, though? Her name is Anissa Johnson. Hana stayed over on a few nights." Then, "You came to see me because of your stepdaughter. What does she have to do with any of this?"

Beth shrugged. "Maybe she knows Anissa Johnson."

Pierce blushed. "Oh…were you afraid your stepdaughter was having an inappropriate relationship with her?"

"Stranger things have happened. Lesbianism is not a new thing in this world."

He nodded. "Just so."

"Do you have the address of the house where I can find Hana?"

"Yes. It's about an hour's drive away."

"Thank you. Please send the bill for everything to my accountant in London. I certainly wouldn't want it to go to New York."

Beth mostly ignored the beautiful countryside as the chauffeur drove along. She needed to figure out what to say once she came face to face with Anissa Johnson. She couldn't just say, "Hands off Hana, bitch! She's mine!" No, that wouldn't do.

By and by the driver said, "This is it, madam. The house you wanted to see. The main entrance is up the way a bit."

Beth got out and walked until she reached an unlocked iron gate. She let herself in and headed towards the main house, hoping no big mean dog would come upon her. She reached the house and peered into the front window.

"May I help you?"

Beth grabbed her chest to quiet her pounding heart as she spun around and said, "Hana!"

"Beth. Let's go inside. It's cold out here."

Feeling beyond sheepish, Beth nodded and followed Hana into the living room. Presently they sat and sipped brandy. "I'm not going to ask how you found my address," Hana said. "It really doesn't matter."

"I would give ten years of my life and every dime of my money," Beth said in a quivering voice, "if I could turn back the clock several hours and decide not to come out here."

"Do I mean that much to you?"

Beth let out an agonized little laugh. "More than

you could possibly begin to know." Then, "I know that there is someone else. She is young and very beautiful, and I am *so* jealous of her. I have pictures." She reached into her bag and withdrew the photos. She handed them to Hana, who perused them with a frown. "How did you get these?"

"A private investigator took them. The woman's name is Anissa, right?"

Hana nodded. "I think it is time that you two met."

Beth shook her head. "Not necessary."

"Oh, I think it is." She called out, "Missus Robotham, will you bring Anissa in here? I have a friend sitting here and would like the two of them to meet."

An old woman came in and said, "I'll do my best to get her away from the telly." She disappeared and came back with a tall, gorgeous, scowling blonde who looked to be about Summer's age.

Hana gave her a gentle smile and said, "Anissa, I want you to meet an old friend of mine. Her name is Missus Sellars."

Anissa flashed a big blonde smile at Beth, then turned to Hana and said, "Can I have some chocolate cake? Missus Robotham just baked one but she says I can't have any till after dinner."

"If you want some cake," Hana said, as if speaking to a small child, "you'll have to ask Missus Robotham. If she says the cake is for dessert, well, I guess you'll have something yummy to look forward to for after dinner."

"But I want my bloody cake now! I fancy something to snack on, and I don't want any more of those dodgy cookies she makes!"

324

"Go back to your telly," Hana said.

The girl kicked at the air. "Is that lady going to stay for supper?"

"Would you like it if she did?"

She threw her arms into the air. "I don't care if she stays or goes. Will you read me a bedtime story? I want a new one, not the old ones." Then she scampered out of the room.

Beth watched Anissa disappear, then said to Hana, "She's a beautiful woman, but she acts like a twelve-year-old. What was all that about? Was she just putting us on?"

"She was just being herself. She's a ten-year-old child trapped inside a woman's body."

"And is she really your lover?"

"No, she's my daughter."

Beth's mouth opened but no words came out. Hana said, "Drink your brandy." Beth nodded and knocked it back. Hana refilled their glasses.

"Hana, what is her chronological age?"

"Thirty-one."

"But she looks so young."

"That is because she is a child who has no grown-up worries."

"Will you tell me about her?"

"Yes, if you'll stay for dinner. You should dismiss your car; I will drive you back to town myself."

Dinner was leisurely and, for Beth, eminently enjoyable. Now that she understand Anissa's relationship to Hana, Beth felt free to enjoy the daughter's company. Anissa chewed her food with her mouth wide open and gabbled on for an hour. Beth marveled at her spectacular beautiful and felt sad that such a magnificent face and body were wasted on a simpleton.

After dinner, Hana fed the fire and said to Beth, "She is beautiful."

"More than beautiful. Ravishing. I can see much of you in her, except that her coloring is different. Her father must have been a handsome man."

"Maybe. I don't know who he was." She told Beth about being raped by Russian soldiers and added that she was currently struggling with financial issues.

"I can help you with that. I have more money than I could spend in a dozen lifetimes. I've decided to leave most of it to my foundation, but who's to say I can't do some good with it while I'm still alive? I'll give you a chunk of it so that you and Anissa can live off the interest."

They made love that night, and as she lay in Beth arms, Hana said, "Beth, you are too good to me. I want our love to last forever."

Beth kissed her, thinking that she loved Hana also and would spend the rest of her life treating Anissa as the daughter she had never had.

26

Wade kept throwing sevens and laughed at his great luck. He'd had such luck for the past few days and decided to quit while he was ahead, so he went in and cashed in his chips. He had won fifty-five thousand dollars. This trip to Monte Carlo had been good to him.

At Cannes, he had found the picture he wanted to take back home and share with American audiences. A two-hour-long drama about a restless young woman who has a fling with an older man. They have a son, and the woman skedaddles to Houston, where she makes do as an "entertainer" in some funky joint advertising LIVE NUDE GIRLS. Her older boyfriend and their son track her down and the man buys time with her in a booth where she tells him her version of what happened to them. Wade was moved by the marvelous acting of the two leads—the jilted man was played by a legendary character actor and the booth girl by an intense, unconventionally beautiful European-born actress. Not exactly the most commercial of films, Wade admitted to himself, but a really fine artsy-fartsy movie that would surely get a new Oscars and compel the movers and shakers to take him more seriously.

He was also going to divorce Beth. He would thank her for all she had done for him and add that he hoped he in some small way had been good for her, too. Of course, their breakup would send Beth running back to her lawyer to cut Summer out of her will...but so what? Wade had married Beth to get financial security for Summer—and where was his daughter now? Shacking up in the Beverly Hills Hotel with Colton Thomas, an aging married womanizer with a toddler son. Thomas, like virtually all other highly successful men, had always put his work first; Summer doubtless knew that his wife and kid came second and she placed third. She had moved into his life knowing how it all was, and accepting those realities. She didn't want life served to her on a silver platter, and Wade respected her wishes. He himself couldn't bear another year of Beth and her hoity-toity bullshit, her dinner parties and gossip and endless fretting about the condition of her breasts and butt. Once back in Manhattan, Wade would see about reclaiming his old suite at the Plaza and inviting Summer to move in with him. He thought about her desire to share an apartment with him and how heartbroken she'd felt when he said, 'Too late; I've married Beth.' Well, maybe he and Summer *could* become roomies after all. Stranger things had happened.

Half a dozen times he had called her at the Beverly but hung up as the phone rang. He made sure that his acquisition of the Houston picture had gotten generous coverage in *Variety* and *The Hollywood Reporter*. He sent Summer links to those trade-paper articles but included no comments of his own.

Wade and Beth planned to fly to New York at the end of the week. Two days earlier, he made a very brief trip to Switzerland and deposited half a million dollars into a savings account. He contacted the Plaza to reserve his old suite at the end of the month. He would wait till he and Beth arrived at the Amsterdam, then say, 'We're through' and move back into the Plaza.

On Thursday afternoon, Beth ran around Paris buying this and that. Wade went for a walk and saw a movie producer he had always disliked. The man invited him up to his suite to play poker. Wade at first said no, but then thought, 'Why not?' The producer was a famously astute poker player, so Wade wanted to see just how good the guy really was.

He left the producer's suite a few hours later with twenty thousand dollars of the man's money. He went to Cartier's and bought Beth a watch with a leather strap. He gave it to her during their ride to the airport. She kissed his cheek and thanked him. He thought, *Maybe I should tell her now and let her know that I want out. But maybe I better keep my mouth shut. It would be a long flight if all we did was bicker about our joke of a marriage. Besides, none of this is her fault. She went out an bought herself a gigolo, a male whore. But now her whore has decided it's time to be a man again.*

They left Cannes and boarded their flight at Nice. Wade and Beth sat across from each other and he opened the champagne and caviar he had bought with his own money. He was ambivalent about splurging in such a way because "champagne and caviar in the air," as he called it, was something he normally did only with Summer.

Beth held up her glass and smiled at Wade. "To Cannes and all your friends there."

He smiled back and said, "To you—and your wonderful taste in men."

They both laughed.

Beth thought of Hana, who was on her way to New York, and the glorious times that lay ahead for them. She believed that her marriage to Wade was virtually over—she would be open and candid with him about who she was and what she wanted, and if he refused to let her be herself, someone would divorce him or allow him to divorce her—and such a scenario comforted her. Life was too damned brief to play games and tell lies. She didn't mind if Summer ended up getting millions of dollars of Beth's money. As they old saying went, you couldn't take it with you. Well, she didn't want to take it with her; she just wanted to live while she was alive, and to do that living with Hana. Yes. Hana was life; Hana was love.

The plane heaved and struggled like a ride at an amusement park, but Beth neither screamed nor cried; she simply shut her eyes and braced herself for the inevitable. Wade's drink now lay on the carpeted floor like a Rorschach stain. The flight attendant hurried over, but Wade waved him off and wiped off his briefcase which held the contract for the Cannes movie plus a large amount of American cash. The money would be enough to get him ensconced in an office and started again as a Hollywood player.

The airplane bucked and rocked like a toy held by a temperamental child. Wade laughed. "Hold on tight. Looks like we're hitting some weather."

Presently the pilot said on the public-address system, "We're going in for a crash landing. Please remove your shoes, unstrap your seatbelts and assume a kneeling position on the floor…"

The flight attendant hid his face in his hands. "Now I will never see America. We're all going to die."

Wade Sellars, lifelong gambler and seeker of luck, leaned forward, knowing with a strange calmness that his had finally run out. He grabbed the bottle of champagne and took a long swallow, grateful for the good times he'd had and not a bit regretful of the bad ones. Just before the Learjet broke apart and tumbled back to earth in a hundred jagged pieces, he thought of Summer. He would never have the chance to apologize to her and remind her of how much he loved her—but had he *really* believed that opportunity would come? When the aircraft's disintegration began and the cabin started to fill up with frosty mountain air, his very last thought was the hope that his fatal fall to earth wouldn't hurt too much…

27

Summer sighed as the jumbo jet landed at LaGuardia Airport. She wished the huge aircraft would just fly all over the world and never come down anywhere. New York City held no charm for her when she knew that Wade wouldn't be there to greet her. He would never be in New York, or anywhere else, ever again.

Less than an hour after Wade's Learjet disintegrated, killing all on board, CNN reported the news to the world. Fortunately, Stephen Rogers' father George called her with the tragic news so she wouldn't have to learn about it from the TV. Stephen got on the extension and the two men pelted her with specific questions about funeral arrangements and whatnot till she hung up the telephone as they spoke. Then she sat for the longest time, wondering why the birds were still chirping and the sky hadn't fallen. Wondering why she was still living and breathing...

At some point she began to scream. She knew was screaming, and not someone else, and she couldn't have said precisely when she would stop. Colton held her in his arms, eyes twitching with anxiety, begging her to tell him what was wrong. Then telephone kept ringing and Colton called down and ordered the operator to make the noise stop. He turned around and looked at her, and she could see that now he knew why she had been screaming. But, presumably by God's wish, the world kept turning and Summer remained alive, though she wished more than anything that she could simply lay down and die.

Colton led a kind doctor to Summer, and the doctor gave her a shot that made her feel dreamy and unreal, and at first she thought he might be trying to accommodate her wish to die, and that her weird, goofy feeling was, indeed, death. She smiled as she gave herself over to death, and felt grateful that Colton hadn't prevented the kind doctor from killing her. She closed her eyes and wondered when, or if, she would see Wade in this new place where she would spend eternity.

But she did not die. When she awoke, Colton sat at her bedside, and after feeling a moment or two of disappointment over remaining alive, she asked him: Was it true? Had her father been killed? He nodded, but she didn't cry, because she had no tears left.

Colton had made sure the telephones were turned off. He had taken Rikia call and declined her offer to fly out there right away to collect Summer. George and Stephen Rogers had made the same offer. Colton, believing that Summer was accomplishing nothing by hiding out in his bungalow, booked a seat for her on United's noon flight and personally deposited her into her first-class seat.

Summer looked at him with big, panicked eyes. "I don't want to do this alone. Come with me."

He offered her a small smile and said in a quiet voice, "I'm as close as your cell phone, sweetie. But you need to do this alone. George and Stephen will be waiting for you in New York."

She took a deep breath. "I don't want them to be there. I don't want any of this to be happening."

He shrugged. "It is what it is. We need to play the cards we're dealt." He added, "We're in a weird situation. We're both public figures. I *am* a married man, and George and Stephen actually believe that you've been out here doing an *In* story on me, not riding my dick. Not that I give a rat's ass what *they* think; it's you I'm concerned about. There will be reporters at La Guardia waiting for you."

Summer frowned. "Reporters? Why?"

"For one thing, you father was quite a curious and colorful character, and your stepmother was one of the world's richest women. For another, they died because their Learjet came apart in midair, and as the saying goes in journalism, 'If it bleeds, it leads.'"

"Colton." She reached out an squeezed his hand. "Come out to New York and help me through this. *Please.*"

He squeezed back. "Would if I could, babe. But there's less than zero I could do for you if I made Thanksgiving trip for you. I'd have to hide out in some hotel while you did all the things a survivor has to do after a loved one dies. Furthermore, the media would love it if they found out that you had flown back to New York with your married lover—who happened to be named Colton Thomas. Also, I'm *way* behind in my writing. The studio is all over my ass; they're saying, 'We agreed to let you be the boss about adapting your novel to the screen, so where the hell is your adaptation?' Lately I've been too much of a lover and not enough of a writer."

She pulled him into her arms and he said, "You go there and do what you need to do. Just remember that if you need me, day or night, just think of me and I'll be there."

Her flight eased itself down onto the runway as Summer thought of that trade-paper article Wade had emailed her without a note of any kind. Why no note? Was he still angry at her? If so, he wouldn't have sent her the clipping at all. No, she decided, he had overcome his anger and sent her that article as his way of saying that he had resumed his showbiz career and everything would be all right. Yes! That was it.

Her jumbo jet landed and within a few minutes the other passengers crowded into the aisle. She sat back and took her time, content with the idea of being the last person off the aircraft. When her time came, she gathered up her things and traipsed past the smiling flight attendants and into the jetway, wondering how strange life was: Your life implodes around you yet the rest of the world carries on as if nothing has happened. She saw the photographers but did not realize that they had come to see her until they started taking pictures of her. Then Stephen and his father jumped in and hustled her into a private room.

She felt tearful on the ride back into Manhattan, the same trip she'd taken with Wade so many times. Much of the city was the same as it had always been, but now Wade was gone…and to her, that made all the difference.

"Are you all right with that, Summer?" Stephen was asking.

"Didn't hear you."

"We think," said George, "that Beth's estate will

take months to settle due to its size, and that ultimately its assets will go to her foundation. In the meantime, we think you should stay in her suite at the Amsterdam. How does that sound?"

She shrugged. "I have my own apartment."

"But you'll have absolute privacy at the Amsterdam."

"Won't I have 'absolute privacy' at my apartment, too?"

"No. The media will be drooling all over this story for days, unfortunately. When this story first broke, a reporter called me for a comment about Beth's estate, and I'm afraid I mentioned that you were to receive a billion dollars."

"Me? Why did she leave me all that money? We really didn't like each other very much."

George Rogers smiled at her. "She and your father loved each other very much, so I'm sure she wanted to share her wealth with you in order to please him. He also wanted very much for you to live at the Amsterdam."

Summer made a face. "How do you know what he wanted? You hardly knew him."

"*I* knew him better than you think," Stephen told her. "He and I spoke at length in Florida about you while you were in Beverly Hills working on that magazine assignment. He told me how much he hoped you would get married; I reminded him of my feelings for you. He told me to give you your space and not to pressure you into an engagement. He really hated the fact that you were living in that cramped apartment when the Amsterdam was available."

Summer wiped tears from her cheeks. "All right, Stephen—I'll move into the Amsterdam."

Over the next few days, Summer made a zombie of herself with prescription meds. She even went to Doctor Simonyi for a shot of speed. The physical aches and pains were something she could endure because they were temporary; but the loss of her father was quite another matter.

Stephen sat beside Summer during the memorial service for Wade and Beth. Her face was blank, her lips dry. His father sat on her other side, and George Rogers' wife sat next to her husband, dressed in black, clutching a hanky and looking fashionably bereaved. Many of Manhattan's most celebrated people had packed into the church and the media covered the event from the curb with satellite vans. A dozen or so of Beth's friends from Europe had hired a jet so they could sit in and say goodbye to her.

"Hana, marry me. You have money; so do I. We could have a happy life together with Anissa—"

She pressed her finger to his lips. "Yes, I'm sure you have money and we could have a good year together."

He frowned. "Meaning…?"

"We would last a year at the very most. You would see your little Summer marry and all that money she got from Beth and the good times the two of you could have had and how much you were still in love with her." She shook her head. "No, Stephen, you and I were not meant to be. I must be with Anissa. She needs so much time to learn the simplest things, and only I can do this for her. Summer needs you more than you know."

"I need you," he told her. He moved towards her, arms wide open.

"No, Stephen—"

"If you're sending me away, can't we be together one last time?"

"No. It would only make this goodbye that much more difficult."

He sighed. "So you are sending me away again."

"But this time I am doing so with love."

He walked to the door and suddenly she ran to him. "Stephen, be happy! Promise me you will be happy…happy enough for both of us…" He looked down at her and saw tears streaming down her face. Then he hurried out the door so as not to let her see his own tears.

28

Summer had been too stoned on sedatives to remember much of Wade's memorial service, except that Stephen had sat by her side and a veritable who's-who had packed into the church. She recalled thinking, 'He would have loved this—a full house, maybe even standing-room-only, and all of it for him.' But she felt thoroughly detached from it all, and indifferent to the spectacle as she and Stephen exited the church to the shouts of her name and news cameras pointed at her, as if she'd just sat through the service for a head of state she had never met.

Back at the Amsterdam, she'd been amazed by the large number of mourners in her suite and amazed by their raised eyebrows and expectant smiles as if she were the designated greeter at one of Beth's pretentious parties. When her mouth got too dry and her voice tired from answering people's nosy questions, she disappeared into her bedroom and popped some more pills.

The following days were just as unreal. She sat in George Rogers' fancy office, Stephen two feet away, nodding and trying to smile as George reminded her that Beth had willed her one billion dollars. *One billion dollars!* Summer, who had always lacked other people's lust for money, failed to see what she had to get excited about. Would it bring Wade back? Would it erase his fistfight with Colton from her memory?

She endured her days and nights despite wishing at bedtime that she would never wake up. Stephen took her to his parents' home for dinner each night, where Summer mostly picked at her food as Missus Rogers smoothed out her gray hair and groped for questions that Summer might enjoy answering. Every day she swallowed hard and licked her lips as she stood surrounded by countless unfamiliar faces who thrust voice recorders into her face and asked blunt questions about her father. Throughout each meal, she smiled with gratitude at Stephen for helping her through this ordeal.

Nighttime was a relief. She would take sleeping pills and die for eight to ten hours. Sometimes she would dream of her father, then wake up in a daze she found not altogether unpleasant. But when she went back for more pills, her doctor said, "If you were a widow or an older woman, I might say yes. But you are a beautiful young woman with an adoring fiancé, so my advice is to stop taking pills and start to rejoin the human race."

She thrashed about in sweaty torment that night. While in the bathroom, her muscles quivering, she opened Beth's medicine cabinet and nearly wept with relief at the sight of so many pill vials—Seconal, Tuinal, Percodan—which she hid in the bedroom.

After a few weeks, the pills stopped working. She would sleep for a few hours, then wake up and fail to fall asleep again. She called Colton.

"Summer," he said, "it's two in the morning."

"Well, at least I'm not interrupting your writing."

"No, but you woke me up. You see, I'm having some trouble adapting my novel to the screen—I'm not used to this sort of work and I'm not sure I'm that good at it. The studio's all over my ass about it and I need my sleep. Understand?"

"Well," she said, "I have good news. This insanity of Beth's will is going to be over soon, and then I can move back into the bungalow with you."

After a long pause, he said, "I think we should wait for a while."

"Why?"

"Because if you fly out here now, you won't be able to move in with me."

"Why not?"

"Haven't you been following the news?"

"Nope. Been too busy with other things."

"Well, you're right in the middle of your fifteen minutes of fame. The media are *very* interested in you as Beth's stepdaughter and billionaire heiress."

"You sound like Rikia…and…um…"

"Summer, are you stoned?"

"Kind of. Took some sleeping pills."

"How many?"

"Dunno."

He yawned. "Well, get some sleep. I'll get done with this screen treatment as fast as I can, and then we'll have a nice long talk and figure out what we're gonna do."

"Unh…" She fell asleep, and when she awoke, eleven hours later, she could remember very little of her conversation with Colton. But she definitely had the feeling he hadn't said the words she wanted to hear.

A few days later, she had Rikia up for dinner. The room service meal was delicious, and Sandra the housekeeper chilled a bottle of Beth's best white wine. Summer thought Rikia looked much too skinny.

"I want to have the lean-and-mean look. That's my new thing. You like?"

"I wish you'd shut up and eat a little something."

"Did I tell you that I'm dating Jay Benjamin right now? I know he's no Colton Thomas, but he's won some minor prizes and gets lots of respect. He was in last year's *The Best American Short Stories*. He's considered much too literary and artsy-fartsy ever to make big money as a writer. His collection of short stories has sold fewer than a thousand copies. But Manhattan's hip crowd thinks he's some kind of genius. Besides, he's a good fit for me at the moment."

"Don't you want to settle down into a permanent relationship with a man?" Summer asked her.

"Nope. I used to, but now I'm thinking that Number One is the only person who matters. I want to be rich and famous, and I'm going to spend the rest of my life trying to attain my goal." Then, "So, what's the deal with you and Colton?"

She shrugged. "He's very busy with that screen treatment. He's a novelist, not a screenwriter, so this project is a little more difficult than he'd anticipated."

"Once that's done, are you going to move back in with him?"

"No."

Rikia raised an eyebrow. "Really? Is it over? Well, if so, don't sweat it. With all the money you're about to inherit, you don't need him anymore."

Summer shook her head. "We're not over, and I need him more than ever. But with all this publicity I've gotten, Colton says I can't just fly back out there and move back into his bungalow."

Rikia swallowed a mouthful of food and said, "Well, go out there and rent a house. Rent a mansion. Once they deposit that cool billion into your account, you can do pretty much whatever you want. Hire a top agent who'll get you invited to all the best showbiz parties and maybe even throw a few parties yourself with that cool billion you're going to get. Then Colton will probably think twice about getting a divorce."

"Rikia, nobody's said anything about divorce."

"Summer, lets face it—you're a child. You need a man. You want it legal and traditional, too—this 'shacking up' thing just doesn't cut it for you. Also, you told me that Colton is sweating this Hollywood writing project because of his financial obligations, especially that Manhattan condo you two are buying. Well, things have changed just a little bit for you; he doesn't need those Hollywood bucks because you've inherited all that money, so the cost of that condo is chump change. You can offer his old lady a nice fat sum of money to walk away and I'm sure she'll say, 'Cool!' She'll even let you and Colton have custody of their kid, but if you're so inclined, you can give that kid a baby brother or sister." She paused. "I mean, I've just summarized what you want in life, right?"

Summer shrugged. "I suppose. Yeah, you're right. I should talk to him about it tonight."

Rikia nodded. "You're a billionaire. Most of the goodies in this world are for sale, and you can afford them." She pointed at the pictures of celebrities on the table. "Did Beth really know *all* those people?"

"All."

"I rest my case."

Summer took a nap until her cell phone awoke her. She grabbed it and said hello.

"Now *you're* the one who was asleep."

"*Colton!* I was going to call you later, when I knew you weren't working."

He laughed. "Since when have you cared about whether you're calling me at an inconvenient time?"

"Huh?"

"You've called me at every hour of the day or night—literally. You've called me a dozen times on some days, and *now* you're worrying about calling me while I'm working."

"It's just that whenever I feel sad and lonely, I just pick up the phone and dial your number without thinking about the time of day. I can't stand being without you. I'm going to fly out there tomorrow."

"Don't bother. I'm about two minutes away—in my hotel, which is right across the street from yours."

"Then get your ass over here, or I'll throw on some clothes and go to your room."

"Negative! I'm very tired and have a nine-o'clock meeting with my publisher tomorrow."

"Well, when can we hook up?"

"We'll have lunch tomorrow."

"I can't wait that long!"

"Oh, I'm sure you can. Tomorrow morning my lawyer and I are going to meet with the publisher to work out matters concerning my next book. After that, I'll need to relax and get buzzed. So what do you say tomorrow at twelve-thirty at Bea's?"

She sighed. "O.K."

"And don't bring a birthday cake."

He stood at the bar as she strode into the restaurant. Friends and acquaintances crowded him as he bought them drinks. Then, spotting her, he pushed away some of those people and squeezed her in. After hugging her and kissing her forehead, he introduced her to his friends. She giggled at how everyone shut up as soon as the big man spoke. "Want some white wine?" he asked her.

"Whatever you're having," she said.

"Jack Daniels over ice," he said to the barman. "She and I are going to sit over there, away from these cretins."

As everyone laughed, he led her to a table nearby.

"I've finally finished that movie treatment. Now the studio wants me to change the ending."

"Colton, you can't do that."

"Oh, but I can and must. If I refuse, they'll bring in someone who will." Then, "I took their money, so I'm basically their employee. That means I have to do as they say."

"Not really. You have more leverage than that. The love of your life is about to become wonderfully stinking rich. You can tell Hollywood to kiss your ass. We'll move into our condo and you can write all those great novels—"

He reached over and squeezed her hand. "Summer, I pulled out of that condo deal."

She gulped. "What? Why?"

"Because," he told her, "we've been apart for a little while now—I've been in Beverly Hills and you've been here. I've done plenty of thinking and

I've done marathon writing sessions. I couldn't have done that with you in that bungalow with me. I can write, or I can be with you. One or the other. Not both."

"Colton!"

Just then their server appeared and handed them each a menu. As Colton perused his, Summer glowered at him. How could he eat after what he'd just said to her? How dare he treat her that way!

"Try the prawns," he said to her. "They're always good here, and I know how much you like seafood."

She shook her head. "I'm not hungry."

"Then two cheeseburgers," he said to their server, handing back their menus. "Make mine rare. How do you want yours?"

Summer shuddered. "I don't want one."

"Two rare cheeseburgers, then."

As the server left, Summer leaned towards Colton, her eyes blazing with rage. "What do you mean, you can't write when I'm around? Of *course* you can! Maybe not in that hotel bungalow, especially when you're shitfaced on booze, but in that big condo we were going to buy? Well, you'd have all the space in the world. I wouldn't be in your way."

"Oh, but you would. Your presence in my home would be on my mind all the time and I would be unable to work because of you. I'm pushing sixty now, and while everyone is saying to me, 'Hell of a career, Colton! You've done so much fine work, and you're still doing great!' but I know the truth, which is that I've written maybe one-tenth of one percent of what I was *capable* of writing. What got in my way? What prevented me from becoming the writer I could have been? Booze and broads, I think. I've loved and

346

made love while I should have been writing. I was put on this planet to write, not booze it up and ball broads. You're just the latest in the succession of women to say, 'Oh, Colton, be with me forever! You can write and be with me!' Well, no, I fucking can't do that. I need to do what is best for me, not do the thing that will make you happy."

She closed her eyes and pulled in a deep breath, determined not to give him the satisfaction of seeing her weep. "But don't you love me?"

"I'm not sure I know what 'love' means."

"When you said you loved me…were you lying?"

"No. I meant it at the time."

She let out a small, bitter laugh.

He nodded. "Yes, I meant it at the time. It wasn't just some 'I've just fucked a chick' bullshit that guys say sometimes. So, yes, I meant it when I said it. But things have changed."

She shook her head. "Things haven't changed at all."

"Then maybe *I've* changed. *Time* has changed, too. You're twenty-one, which means you've got your life in front of you. Youth is a wonderful gift; you need to appreciate it and enjoy it with a man who's also young. You're young enough to be my daughter, and I don't think a man should marry his daughter."

Their cheeseburgers arrived. As Colton devoured his, Summer said, "Colton, you said we had a good year or two together. Right?"

He chewed away and nodded.

"Well, let's continue to enjoy our time together."

He swallowed. "Our time is up. We can sit here and talk all we want, but I still have to get back to my Beverly Hills bungalow and do some more writing.

After that, I have to write and write and write some more—"

"Colton." She paused to figure out what she wanted to say and how loudly to say it. She felt that everyone in the restaurant knew Colton Thomas was sitting there having a meal with a much younger woman. Those other guests were probably doing their best to eavesdrop, and Summer thought her conversation was none of their damn business. "Please don't leave me now. I've inherited a billion dollars. Our options are wide open. Just don't leave me. You're all I have left. You're the only person I care about."

He frowned. "You're twenty-one, beautiful and smart, with a billion dollars—and you say I'm the only good thing in your life? I'd say you're really underestimating yourself and your situation."

"But you're all I want." She wiped a couple of tears from her cheeks.

For a few minutes they said nothing. Then Colton said, "O.K., if what we have means so much to you, we'll keep going and see how it plays out. It's going to be difficult, but we'll try."

Summer mouthed, *Thank you.*

"Now finish your food, because you need to start packing. I have to fly back tomorrow morning."

She picked at her food. Later on, they had cappuccino. He said, "Well, I hope you'll like my bungalow more than you did last time."

"Is the weather still bad out there?"

"Hope not. Bad weather makes me cranky."

"Maybe you don't want me to go with you."

He shook his head. "You're not the problem. That fucking movie script is. Like I said, I'm a

348

novelist, not a screenwriter. This isn't the kind of writing I do. It frustrates the hell out of me."

"Then just say, 'Find someone else.'"

He sighed. "I told you, I can't do that."

"Because…?"

"They've paid me nearly a hundred thousand dollars to do this."

She rolled her eyes. "I have a *billion* good reasons why you could tell them to piss off."

He shot her a sidelong glance. "Is this the first time you've talked that shit?"

"Meaning…?"

"You're buying me off. Everyone has his price, so now you're paying mine, like you're buying me at auction."

"Colton, I want you to be my husband. I want us to be together always, and that's what the money is for. You don't have to hole up in a Beverly Hills bungalow and torture yourself writing that Hollywood crap you loathe. You can spend the rest of your life being the kind of writer you want to be. Mostly, I want us to be together and be happy. That's the whole point of life, isn't it?"

He shook his head. "Summer, it's not going to work. What we had in that Beverly Hills bungalow was wonderful, but it was a temporary thing between two people. It wasn't meant to last any longer than it did. When we met, I was a has-been who needed some love and inspiration, and you were there to give me that. You went to bed with me and helped me believe that I was some kind of stud, and I will always be profoundly grateful to you for that. But none of that means much now, so I'll just keep writing and you have a nice time with the billion bucks that

Daddy squeezed out of Beth for you."

"I have huge money. I'll buy us a mansion in France so you can write all you want—"

He sighed. "Summer, I'm Colton Thomas, not Wade Sellars. I'm not for sale."

"Meaning…?"

"Just what I said."

She spilled her drink as she got up and ran out of the restaurant.   .

29

Summer slept for most of the next three days. Sandra, her housekeeper, arrived with trays of food and beverages, but Summer waved her away, mumbling about feeling unwell. When Sandra threatened to call Doctor Simonyi, Summer explained that her moodiness and lethargy were due to nothing more than menstruation. Sandra said to Stephen, "Miz Summer is feeling poorly; it's a female thing."

After a while, the pills failed to deliver the long, mindless bouts of unconsciousness she craved; they just left her too lazy and confused to do much of anything. She knew she had to be mentally together the following evening when she and Stephen joined his parents for dinner. She would have no excuses left about her health; menstrual problems lasted only five days.

She often lay on her bed and relived her last weeks with Colton. Was it her own fault? If so, what had she done—or failed to do? She kept remembering his kind blue eyes and big warm smile as he said, "I need you. I can't live without you." But that was in February, and by June he'd asked her to leave. She knew she needed to continue living and working and doing her best, but those damn pills made it so *easy* for her just to lie there like a zombie. She always felt the temptation to overdose and float away forever. She thought back to her days in Switzerland as she learned to walk again, all those painful days and long nights—and now this! Was God saying to her, "Yes, that time in Switzerland was quite bad for you, but I wasn't done with you. You needed to suffer some more, so deal with *this*."

Colton had said to her, "You have youth, beauty, brains and a billion dollars, so stop feeling sorry for yourself." But those blessings suddenly meant nothing to her, or at least they meant less to her than they did to everyone else. The telephone rang and Sandra answered it. "No, Mister Hughley, I'm afraid she can't come to the telephone—"

"I'll talk to him!" she called out, jumping out of bed. "Robertson! Where the hell are you?"

"In your lobby. I was passing through and thought I'd invite you out to lunch."

"I'm not hungry, but come on up."

Presently he sat on an easy chair in Summer's bedroom. "Can I get you anything?" she asked. "A drink? Sandra can cook you a steak."

"I'd really like it if you'd pull on a pair of Levi's and a sweatshirt. We could go out and find a burger joint."

"No. I don't feel so great. I'm on the rag."

"Like hell you are."

"Excuse me?"

"The only time you spent so much of your day when you were with Colton was to boff him." She scowled at him but he just smiled. "I spoke to Colton just before he flew back to California. He told me about your conversation at Bea's. Your thing with him had to end. All of his relationships are temporary. He is a writer; he can't be anything else. He certainly can't be a husband and father."

She thrust out her chin. "He loved me. He even made me choose between my father and him."

Robertson nodded. "He told me about that. Said it was the dumbest thing he'd ever done. By making you choose, he was making a commitment to you, and he definitely wasn't into commitments, except to his work. He said you finally ended it. You literally walked out on him."

"Yes. There was nothing more for me to do."

"I agree. But Colton feels you gave him his life back. You relieved him of whatever obligation he had to you—"

"Robertson! Colton loves me! He really does! He said he couldn't live without me!"

"Oh, I'm sure he did say it and I'm sure he meant it when he said it. I've said the same thing a hundred times to this or that woman—and I meant every word of it at the time. Men mean what they say to a woman when they're saying it, but women need to understand that men, later on, may feel differently. You see, Colton's a writer and an alcoholic. You were crowding him so much that he had a hard time breathing."

Summer crossed her legs. "And your point is…?"

"That I care about you and want you to be happy. I came up here to say hello but didn't expect you to be in bed, looking like a fucking corpse."

"Colton will come back to me," she said.

"Negative. That's a done deal. Now get your shit together and rejoin the human race."

"I have a billion dollars," she said. "I live in a palace. But I can't make love to a billion dollars. I have everything in the world except what really matters."

"If you want to do some constructive work, prove that you really loved your father."

"What?"

"You heard me." Then, "Look, I understand that this Elizabeth Rogers Stainton was a nice lady, but it's no secret that Wade Sellars shacked up with the most beautiful women around. So he goes and marries Beth Stainton, and you end up inheriting a billion dollars. Do you think she left you that much money because she loved your sunny blonde smile?"

Summer shrugged. "I have no idea at all why she left me all that money."

"Well, I'll tell you. Your father wanted you to have the best of everything after he died, and as the old saying goes, 'The easiest way to become a billionaire is to find someone with a billion and marry them.' Well, Wade Sellars spent the last year of his life trying to please a women who was probably pretty damned impossible to deal with most of the time, and he did it all for you." He watched as tears streamed down her face. "Stop your crying. Hear me? Get dressed and go have some fun. Your old man is up in heaven right now, thinking, 'I didn't get her that billion so she could lie in bed feeling sorry for herself.' He would be so disappointed that you're crying all the time over a man who doesn't want you."

She smiled and wiped away her tears. "Robertson, it's too late tonight to go out because I took a few sleeping pills and I'm feeling like a zombie. But do you want to have dinner tomorrow?"

"No."

"Why not?"

"Because I came by just to tell you what I thought. Now that I've said it, I have nothing more to say to you."

"Well, can't be we friends?"

"Yes—but *just* friends. I'm not Wade Sellars or Colton Thomas."

She laughed. "But you *are* a handsome man."

"That's what my girlfriend says."

"I think my father wanted me to marry Stephen Rogers."

"Do you love him?"

"I'm ambivalent. Of course, I've never really given him a chance. We started going out, but then I met Colton and that changed everything."

"You need to give yourself another chance. A hundred chances. Meet handsome men and date them. Dance your ass off. Enjoy your billion dollars. That way, your father can rest in peace."

Summer began dating Stephen again. Stephen's mother told her that Beth Stainton and Wade Sellars, wherever they were, would feel that Summer had done quite enough mourning and needed to start living life and having fun. He dragged her off to Manhattan's chicest nightspots—no doorman would turn him away, especially when he was with her— where she met his many friends and blushed as they felt her up on the crowded dance floor. Throughout each evening, she mostly looked forward to getting home and taking a couple of pills that would make her feel dreamy and then knock her unconscious as surely as a boxer's punch.

One day became virtually indistinguishable from the next. The sexy young women she had met at nightclubs called to invite her to lunch at Manhattan's most exclusive restaurants. She accepted, although she would have much rather stayed home, and smiled as they told her what they knew of who was dating whom and which hip stores were selling clothes an accessories worth buying. Summer nodded, knowing that the world was full of goodies and she could have as many as she wanted, and a hundred times more.

By the middle of June, she told herself that she couldn't just sit and sweat in the sweltering heat; she had to make some plans. Stephen tapped his toes and checked his watch, telling her that he would go wherever she wanted, but they had to decide soon. Other people called her every day or every other day, including a handsome actor, a sociable Spanish family and a man who worked at a financial firm that competed against Stephen's.

They called; they sent empathy cards. She thanked them for their kindness but in truth she felt indifference towards them. She learned online that Colton had finished his movie treatment and gone to Big Sur for a week or more to chill out. She wondered: Was he still married to Jennifer? Did he go there with her or had he found a new lover?

Rikia, too, was leaving town for a while. She had made reservations for somewhere in Rhode Island so she could unwind and her new man could sit with his computer on his lap and write.

Just then she had an idea that made her smile. When had she last felt wonderful? Those shots! Doctor Simonyi had stuck those needles into her arm and she felt born again! She threw on some clothes and headed out to his office. Presently she was on her way to an examination room when a man threw his arms around her. "Heiress!" he cried.

"Hank?" Summer asked, bewildered. "Why are you here?"

"I'm in the cast of *Butterfly*," he told her. "Have you seen it?"

She shook her head. "I've been busy with…other things."

"I've read about you lately. That you've come into some heavy money. Don't know why *you* need to get shot up with speed."

She shrugged. "Heiresses get lethargic, too."

He snapped his fingers. "Hey--I've got an idea. We're having a party tonight. Wanna come?"

She nodded. "O.K., but first I need my needle."

"Then I'll wait for you. I can't wait for you to see the show. I'll be naked, you know."

"I'll try not to look at your stuff."

30

Summer sat open-mouthed by the terrible energy of the show. Hank had only one song, which he mostly talked, and she felt surprised that he wasn't really very good; somehow his charisma didn't float from the stage and cover the audience the way she thought it would. The show included one show with frontal nudity. Hank was in there, too, as naked as the others, and Summer presently observed that all their penises were essentially the same size. Stephen's was that size as well. She guessed that nearly all males were born to have the same size members, and the few who had much bigger ones, like Harry Reems and John C. Holmes, ended up in porn movies. Then there were the guys like Colton—poor Colt! Big man, not so big down there. She began giggling, thinking of penises and lovers as she sat in the dark, dank playhouse.

Wade was dead. She could think of him now that way and accept it. She knew he had lived a full, satisfying life, at least until his final year. As some had told her, he had lived his last year for her, so that she could live many happy years after he was gone.

www.ingramcontent.com/pod-product-compliance
Lightning Source LLC
Chambersburg PA
CBHW020325180626
46812CB00001B/59